Outstanding praise fo[r]

"With *The Girls' Globa[l]* [de]livers a brisk, funny, keenly [observed tale of a woman who] wants more out of life than a soul-killing job and a tepid romance—and finds it on exotic shores."
—Kim Green, author of *Paging Aphrodite* on
The Girls' Global Guide to Guys

"Alan does a masterful job . . . As the three women face the trials and triumphs of life, they assist each other in ways that only best friends can—through unconditional love, unrelenting humor and unwavering support. Reminiscent of *Bridget Jone's Diary* and *Divine Secrets of the Ya-Ya Sisterhood*, Alan's is a novel to be savored like a good box of chocolates."
—*Booklist* on *Who You Know*

Outstanding praise for the novels of Carly Alexander

"An entertaining read that will get you in the holiday spirit."
—*Romantic Times* on *Ghosts of Boyfriends Past*

"In *The Eggnog Chronicles* Carly Alexander serves up laughter and tears, friendship and romance. It's one of the smartest and most satisfying books I've read in some time!"
—Holly Chamberlin on *The Eggnog Chronicles*

Outstanding praise for the novels of Holly Chamberlin

"Looking for a perfect summer read? Ms. Chamberlin has written it!"
—*The Romantic Reader's Connection* on
The Summer of Us

"Fans of *Sex in the City* will enjoy the women's romantic escapades and appreciate the roundtable discussions these gals have about the trials and tribulations singletons face."
—*Booklist* on *Living Single*

Books by Theresa Alan

WHO YOU KNOW

SPUR OF THE MOMENT

THE GIRLS' GLOBAL GUIDE TO GUYS

Books by Carly Alexander

GHOSTS OF BOYFRIENDS PAST

THE EGGNOG CHRONICLES

THE SECRET LIFE OF MRS. CLAUS

Books by Holly Chamberlin

LIVING SINGLE

THE SUMMER OF US

BABYLAND

Published by Kensington Publishing Corporation

SEX AND THE SINGLE WITCH

Theresa Alan

Carly Alexander

Holly Chamberlin

KENSINGTON BOOKS
www.kensingtonbooks.com

KENSINGTON BOOKS are published by

Kensington Publishing Corp.
850 Third Avenue
New York, NY 10022

All Kensington titles, imprints and distributed lines are available at special quantity discounts for bulk purchases for sales promotion, premiums, fund-raising, educational, or institutional use.

Special book excerpts or customized printings can also be created to fit specific needs. For details, write or phone the office of the Kensington Special Sales Manager: Attn. Special Sales Department. Kensington Publishing Corp., 850 Third Avenue, New York, NY 10022. Phone: 1-800-221-2647.

Kensington and the K logo Reg. U.S. Pat. & TM Off.

ISBN 0-7582-0931-2

First Kensington Trade Paperback Printing: September 2005
10 9 8 7 6 5 4 3 2 1

Printed in the United States of America

CONTENTS

The Trouble With Witchcraft

Holly Chamberlin

As always, for Stephen.
And this time also for Emily.

* * *

I thank Douglas A. Mendini for his exemplary friendship. I would also like to honor the memory of Janet Louise Chamberlin Smith. Last, but never least, I thank John Scognamiglio for his ceaseless support.

1

Take a pinch of dried Liverfew and drop it into the pot of boiling oil. Be sure to stand well back, as Liverfew has a tendency to explode if the oil has even the slightest trace of rancidity.

"I mean it, Haven, if I don't have sex soon I'm going to—I swear I'm going to give it all up and become a cloistered nun."

"No, you won't," I said.

Lia considered, then spoke more reasonably, more like the Lia I knew. "Well, maybe not. I'm not keen on the idea of a habit; I'd just get lost in it. Look, I've never asked you for magical help before," she reminded me, as if I'd forget that impressive fact, "but I'm really desperate. You have to help me, please."

I wasn't sure I had to help her—I'm under no official compunction to help anyone who asks for magical assistance—but Lia Brock is my best friend and the only simply human who knows what I am, which, and by now you've guessed this, is a witch.

Lia discovered my secret in college. One night she walked in on me while I was concocting a potion to help clear up a cold. It was my fault, of course, that Lia found me surrounded by smoking vials and dusty old books; I'd forgotten to lock the door.

It's never mattered to Lia that I am a magic-making person. Her feet are so firmly planted on the ground, her eyes are fixed so straight ahead that I wonder if she'd know the moon in the sky if someone forced her head up to see it. In fact, if she weren't so deeply rooted in the mundane, I'm not sure I would like her so much. Lia is an antidote for the rest of my life, stability where there's often instability, rationality where there's only irrationality, calm where there's mostly chaos.

Rationality? Calm? That evening I saw neither in the woman slumped on the couch in the living room of my downtown apartment. Her suit was rumpled; her face wan. I noticed with alarm that she'd taken to biting her fingernails.

"Can I get you something to eat?" I asked.

Lia shook her head. "I had a business lunch. It went on until three. Steak, potatoes, the works. The client is from Texas."

I've never been on a business lunch. Lia, however, as a rising lawyer in a medium-sized firm handling interestingly large cases, "does" lunch regularly.

"You don't want to lose more weight," I said. Why did I want Lia to eat? So she'd be distracted from the topic she'd come to my apartment to discuss.

Lia just shook her head.

"She's not dumb."

The voice was that of Harold, my familiar, a large black-and-white Maine coon cat. At the moment he was sprawled on his back with all four feet in the air, airing his magnificent belly. I should point out that I heard Harold's voice in my mind; he might be magical, but he still has a feline anatomy.

"No," I told him, in a voice inaudible to human ears, "she isn't."

In fact, Lia is probably the most intelligent person I know. She's also funny and quirky, and though, by her own admission, she has maybe the worst hair ever—it's a strange, pale brown that frizzes oddly in the least humid weather—and struggles mightily to keep from looking skeletal, Lia has attracted a fair share of men since college.

Why, I wondered, was she feeling so desperate?

"Love spells aren't my specialty," I said bluntly.

Lia rolled her eyes. "What, you've accidentally turned a prince into a frog?"

My heart speeded up dangerously. Lia had come far too close to the truth.

"Don't do it, Haven."

I looked askance at Harold and said, "I know what I'm doing."

Harold, knowing better than anyone that I most certainly did not know what I was doing, rolled from his back onto his stomach and made a disgusting and pointed hacking sound.

"What's wrong?" Lia asked, wrinkling her nose. "Does he have a hairball?"

Lia knows that Harold and I can communicate in an unusual way, but I've left the details of our "verbal" relationship a mystery.

"He's fine," I said firmly. Harold stood to his full height, his back an impressive two-and-a-half feet off the ground, and with a twitch of his massive fluffy tail stalked out of the room.

"So, what do you think?" Lia persisted.

"I don't understand why you need my help now," I said. "Everyone goes through a dry spell once in a while."

"Haven," she retorted, "this dry spell has lasted for six months. It's no longer a spell, it's an era."

"Oh," I said. My own latest dry spell had lasted almost two years. What did that make it, an official period of history?

Lia scooted forward to the edge of the couch and clasped her hands before her chest. "Here's the deal," she said. "I want to get married. Not necessarily tomorrow, but soon. And at the rate I'm going, I'll be lucky to walk down the aisle at sixty. Please, I just need a jump-start, a magical kick in the pants."

Poor Lia. I'd never seen her so worked up over anything. "I promise I'll think about it," I said.

Lia's tiny face broke into a lovely smile; her smile is one of her best qualities. "You're the best friend a girl could have," she told me.

I wondered: Would she still think I was such a good friend when I accidentally turned her into a wolverine?

2

Sprinkle liberally with crushed pine bark and stir. Take extreme care when applying the rough mixture to the skin, as too vigorous an application may result in the sudden appearance of large, oozing pustules. Results vary.

I am a witch. This is an unavoidable fact of my life, like having blue eyes and red hair. But even those genetic predispositions can be disguised by colored contacts or bottles of dye, whereas no matter what I do or how I try, I will always be, right down to the core, a witch.

So, you're thinking, what's wrong with being a witch? Witches can just "zap" up anything they want, like diamond bracelets and lavish couture; witches can punish their enemies without their enemies ever knowing who's responsible for their sudden and complete financial ruin; witches can banish diseases, everything from the common cold to cases of advanced cancers, just by mixing a steaming purple potion.

Sounds like a pretty good deal, doesn't it?

Well, it doesn't work like that, not most of the time.

Witches, in some respect, are citizens of two worlds. We're obligated not only to the city, state, and country in which we live, but also to the coven to which we belong and to all the larger governing bodies of the witchy world—about which I'm forbidden to tell you.

Witches are burdened with ethical concerns, too. For example, if you do manage to produce an Audi A8 for your driving pleasure, you can be sure it came from somewhere, meaning the rightful owner is now without his Audi A8, which means, in effect, that you are guilty of grand larceny.

And, of course, there are limitations on a witch's powers. For example, most witches can't just snap their fingers and summon up a complete turkey dinner—one that's fit for consumption, anyway. Only very, very few witches can effect transmigration of both the body and the spirit. And no witch, no matter what wild rumors abound, can bring a dead thing back to life, not even an insect.

All witches are, however, painfully aware that a large number of people don't believe they exist, or think they're all just a bunch of crackpots, not magical but certifiable.

Thankfully, the old stereotypes of witches as ancient, craggy crones with green skin, pointy chins, pointier hats, and warts have largely fallen by the wayside. Still, being a member of a marginalized group can be unpleasant as often as it can be exhilarating.

Two or three times back in college, feeling a little left out, I tried to ignore the fact that I see auras around every living thing as naturally as a simply human puts one foot in front of the other. But each attempt to "fit in" failed miserably.

I remember one Halloween night in particular. Someone from down the hall produced a Ouija board. I knew it was not a good idea for me to be around a divination tool (or game, as the simply humans regarded it), what with my powers, such as they are, but I thought, if I make my mind a complete blank, maybe I can hide my witchiness and, at least for half an hour, be part of the normal crowd.

But when the planchette lifted off the board all by itself and began to tremble violently while pointing directly at my forehead, I had to get out of there fast. Lia followed, tossing off some excuse that we were catching a late show at the local art house, but still, I felt the suspicious and frightened stares of my floormates follow me all the way to the elevator.

It's a universal truth that you're forever stuck with being who you are. I guess that's not so bad if who you are is brilliant or beautiful or rich or even just self-confident. I am none of those. Who I am is a witch with deep self-esteem issues.

This problem, of course, is traceable to my parents.

Howlite and Topaz Castle are seriously powerful workers of magic. They are the Nick and Nora Charles of the international magical world, the glamorous, power couple extraordinaire, as successful and famous as Siegfried and Roy, as watched and pursued as Princess Diana and Dodi Fayad.

Like those other mythic couples, whether fictional or real, dead or alive, Howlite and Topaz are totally and completely devoted to each other, to the exclusion of everyone else, including their daughter, me, Haven Castle. This devotion, while in some ways admirable, resulted in my feeling like a third and largely unwanted wheel since the day I was born. Well, since shortly thereafter.

When I was very young, I was, of course, ignorant of social dynamics. But by the time I was nine or ten, I'd figured out that most of my classmates liked me because of my glitterati parents, not because I had a nice smile or was good at jump rope. Being popular by association isn't all it's cracked up to be, I can assure you.

I've seen my parents only once in the past five years.

They came to the city for a memorial service; one of their oldest friends had finally died, at the overripe age of 105. We met for lunch before the service, at an extremely high-end restaurant chosen by my father; when the check came and neither of my parents reached for a wallet, I reached for mine. For a month afterward I ate nothing but ramen noodles.

I'm sure my parents had no idea of my financial situation; either that or they just didn't care. You see, they were severely disappointed when I decided not to pursue magical graduate studies at a prestigious "secret" institute. Really, I thought, what was the point when my native talent was so meager?

Just when my parents had gotten over the first rush of disappointment, I announced that instead of pursuing some more pedestrian but still lucrative profession, like medicine or the law, I'd decided to take a job at an antique clothing store. At that point they permanently withdrew any and all financial support—and pretty much stopped calling.

Well, life at Anastasia's Attic is not one my parents would have chosen for me, but it fits me perfectly. The store is owned by a wonderfully eccentric witch named Fabula Luna. Fabula named the store after her favorite aunt, a woman who lived and died under extraordinary circumstances. I understand that Anastasia's final hours involved a handsome, deposed prince of state and a rare South American bird.

I met Fabula shortly after I graduated from college. She helped me get accepted into the coven and adjust to urban life; she even helped me find an apartment I could afford that wasn't rat infested or adjacent to a crack den. I don't know why she took me under her protective wing, but she did, and I think that without her I might not have survived those early years on my own. I told her that once and she laughed. "Of course you would have survived, darling," she said. "What choice is there but to survive?"

Fabula's eclectic and unique taste is amply represented at Anastasia's Attic, where you can find vintage clothing from every decade of the twentieth century, as well as occasional pieces from the eighteenth and nineteenth centuries. You'd be surprised by how popular corsets are among the witch community, though I personally don't find them very comfortable, but maybe comfort isn't the point. Until quite recently my own style, if it could even be called that, tended toward the un-obvious and the self-effacing.

It should come as no surprise that I liked being a staff of one. There's something safe and secure about dealing with the world from behind a counter; as Fabula's employee, all I had to do was maintain the systems she'd established. Fabula, on the other hand, had the exciting job of traveling the globe in search of exotic pieces—vintage Schiaparelli designs; elaborately embroidered waistcoats reputed to have once belonged to George Gordon, Lord Byron; and beads and baubles from the ruined estates of Southern belles.

Thanks to Fabula, I've spent many, many days cocooned by swaths of luxurious silks and old coats of glistening mink; stacks of tartans and robes of brocade; and cases of sparkling paste and crystal jewelry—rhinestone tiaras once worn by turn-of-the-century divas, massive amethysts set in scrolled silver, original Schlumberger enamel and gold pieces from the 1960s, cameo brooches and jet earrings from the 1890s, and strands of lustrous old pearls.

And, of course, hats are always piled high around the store—pillboxes from the 1960s, cloches from the 1920s, sequined caps from the 1970s, and tiny fur pieces with bits of net from who knows when.

Such was my life amidst the artifacts of lives past. Every morning at nine-thirty I left my apartment and walked the few blocks to the store. Harold rode regally in my bright pink backpack, eyeing the people we passed with critical curiosity and the dirty gray pigeons with disgust. Harold is a discerning feline; if he needed to hunt, he certainly wouldn't waste his time on pigeons.

Once at the store, I'd spend the day taking inventory; dusting shelves; rearranging complicated displays; chatting with customers, both witches and simply humans; and maybe, luckily, ringing up a sale. At seven each evening I closed the store, and Harold and I headed home.

Most nights we ate dinner in front of the television; Harold is a big fan of HBO. On occasion, Lia, Harold, and I would go to one of our favorite bistros for dinner. I was usually in bed by eleven.

If my life was somewhat dull, especially compared with that of my parents, it was also pleasant and, in its way, satisfying.

And then, Jared Cragmere happened.

3

Under no circumstances shall you interfere with another witch's will in matters of the heart.

Jared Cragmere, thirty-one years old at the time he relocated from the West Coast, took our city by storm. Within two weeks of his arrival he'd started a monthly magazine called *Perception*. By the publication of the second issue, *Perception* was the must-read magazine of every urban witch with an interest in politics, art, and fashion.

And if the publication was a success, its publisher was an even greater hit. Some of Jared's social success had to do with his generous personality and formidable intelligence. Most of it had to do with his astonishing good looks. Jared Cragmere is beautiful; he has the kind of beauty that will last, not burst into puffiness or collapse into cadaverous folds. Jared has structure beneath the fine surface.

Everyone was crazy about Jared. The older straight male witches, disappointed in their own average offspring who were more interested in what they wore than in what they wrought, wanted to adopt him as their son and heir.

Younger straight male witches wanted to be Jared's friend. I'm sure they hoped that some of his magnetic charm would rub off on them.

The senior gay male witches tried to buy his affections; young gay male witches were alternately jealous and adoring of his beauty.

The coven's older female witches divided into two camps concerning Jared Cragmere: one camp wanted to mother him, and the other wanted to make him their boy-toy lover.

And, of course, the young female witches among us were universally smitten. Suddenly, best friends were sworn rivals. Nothing mattered more than being the object of Jared Cragmere's affections. Twins, formerly inseparable, came to blows one night at Talisman, the club our coven operates. One swore Jared had winked at her; the other was convinced he'd winked at *her*. It turned out that Jared had winked at neither; he'd gotten a speck of dust in his eye.

Occasionally, I spotted Jared outside the confines of the coven and its stomping grounds, and I wasn't surprised to see that simply humans were as compelled by his presence as witches. People stared after him, stupefied with lust; some even followed him, but rarely did anyone actually approach him. Once I saw an elderly street person put her hand out to him; Jared held her hand a moment before giving her a folded bill.

He was beautiful and kind. And, hopefully, unaware that he was being watched by Haven Castle, witch unextraordinaire.

Being unextraordinaire, I was afraid that someone as magnetic as Jared would never notice me, particularly with a witch like Angora Slate hanging around.

Angora Slate is to the female sex what Rolls Royce is to the world of automobiles; what Chanel is to the world of fashion; what the Hope Diamond is to the world of gems. Her hair is long and light brown with natural blond highlights. Her eyes are bright blue, and her skin is an enviable, natural tan. Angora could easily have been a professional model, but I don't know that modeling would have given her anything she didn't already have—money; urban fame; and, most importantly for Angora, romance without the tediousness of a domestic commitment.

Another thing I should mention: Even more than her stunning physical beauty, Angora's biggest claim to fame was never, ever to have used magic in matters of sexual conquest. And her conquests were many. According to her own legend, Angora had taken as her lovers several members of the European royal families; a South American business tycoon and his former Miss Universe wife; two Oscar winners; innumerable politicians, of all parties; one very dashing member of the Catholic clergy; and, most shockingly, an underage protégé of the urban art world, a boy barely fifteen.

I used to wonder how all those lovers felt about Angora's familiar, a large porcupine with a nature as prickly as his physique. Aptly, if not originally, named Spike, he loathes and despises everyone except for his witch, to whom he is absurdly devoted.

But back to my story. Months passed and, amazingly, Jared seemed immune to Angora's charm. A small flame of hope reignited in my breast, a hope that I might actually be the one for the elusive Jared Cragmere . . .

And then the coven was abuzz with the news that Angora had finally slept with Jared, and I knew that any tiny chance I might have had with him was gone forever.

So, I did it. I did what I shouldn't have done, but I swear I had no idea how horribly wrong things would turn out. It was the act of a desperate woman, a woman with no belief in her own ability to attract a man as beautiful and compelling as Jared Cragmere.

I, Haven Castle, cast a love spell on Jared. It was meant to make him notice me. Instead, it made him disappear—

entirely, completely. One minute he was just yards away, selecting an apple from a fruit stand on Pinter Street, his familiar, Mercury, at his feet, and the next minute he and Mercury were gone and no one, least of all me, had any idea of where they were.

4

In times of unusual stress or persecution, it is acceptable, even advisable, to wail, howl, and tear your hair and even, on occasion, the hair of others.

Harold was sprawled on the hardwood floor of my bedroom, his green eyes just slits, watching me have yet another meltdown.

"You're not being very helpful," I snapped, which was totally unfair, because Harold was doing all he was able to do, which was to admonish and advise. It wasn't his fault that I'd ignored his warnings and gotten myself into such a mess. "I'm sorry. It's just that I'm—"

"It's all right," he said, magnanimously. "Just remember, I feel your pain."

I smiled ruefully. "I doubt it, but I appreciate the sentiment."

The fact was that by the time I got back to my apartment that dreadful day I was absolutely frantic. Was Jared Cragmere dead or alive? I'm not an expert at divination, but every witch knows one or two methods well enough to use in an emergency. This was an emergency. I reached for my set of—of course, I can't tell you any specifics of magical methods. After a few fumbling attempts, I managed to learn that Jared was still alive.

At least I hadn't killed him, and while that information comforted me, it wasn't exactly helpful.

I didn't sleep at all that first night. I could have taken a sleeping potion, but I hoped that if I just stayed alert and thought long and hard enough, by morning—at least by lunchtime—I'd have found a way to bring Jared back. Well, I thought long and I thought hard but all I came up with over and over again was the realization that I had made a serious error, one with consequences I was not prepared to handle.

Twenty-four hours after Jared and Mercury disappeared right before my eyes, I was still no closer to a solution. I felt trapped, like a poor little fox backed into a hedge by a passel of yapping dogs.

I couldn't go to my parents for help, although I knew that if anyone could find Jared and bring him back it was Howlite and Topaz Castle. See, I wasn't at all sure they would help me; in fact, I was almost certain they'd lament my incompetence and advise me to clean up my own mess. I am an embarrassment to my parents; I know they wish their only child had been someone extraordinary and not someone who fumbles even the most basic of spells.

"Stop whining about your parents," Harold commanded. "Start reading your spell books."

And so I did. For days I pored over my spell books, but I had no luck finding just the right combination of words, the perfect formula to reverse my particular spell gone wrong.

Things were bad.

For days, and then weeks, and then months I tried every way I knew to contact Fabula, but to no avail. After a while I wondered if she was deliberately hiding herself, off enjoying a romantic interlude; her affairs were many but always discreet. Finally, I concluded the reason I couldn't locate Fabula was because I lacked the talent to locate her.

I grew very afraid. See, most of the coven members suspected that Jared's disappearance was due to foul play. Witches are a vindictive, unforgiving, and begrudging lot, and ancient rivalries never really die. The famous Hatfields and McCoys have nothing on the feuding families and covens of the magical world.

How, then, would my fellow coven members react when they learned that one of their own was responsible for the disappearance of their golden son?

I knew that I should admit to having botched a simple love spell any halfway talented novice should have been able to cast successfully. Surely one of our coven members would know how to find Jared and bring him back.

But I just couldn't do it. See, the botching part wasn't the worst part of my misdeed. Within the magical world, and particularly in our somewhat self-important, terminally hip urban coven, it's just not acceptable to coerce someone into falling in love with you. A witch who casts a love spell, particularly on another witch, is just pitiful.

Hence, the magnificence of Angora Slate.

I just knew that if I confessed to having cast a spell on Jared I'd be ostracized from the coven that was the only home of sorts I'd known since leaving my parents' house.

I couldn't even bring myself to tell Lia what I'd done. I was too ashamed and anyway, what could she have done to bring Jared back?

About a week after Jared disappeared, Lia and I were having dinner at a little Italian café downtown. "So," she asked, her eye on the plastic-coated menu, "what's going on with this Jared person?"

"Nothing," I replied, feigning nonchalance, "nothing's going on at all. He, um, he moved out of the city."

Lia glanced up at me, then looked back to the menu. "I thought he moved here just a few months ago."

"Maybe he's a rolling stone." And, desperate to change the conversation, I then said, "What are you having? I've heard the pasta primavera is good."

Lia frowned and shook her head. "Not enough calories. I've lost another pound. Do you know how much money I spend at the tailor? I think I'll have the antipasti and the lasagna. And then the tiramisu and a bottle of wine and some bread."

"I didn't realize being thin was so expensive," I said.

Lia laughed. "That old expression is only half right. You can be too thin, but you can never be too rich."

"Don't you think there are some very wealthy people who feel burdened by their money?"

"Enough to give it all away?" Lia shook her head. "I'm not so sure. Hey, have you read that article in *Vanity Fair* this month, the one about the Senate scandal?"

"No," I said, glad to be so far off the topic of The Mysteriously Disappearing Jared, "I haven't."

5

Next, apply the poultice to the festering wound. At first, there will be a powerful smell of corruption. Ignore the odor, as usually it will pass in an hour or two. If, however, the odor persists for more than a day, see Disaster, Avoidance of, p. 2006, or risk the permanent loss of all sensation from the neck down.

"You never learn, do you?" Harold was perched on top of the tall armoire against the only windowless wall of the living room. He looked like an avenging angel or a grim gargoyle, some generally unpleasant creature looming menacingly over my head.

I placed several candles around the living room in preparation for the brief casting ceremony. Candles were not germane to the spell, but simply humans—even utterly prosaic ones like Lia, I assumed—expect witches to be surrounded by burning candles as they conjure and cast. Besides, I thought, maybe by enhancing the mystical atmosphere of the room my own meager magical talents would feel inspired.

"Why are you angry with me?" I said, not looking back up at Harold, though, of course, I knew the answer.

"Because you're about to act against my advice—again—and I might not know everything, but there are some things I do know, and about those things you should listen to me. It's what I'm here for, remember? At least, it's part of what I'm here for."

To advise. To admonish. To annoy.

And Harold had advised me, strongly, not to work a love spell for Lia. So, what possessed me to go ahead?

Lia is my best friend. She has done so many nice things for me; most importantly, she's kept my secret for close to ten years. Not once has she forgotten my birthday, which is more than I can say for my parents. And when I'd gotten a terrible bout of the stomach flu one winter, she'd spent an entire weekend working at the store in my place. The least I could do for her, I told myself, was help her find a date.

Lia arrived at six o'clock, exactly on time. Harold leapt from the top of the armoire, a good seven feet to the floor; his heavy landing made me jump. He then repositioned himself on the arm of an upholstered chair.

Lia looked to Harold, then turned to me with a frown. "Is something wrong with Harold?" she asked. "He looks, I don't know, sick or something."

"He's fine," I said shortly. "He's just mad because I forgot to buy frozen shrimp at the grocery store."

Harold turned his back to us then; I wondered why he just didn't leave the room.

"Because I want you to be aware of me," he said. "I am a reminder of the fact that what you are about to do is wrong and dangerous."

"So," Lia said, "I'm ready. What do we do first?"

I took a deep breath.

6

*If you follow these instructions to the letter, you should at-
tain success. However, even one minor variation can cause
irreversible disaster, in which case, remember: You have
been warned.*

"Anastasia's Attic," I said into the receiver of the black
lacquer Art Deco phone. It was shaped like a swan; the eyes
were made of rhinestones.

"It's me," replied an excited voice. "Lia."

"Hi," I said. "What's going on?"

"This is unbelievable, Haven!"

"What's unbelievable?"

"The spell! It's only been a few days and already I've got
three dates lined up for the weekend."

"That's great," I said enthusiastically. I dared to think
that after so many years I'd finally achieved some success in
witchcraft. It didn't make up for what I'd done to Jared
Cragmere—nothing would—but it gave me some hope that
someday I might find a way to rectify my grand mistake.

"By the way," Lia said, her tone suddenly more businesslike, "how long does this spell last?"

Had we really not talked about this very important aspect of the spell? "Forever," I said. Forever, I thought, was a very, very long time.

"Excellent! Look, I've got to go, but thanks again, really."

Before I could respond, Lia was gone.

I returned to folding lace handkerchiefs. Before many minutes had passed what small bit of joy I'd felt was replaced by doubt. Lia had said she wanted to get married; getting married involved choosing one man or woman over all others. But this attraction spell lasted forever; at least, that's what the spell book said.

How, I wondered, would Lia's future husband feel about his wife's inordinate popularity with the opposite sex? How would he tolerate men flocking after his bride as she made her appearance poolside at their romantic island honeymoon resort?

I folded the last handkerchief and returned the tray to a shelf in one of the low glass cases. As I did this, I noticed Harold, now resting on a large maroon velvet pillow; he looked like a pasha, satisfied, content.

"I told you," he said, "to consider all the consequences before casting the spell."

"How could I consider all the consequences?" I retorted. "How could I possibly imagine everything that might possibly happen in a possible future?"

"A spell lasting forever is a pretty obvious consequence. Do you even know what 'forever' means in this case? Does 'forever' end when Lia passes from this world, or does it continue on into the next and the next? If I were you—"

"You're not."

"But if I were, I'd start looking for a reversal spell now. Just in case."

Just in case . . .

"I need some fresh air," I told Harold. "Are you coming?"

Harold rose and stretched as only a cat can, with deliberation. "While we're out, I could use another packet of catnip."

"I just bought one last week," I said, reaching for the keys to the store.

"It's gone stale; you didn't reseal the packet properly."

I wondered: Was there anything I could do properly?

1

Remember that even the most gifted and practiced witch will, on occasion, encounter the unexpected. When this occurs, it is wise for the witch to accept the surprising turn of events and learn from it. Growth comes only from change.

"If you're not going to finish that . . ."

I reached around and handed Harold what was left of the monster chocolate chip cookie I'd bought at the bakery down the block from Anastasia's Attic.

Yes, I handed the cookie to Harold; unlike the average cat, which in almost every way he is not, Harold has extraordinary dexterity.

It was a beautiful day in late September. The air was warm and mellow; the harsh heat of summer had gone, and the bitter cold of winter was still long off. I did feel less gloomy than when Harold and I had set out from the store.

"I know you're enjoying this jaunt," Harold said, "but we should get back to the store. You're not being paid to play hooky."

"Okay, okay," I said, "but I'm taking the scenic route."

At the next corner I turned onto Pinter Street—and stopped cold.

Across the narrow street stood a mountain man. That was my first thought: A mountain man, just down from the wilds, complete with long, matted beard and a cracked leather backpack.

Something about the incongruous figure struck me as familiar. I tried not to stare; the wild man could very well have been a deranged homeless person who would fly at me, teeth bared, if he caught me eyeing him.

Harold was repulsed. "What's so fascinating?" he asked. "Move on, Haven. That—thing—is a walking plague."

I did try to move on, I did, but something made me stop after only a step and look again at the poor man.

It couldn't be. Or could it? Could this poor, wrecked soul really be—Jared?

I closed my eyes, opened them, shook my head, and took another step. But again, I stopped, then shot another look across the street. Could Jared really have returned without anyone from the coven knowing?

Maybe, I thought wildly, maybe I wasn't responsible for his disappearance after all! Maybe he'd just decided to take off, go on an adventure. Maybe he was incognito right now, just back for a brief visit, preparing to mysteriously take off again.

Of course, even as I entertained these thoughts, I knew I was fooling myself. First, I'd witnessed the moment of Jared's disappearance. Second, if the dirty, filthy mess was indeed Jared Cragmere, there was no way he was dirty and filthy on purpose. I watched as the man stuffed a hot dog loaded with all the works into his mouth as if he hadn't eaten in months, and for all I knew he hadn't, not hot dogs, anyway.

Jared Cragmere, the hot dog type? No, I thought, it couldn't be.

Suddenly, I felt Harold stiffen to attention. "It can't be . . ."

"It isn't," I said, with absolutely no conviction.

And then I saw Mercury, that stocky little pug, emerge from behind the vendor's cart, and I knew for sure that the man with the long shaggy hair and the beard down to his collarbone, the man now on his third hot dog, was Jared Cragmere, back from whatever hellish place he'd been banished to by me, Haven Castle, witch unextraordinaire.

8

In the case of exposure, do not at any cost reveal your own involvement in the aforementioned scandal. Revelation has been known to lead most rapidly to death.

"If I had taken your advice and not cast the spell for Lia, Jared wouldn't be back in the city."

Harold lowered his leg from behind his head and yawned widely. When he was once again composed, he said, "It's possible your spell brought him back, but you can't know for sure if you're the responsible party. You also don't know what else might have happened as a result of that ridiculous attraction spell. Jared's back and that's a good thing, but are you sure no one else has mysteriously disappeared?"

"Can't you let me be happy even for a moment?" I asked.

"I'm sorry," he said. "Be happy. And then, when you're done singing and dancing, you might think about what's going to happen next."

"What do you mean?"

"There's a very good chance that Jared wants to know who tossed him off the planet for a year."

"We don't know he was tossed off the planet," I said lamely.

Harold issued a feline grunt. "Does it matter where he was, exactly? He wasn't where he wanted to be, and I'm pretty sure that's all that matters to him."

We talked no more that night, but I thought seriously about what Harold had said. Jared was back and, like a wronged warrior in a martial arts movie, he might very well be looking for revenge.

For about a week I avoided the coven's hangouts. The thought of coming face to face with Jared was terrifying. How, I thought, could I look him in the eye and keep my dread secret? Wouldn't he see the guilt written all over my face?

I might have been able to avoid Jared at first, but being in the store I was privy to all sorts of rumors. Witches come to Anastasia's Attic to talk as often as they come to buy.

Within the first days of Jared's being home I heard that he was insane with rage and determined to uncover the person who'd sent him off to a place I now knew was located in one of the millions of universes alternate to ours.

I heard that he had lost a dangerous amount of weight, and that his closest friend, Axel, wanted to check him into a hospital. I heard that he'd gone over the edge, that he had a nervous breakdown of the first order, and that when he opened his mouth all that came out was angry gibberish.

I heard that he'd caught some dread disease from the alien people he'd been dumped upon, and that it had affected his central nervous system so that at random moments he was subject to strange fits of spastic flailing.

Well, regardless of whether I was ready, I was about to learn the truth about Jared Cragmere for myself.

It was a Thursday. Business had been slow that morning; I'd sold only one item, a tortoiseshell hair comb, to an ancient witch with a penchant for Victorian accessories. At noon I closed the store, as was my habit, and headed for the café where I ate lunch regularly. Café Kendra is small and unassuming and patronized mostly by simply humans. It was the last place I expected to run into Jared Cragmere, darling of the witchy world.

I'd gotten my sandwich and settled at a tiny table in the corner when—

"Haven?"

And there he stood, only feet away, Jared Cragmere, the man I adored, the man I had tortured.

His golden brown hair, the color of a lion's coat, once again framed his beautiful, chiseled face. The beard was gone. His eyes, an unusual pale green, were bright and clear. Gone, too, were the filthy rags. Instead, he wore a dark brown leather blazer, jeans, and a funky print shirt open at the neck; hair slightly darker than the hair of his head grew at the base of his throat. I was overcome with desire. Jared certainly wasn't dying of malnutrition; in fact, he looked even fitter than when he'd first come to the city a year before.

Harold shifted noisily on my lap. "Did he have to bring that—thing—back with him?"

"Harold," I said impatiently, "please." Mercury, standing at Jared's feet, looked up at me with his liquid brown eyes. "Does Mercury know? Does he know I—"

Harold poked one long nail into my thigh. "He might pick up on something if you don't keep your 'mouth' shut. Stick to happy thoughts, Haven. At least until we get out of here."

Jared took a step closer.

"Haven Castle?"

I opened my mouth but nothing came out.

"It's Jared, Jared Cragmere. Remember me?"

How could Jared have thought that I—that anyone!—had forgotten him?

"Of course," I said. My voice was a little too high, as if I were deprived of oxygen. "Of course I remember you. Hi. I heard you were back. Congratulations. I mean, I'm glad."

Jared laughed. His teeth were very straight. "That makes two of us! So, can I share your table?"

"Oh," I said, "sure." Sharing a meal with Jared Cragmere. Was it possible to accomplish such a thing without tearing at his clothes? Without imagining my lips pressed against his stomach? Without—

"Haven!"

I took a steadying breath. Harold settled more firmly in my lap as if to hold me in place.

Meanwhile, Jared had seated himself at the table and twisted open a bottle of water. It was as if nothing terrible had happened to him, as if everything was perfectly fine.

"Was it very awful?" I whispered.

Jared laughed again. It didn't seem the laugh of someone who had gone insane under the pressure of torture or other abominations.

"No, it wasn't awful at all. I mean, not in the way most people mean when they ask me that question. I wasn't poked with pointy sticks or deprived of food, though I've got to say, and no disrespect to the Hebetatians, their cuisine is pretty foul. You know the first thing I did when I got home?"

I thought back to the wild man at the hot dog cart and shook my head.

"I got a large pepperoni pizza and sat there in the store and ate the whole thing in about three minutes flat. I'm a hero in Tony's, you know. Free soda refills any time I come in."

"You're teasing me," I said.

"Nope, you can go ask Tony right now. From pizza I moved on to hot dogs and beer. Thankfully, I'm over the junk food jones."

As Jared took a large bite of his roasted vegetable sandwich, I thought about all the things that had happened in the past year. I thought of Jared's own birthday—had he been alone on that special day?—and of the movies that had opened, and the songs that had first been sung. I thought about the wonderful April we'd had, the air sweet and warm, and then about the spectacular ice storm that had hit the city in late January, virtually shutting it down for two days and suspending all of us in a sort of romantic wonderland.

"You missed so much," I said, and tears pricked my eyes.

"Did I?" Jared put down what was left of his lunch and wiped his hands. "I've been reading the papers from the past year, trying to catch up, and mostly it just seems like more of the same. Maybe our world's a bit more ugly than it was when I left, but so far I haven't found anything all that shocking." Jared laughed, and now it sounded a bit sad. "What does that say about me?"

That he'd lost all hope as a result of his banishment from home? That he now saw the world as a cruel and unfair place?

"That you've become a pessimist?"

"Nah." Jared smiled again, a smile more powerful than my parents' magic. "Just a realist. Love is as real as hate. I acknowledge both. You're not eating your sandwich."

I'd completely forgotten the sandwich, and now I was embarrassed to eat with Jared watching me. What if a piece of lettuce got stuck in my teeth? What if the tomato slid out of the sandwich and onto Harold's back?

"Oh," I said, "I'm not really hungry right now. I think I'll take it back to the store for later."

"I'll have it wrapped up for you." Jared was out of his

seat and carrying the sandwich to the counter; I watched as the server wrapped it in cellophane and dropped it into a paper bag.

"You're acting like a high school ninny."

"Thank you," I told Harold. "I know."

Jared was back; he handed me the paper bag but remained standing.

"I should be going," he said.

"Me, too." But I stayed seated; I suddenly felt as awkward about walking out of the café with Jared as I had felt about eating my lunch in his presence. What if I tripped? What if I fell?

"Would you like to have dinner with me tomorrow?"

It was absolutely the last thing I expected to hear from Jared.

Was his invitation a cruel joke? Was it a clever way to humiliate me? I'd say, "I'd love to have dinner with you," and Jared would say, "Do you really think I'd ask you out after you screwed up my life for a year? You're more stupid than I thought."

"Harold?" I said.

"Ah, now she wants my advice . . ."

"Just tell me. Is he being sincere?"

"I believe so. For some strange reason he's attracted to you."

"Remember who feeds you," I said testily.

"Do you really doubt my ability to open the cabinet below the microwave and pop open a can of Fancy Feast?"

I looked down at my familiar's large, placid, intelligent face and didn't doubt his ability to do anything he was determined to do. Why, I wondered, couldn't I be more like my cat?

"Okay," I squeaked, and Jared smiled.

"Great." Then he looked at me, really looked, and I wondered, nervously, what he saw. "You know," he said, finally, "you have a beautiful face. There's something—something poetic about it. You look like a woman from a beautiful poem. Or a woman from a Pre-Raphaelite painting, something by Millais or Rossetti."

"It's the red hair," I said, embarrassed by his rapt attention.

"It's more than that. There's a quality about you." Then Jared shrugged and smiled almost shyly. "Well, I'm not a poet or a painter, so I'd better stop talking before I totally embarrass myself."

I blushed, I know I did; I could feel my cheeks grow warm. "You haven't—I mean, you're not—"

"Now I've embarrassed you. I guess it's time for me to go. So, tomorrow, eight o'clock?"

I nodded; I didn't trust myself to speak. Jared scooped Mercury from the floor; at the door of the café, he turned and gave a little wave. And I fell in love all over again.

9

Should there be an excess of the Newtlize potion, be sure to safely dispose of it (see Hazardous Potions, Disposal of, page 3008), or risk utter destruction of your life and abode, as after a period of roughly twenty-four hours said Newtlize potion will spontaneously combust.

"Haven, I feel like a movie star!"

"Oh," I said.

"My life has become a madcap whirl of gorgeous men, fantastic dates, and expensive gifts. Why, just the other night this guy gave me an Hermes scarf to die for!"

It was later that mind-bending day when Jared Cragmere had asked me to have dinner with him.

"What guy?" I asked Lia, though already there had been too many men for me to keep track of.

Lia laughed. "Oh, I don't remember his name. Actually, I'm not sure I ever knew it. It doesn't matter. I'm not seeing him again. I didn't like his haircut."

This was my down-to-earth best friend talking? The woman who until a few days earlier would have disdained even the notion of a madcap whirl as wasteful and self-indulgent?

What, I wondered, had I created? I'd transformed my sensible, levelheaded friend into a club-hopping, men-trashing, air-headed party girl!

"So," I said, "are you happy?"

"Happy?" Lia laughed again. "Haven, I'm ecstatic! I've never had such a good time in my life! So, what's going on with you?"

I wondered if I should tell Lia about my impending date with Jared. She'd be happy for me, of course, but she wouldn't understand the whole story, how I both looked forward to and dreaded the date. I wished then that I had told Lia the truth about Jared's disappearance, but here's the odd thing: The longer I held the secret, the harder it became to let it go. It had become so much a part of who I was, I was terrified of life without it.

"Just tell her and get some of this guilt off your conscience."

I looked down at Harold; his eyes held mine. I finally looked away.

"Not now," I said, "it's not the right time."

Harold stood and stretched mightily. "Suit yourself. I'm off for a nap."

"Oh, nothing," I lied to Lia, as Harold headed for the bedroom. "Just the usual, work, a few movies."

"You know, Haven, I'm meeting so many guys now I'm sure I could introduce you to someone nice."

"That's okay," I said, mustering a tone of nonchalance. "I mean, I'm kind of fine on my own for now."

"Is it the witch thing?" Lia asked. "Are you more comfortable dating witches? You know, it's strange, but we never really talked about that."

"Actually," I said, "it is the witch thing. When I'm ready to date again I'll find someone through the coven. But thanks for the offer, really. Look, I should go. I've . . . I'm going out to catch a film."

Another lie.

Lia said good-bye. I imagined her turning to her mirror to apply a final slick of lipstick before Bachelor #57 appeared at her door.

Later, I crawled into bed and thought about the look on Jared's face when he'd asked me out, and then about the things he'd said about me, so romantic and so charmingly sincere. There wasn't a dishonest bone in Jared's body; he was so good-hearted he couldn't even see the guilt emanating from my own corrupt person.

And I was going on a date with this paragon.

10

Should it be impossible to lay your hands upon Extract of Fenwick, Extract of Baywick may be substituted, keeping in mind that the results of such an altered concoction could possibly result in permanent blindness.

"I have absolutely no fashion sense! Harold, help me!"

I stared down at the blouses and skirts and pants strewn about the bed, components of a larger, finished picture I just couldn't envision.

"What can I do?" Harold replied. "I don't know anything about putting together an outfit."

I had to smile. "I forgot. You're naturally well dressed."

"I am couture. But let's talk about something else for a minute." As if to emphasize the change in topic, Harold leapt off the floor and landed in the center of the bed, right on top of the nicest blouse I owned. "Let's talk about this date."

"I don't want to talk about it," I protested, "not in the way you mean."

"Haven," Harold said, his tail swishing mightily, "I must

insist you face this. Do you really want to get close to the man who has every reason to hate you? You've heard what the coven's been saying. Jared wants to know what happened to him last year. He's a powerful witch and he's got some powerful friends. At some point he's going to discover you're the guilty party."

I looked down at Harold's massive paws and wondered if his nails were tearing my blouse. "I'll be careful," I mumbled. But was going out with Jared being careful? Or was it delivering myself into the hands of the very person who could destroy me and what little magical reputation I had?

Maybe, I thought, I deserved to be exposed and publicly humiliated and—

"You should tell him right out," Harold interrupted. "It will go better for you in the end."

"Maybe," I said, grabbing a pink T-shirt off the bed, "I'll wear this tonight."

"Ah, so it's true what they say that 'denial is not just a river in Egypt.'" Harold stalked to the edge of the bed and leapt to the floor. "I'll be in the living room, napping."

I tossed the pink T-shirt back onto the bed with a sigh. Deep down I knew Harold was right, but the notion of confessing was more than appalling—it was impossible.

As impossible as canceling my date with Jared Cragmere.

"So," I asked, "will you be starting up the magazine again?"

We sat at a corner table in a tiny bistro called Mauve. The place was dimly lit and rustic; the food was delicious. All evening I'd been careful to avoid the subject of Jared's banishment; I dared to hope he might not mention it, either.

Absurd. All subjects would lead to the lost year. How could they not?

"I already have." Jared's face grew animated; his pale green eyes were like jewels in the candlelight. "Luckily, the financing is still available, and I was able to get back three of the writers I'd hired last year. There are some glitches, but, in general, people were excited about the project when we started and they're excited about it now. I feel very fortunate."

"I'm so glad," I said, "that your life is getting back to normal. I mean, to the way it was before you—"

"It's getting back to normal, sure, but it will never be the same as it was before I—"

"Went away."

"Was sent away," Jared corrected. He leaned in toward me, across the table. "Haven, I want to know who's responsible. And I want to know why he did it. It's just not in me to let it go, not yet, anyway."

"Oh," I said, feebly. I felt Harold shift at my feet. "But what if there is no good reason? I mean, what if whoever banished you did it by accident . . .?"

The sudden look of determination on Jared's face cut me off. "Even so," he said, "someone cast a spell on me for some reason, even if it wasn't to banish me from this world. I want to know why I was his target in the first place. I don't like being used. I don't like being a victim."

I, I thought, *am a victimizer.* I felt as if I would pass out right at the table. Harold put a steadying paw on my leg, but I couldn't hide my agitation.

"Hey," Jared said. He took my hand, genuine concern in his pale green eyes. "Are you okay? I'm sorry. Is talking about this upsetting you?"

His hand on mine was cool and comforting. I noticed, not for the first time, how beautiful his hands were, so fine and yet powerful. "A little," I whispered. "I just feel so bad about what happened to you."

"I appreciate your sympathy, Haven, I do. But you have nothing to feel bad about." Jared squeezed my hand gently. "You didn't banish me to the land of bad food and reeking fens! Try not to let it worry you, okay?"

I nodded; it was less of a lie than my saying, "Okay, I won't worry."

After dinner, Jared walked me home. At the door to my building he kissed me very lightly on the lips and asked if he could see me again. The kiss sealed my fate; of course, I said yes. When I got upstairs to my apartment I peeked out the bedroom window. Jared was there, looking up at me. He waved, then walked off into the dark, Mercury trotting at his heels.

I turned to Harold; he sat upright in the center of the bed.

"I'm going to try to contact Fabula again," I said.

"Why? What can she possibly do for you now?"

"I don't know," I admitted, "but I need help."

Harold yawned. Then he said, "I feel I should remind you that the only person who can help you now is you."

Harold curled into a massive ball and was asleep immediately. I went into the living room and reached out to my friend.

But once again, Fabula did not come.

11

Should you become aware of the fact that you are suspected of an unholy alliance, by all means, do not waste time attempting to deny such an alliance. Simply keep your mouth shut and run.

"So, where did he go for an entire year?"

"Oh," I said, wondering why I hadn't thought through my lie. "He went . . . back home. There was some family stuff he needed to take care of."

Lia and I were having brunch at a popular spot called Jaune. A few weeks had gone by since my first date with Jared. I'd finally decided to tell her about him, at least about our present if not about our past.

"Did someone die?" Lia asked.

Harold made an unpleasant sound in his throat. "Ah, the tangled web we weave . . ."

"Um, no," I said. "Anyway, enough about me, nothing's really happened yet with Jared. What about you? What's going on?"

Lia checked her watch; it was one I hadn't seen on her

before. "What's going on is I have to leave. I'm sorry, Haven. I'm meeting Larry—have I mentioned him?—at some gallery. He wants to buy me a painting. He says he knows art, which is a good thing, because I certainly don't."

"New watch?" I asked.

Lia tossed a few bills on the table. "Yeah, it was a gift. It's not really my style, but since it is a Rolex I figured I'd wear it a bit before selling it. Even a gently used Rolex can fetch a good price."

"Oh," I said. Again, I wondered what exactly I had wrought by casting the attraction spell for my friend. At the very least, I had created someone who was almost a stranger.

After Lia had gone off to meet the latest in a string of enthralled men, I sat alone at the table with Harold and a Bloody Mary and thought back over the past weeks.

Since running into each other at Café Kendra, Jared and I had seen each other almost every day. We took walks along the river and through the park; we visited museums and galleries. He showed me his downtown loft, where he both lived and worked. I brought him to Anastasia's Attic. We had dinner one night with his friend, Axel, a lanky, hyper, jovial member of the coven I'd known only by sight. Axel seemed to approve of Jared's choice in girlfriends; the next day he sent me a dozen spelled tulip buds. I don't know where he found tulips in late September, but then again, witches have their ways. Each hour on the hour one of the buds opened and erupted in tinkling song.

As for our familiars, Jared's and mine, well, Mercury and Harold, while not the best of friends, had come to tolerate each other's company. I gave Mercury a flea bath; Harold deigned to let Jared brush him.

In the third week of our relationship Jared stayed over at my apartment for the first time. I'd thought I was in love before sleeping with Jared; I never dreamed that I could be so much more in love after.

That first night together, after I'd felt so many things I'd never felt before, I stayed awake to watch Jared sleep. My beautiful Jared—his long lashes against his cheek, the beginnings of a dark gold beard along his slightly hollowed cheek and square jaw, his perfect ears. How, I thought, could someone so beautiful want me—someone so average, so plain?

He looked like a young boy; he looked like an old soul. He looked like someone I could only dream of touching, of loving, like an angel; but there he was, in my bed, my worn cotton sheet draped across his waist, his naked shoulders, straight and strong but somehow also delicate.

It was almost unbearable. I'd never been so full of desire in my life, not ever, as I was at that moment, watching Jared sleep. So full of desire and love and a fierce urge to protect this man at all costs from whatever or whomever tried to harm him.

To protect him from someone—like me.

I lay back down and closed my eyes. Jared's breathing immediately quickened, as if he were dreaming about something bad, as if he sensed danger was near. I placed my hand lightly on his chest. I felt his heart. His breathing slowed, and we slept.

"Haven?"

Harold was sitting in Lia's abandoned chair, staring at me from across the table.

"Oh," I said. The memories of that first night had left me feeling unsettled, both excited and afraid. "Sorry, I was just day dreaming."

"The waiter's been hovering like a buzzard. I think it's time we paid the check. And don't overtip. Did you catch the look of annoyance when you asked him for a bowl of cream? Cretin."

"Okay," I said, reaching into the depths of my bag for my wallet, "I'll be reasonable."

12

If upon administration of the brew the subject experiences the rapid and painful eruption of burning boils, followed closely by vigorous projectile vomiting, it would be wise to arrange for clandestine disposal of the corpse, as said subject will soon cease to live.

"Aren't you glad we stayed in the city instead of driving upstate to pick apples?"

Jared and I walked hand in hand along the park. He wore a long wool scarf wound loosely around his neck; old black, lace-up boots under worn jeans; and a black wool pea coat. He was, to my infatuated eyes, a combination of soulful rock star, suffering nineteenth century writer, and swashbuckling hero—everything romantic a man could possibly be.

"I am glad," I said. How could I not be? It's hard to feel sad or worried when the sky is a brilliant blue and you're in love with someone whose presence makes you shiver with delight and whose absence makes you tingle with anticipation.

"Eat, drink, and be merry, for tomorrow you die. I may not be quoting exactly, but I'm sure you get my point."

"Thanks," I told Harold, "I think I will be merry."

The poets, I discovered in those early days of my relationship with Jared, are right. The first flush of love is powerful enough to vanquish all hesitation—at least, to mask it.

"Ah," Harold noted, "look who we're about to encounter, Boswell Van Der Minter in all his sartorial glory."

"Oh," I said. Except for Axel, no one in the coven knew Jared and I were seeing each other. At least, I didn't think anyone knew. Did it matter?

"Bosie!" Jared called out, with a jaunty wave.

Boswell Van Der Minter is a dandy; he is dapper and dashing, natty and neat. I've always liked Boswell, even though he's terribly affected, because he succeeds in being great fun without actually being mean.

That particular day Boswell wore a perfectly tailored suit, a suit Fabula would call bespoke. His silk tie was anchored to his crisp cotton shirt with a gold pin. French cuffs, polished wingtips, and, of course, a flourishing pocket square were all meant to be noted and admired, as was Boswell's familiar, a sleek white ferret named Oscar. Oscar was curled around his witch's neck; that day he sported a collar of coral and green turquoise. Oscar is as affected but as lovable as his witch.

After sharing pleasant greetings, Boswell eyed me with obvious appreciation. "You, my girl, are adorable. I don't know why I've never noticed you before, not really."

I smiled awkwardly.

Boswell looked to Jared with as much if not more appreciation than he had shown me; finally, he looked back.

"Ah," he said, his eyebrows rising to astounding heights, "I think I see now . . . a transformation, an awakening, a blossoming, yes . . ."

Jared laughed. "You're a regular poet, Boswell."

Boswell bowed, ever so correctly. "My dears," he said, "it was lovely running into you, but I must be off." He offered us each his begloved hand for a teeny shake of his fingertips before mincing off, handling his cane much in the manner of Hercule Poirot.

"It's official," Jared said.

I looked away from Boswell's retreating figure. "What's official?"

"That we're a couple."

"Why?"

"Because," Jared explained, "Bosie is the biggest gossip of the century. Trust me, by five this afternoon every witch on the entire eastern seaboard will know that you and I are together."

As I stood there, trying to absorb this interesting news, two women in their mid-twenties, dressed in the height of urban fashion, crossed from the other side of the street. If it wasn't clear why the chicken crossed the road, it was perfectly clear why these women crossed—to get a closer look at my boyfriend. They stopped, they stared, they devoured Jared; there was nothing at all subtle about their naked, voracious interest. Were they wondering: What is that gorgeous man doing with that bland little nothing?

Finally, finally, the women moved on. I dropped my gaze to the dirty gray concrete; I felt ill. There's something macabre and also something brittle about autumn. Things are breaking apart, falling away; things are dying. If you breathe deeply enough, you will smell the rot.

"Haven?"

I looked up again; nothing in Jared's face told me he'd even noticed the two women. Somehow I found the nerve to say, "Is it okay that people know we're a couple?"

"It's okay with me. How do you feel about us?"

"It's only been a few weeks," I said, thinking to give

Jared an excuse to slow things down. "Everything's happened so fast. Are you sure . . . ?"

"I'm sure," he said, and his eyes held mine. "It feels right."

I breathed, then laughed; we hugged tight. "It does, doesn't it," I said into his neck.

Later that afternoon we stopped for coffee at Café Kendra. Mercury settled on Jared's right shoe and was asleep almost immediately. Harold, however, had noticed a sprite-like tortoiseshell feline at a far table and was dedicatedly trying to make her notice him by puffing himself to an outrageous size.

Jared handed me a piece of the brownie he'd bought. "So, Haven Castle," he said, "tell me about yourself."

"There's not much to tell," I demurred.

"I don't believe that. Come on, tell me about when you were a little girl."

Harold was not so taken with the tortoiseshell that he failed to offer a bit of advice. "He's bound to find out some time. At least don't keep this a secret."

Love, I suppose, had given me some small measure of courage, because I said, "My childhood was sort of unusual. See, my parents, well, they're sort of famous—"

Jared nodded.

"My parents," I went on, with determination, "are Howlite and Topaz Castle."

Jared sat back, almost as if he'd been pushed. "Wow. I don't know why I didn't put it together before now . . ."

I knew why: Because no one associated the lackluster daughter with the spectacular parents.

Suddenly, a memory of fifth grade flashed in my mind. One of the most popular girls in my witches-only school invited herself to my house after school one day. I'd thought

Dinora wanted to spend time with me; it didn't take long to figure out that all Dinora wanted was to play with my extensive collection of magical, antique dolls.

One bitter memory followed another. I was fifteen; Marco was sixteen. He came over for dinner one night but spent more time leering at my mother (who savored the adolescent attention) and sampling cigars with my father (who was happy to find such a devoted student) than he did even speaking with me.

"Haven?" Jared was looking at me with concern. "Are you okay? You sort of spaced for a minute."

"I'm fine," I said. "Look, you should know the truth about my parents. They're incredibly talented and incredibly charismatic. They're also incredibly selfish and cold-hearted. I'm not anything like them."

Jared grinned. "I believe you, except for the incredibly talented part."

I shook my head; I wanted Jared to understand that about me. "No, I'm not half as talented as my parents. It's okay. I've accepted my limits."

Jared took my hand and kissed it. "Well," he said, "I'll let the subject go for now. But you should know I'll take generous and warm-hearted over talented any day."

I thought I would cry. I don't think I'd ever felt so happy, so loved.

"Good girl," Harold said roundly. "You were brave, and you trusted him. Now, if only you could—"

"Not now, Harold, please," I begged. "Let me have this moment."

Because, I thought, any moment could be our last.

13

The wisest counsel this writer can give the young and inex-perienced witch is this: Trust no one, not even yourself.

They say there is no perfect crime. Any witch with half a brain will tell you that there's no perfect magic, either.

Magic leaves a trail. Every spell or incantation is trace-able, if not back to the witch herself than to her school of training or her general location—East or West Coast, America or Europe, Asia or Africa. Just as energy never dies and every action ever taken is still causing reactions some-where, somehow, so the wispy, phantom trail of even the most amazing magical act survives for an extraordinary witch to discover.

Jared, by anyone's account, is an extraordinary witch. If anyone could follow the accidental, possibly miniscule clues my spell had left behind, he could. Besides, it wasn't as if he were dealing with a master witch, someone skilled in cover-ing her trail. He was dealing with me. The fatally untal-ented witch who was falling deeper and deeper in love each day.

* * *

We were at Jared's loft one evening after dinner. While he made cappuccinos with a gorgeous espresso machine, I walked through the loft and noted every CD, every photograph, every book. I needed to know everything about Jared; every detail, no matter how small, was of enormous importance.

"Ready." Jared emerged from the kitchen and placed two steaming cups of cappuccino on a small table in front of the couch.

"What's this?" I asked. A tiny ceramic toadstool sat on a shelf next to a battered copy of Kenneth Patchen's poems. It was an odd little piece, charming and a bit grotesque.

Jared laughed. "Something I found in the garden when I was maybe five. I don't know where it came from. Amazing it survived all these years."

I smiled at the image of a five-year-old Jared playing in the dirt of a garden.

"Tell me about your childhood," I requested.

Jared took my hand, and we settled on the sleek leather couch. Harold, having adopted a particular armchair as his own, was asleep in its green velvet depths. Mercury lay on the rug with his head on his paws.

Jared handed me a cup of cappuccino. "I was happy," he said simply. "While my childhood lasted, I was happy."

"While it lasted?"

Jared told me his story. He was born in England to parents of an old, old family of witches and was cherished as an only child born late in a marriage often is.

"I don't recall many details," he said, "just an overall feeling of security and contentment. I suspect my early years were idyllic, right out of a storybook."

But, he told me, the idyll ended abruptly when he was nine and his parents were killed in a car crash. What little money they had went to bury them. For a while Jared lived with his maternal grandfather, and then he, too, died unexpectedly.

"I'm so sorry, Jared," I said, laying my hand on his.

"It's okay." Jared grinned. "I'm tougher than I look. I was twelve when Granddad died and determined not to be dumped in an institution. So, I 'disappeared' from the official radar. I guess you could say I dropped out. For the next few years I made my way across England and Ireland, even got to Wales for a bit."

I sat back, stunned. What courage it must have taken to strike out on his own at the age of twelve; what self-confidence and, also, what trust in the world not to be an entirely abusive place. Maybe Jared's early experiences on his own helped him survive the year he spent with the Hebetatians. I hoped so.

"But what about school?" I said. "What about food and shelter, the basics?"

Jared shrugged. "There were some lean times, but I survived. I met a lot of great witches, people who were willing to put me up for a while in exchange for work, people who were happy to teach me. Looking back, I think I got a far better education on the road than a lot of people I know who spent years in a classroom."

"So," I said, "how did you wind up here, in the States?"

Jared took my empty cup and placed it on the small table. "On a whim, really," he said. "I was eighteen, maybe nineteen, I don't remember. It was a crazy time in my life, very exciting and very frightening."

"But you have no trace of an accent," I said.

"Only when I go home, back to England." Jared smiled. "You'll come with me someday. You'll love it."

I will love it, I thought. I'll love it because it's Jared's home, and I can't help but love everything associated with him.

Then we went to bed and made love. Afterward, while

Jared slept deeply beside me, I watched him and thought about us. We were both, in a way, orphans—Jared literally, and me emotionally. We'd both been on our own for a long, long time. Maybe that was part of what had drawn us together. Maybe we'd recognized each other's essential loneliness.

I remember that just before falling asleep I decided it didn't really matter why we'd come together, just that we had.

I was so happy in those early days. So very, very happy.

14

Under no circumstance is it permissible to take what isn't rightfully yours. Except, of course, when it is truly necessary.

And then, things began to change.

It didn't matter where we were or what we were doing—walking hand in hand along a busy street, or alone together in bed; having coffee with Axel and his familiar, a whippet named Wagner; or watching the stars from the roof of Jared's loft—suddenly, without warning, guilt would stab me like a murderer with a knife.

I was Jared's lover, but I was also his enemy. I was his girlfriend, but I was also a trickster and a fraud.

Not surprisingly I began to suffer the classic symptoms of anxiety—shortness of breath, panic attacks, loss of appetite. I kept these symptoms from Jared.

"You can't hide the anxiety from me."

It was a dark, raw day in October. I'd closed the store early; not one person had come by and suddenly, a place crammed with artifacts of lives already lived out seemed just too depressing. Now, Harold and I were at home. I'd brewed a tea purported to soothe dark spirits, but its powerful herbal flavor made me feel nauseous, so I'd tossed the murky liquid down the kitchen sink.

I stood, arms folded, at the living room window; the view was bleak, bleached of most color.

"I know," I said, "I'm a wreck. I mean, I'm in love and it's wonderful, but I feel like—"

"No need to explain. Frankly, I don't know how you've stood it this long."

I laughed bitterly. "It's better to be with him and suffering than to be without him and suffering. I know, I'm being terribly selfish."

Harold leapt onto the windowsill.

"Yes, you are," he said, "but it's understandable. Love is selfish; a lover only thinks of his beloved's needs after his own have been met. Humans and witches pretend love is kind but it's not, not without a lot of effort."

A skinny pigeon, its feathers dark and oily, landed on a fire escape on the old red brick building across the street. Just beyond the building's roof rose a billboard ad for designer underwear.

"That sounds so sad," I said.

"It is. But there's no point in arguing the facts of human and witchy nature." Harold's impressive whiskers twitched, as if he'd sensed something unpleasant in the air. "All in all, being a feline, even a magical one, is far easier."

"Tell me something, Harold."

"If I can."

"Do you and Mercury talk about us? About Jared and me?"

"If by 'talk about' you mean do we discuss the nature of your relationship as witnessed by us? Then, no, we don't talk about you. I am, as always, the epitome of discretion. And, to give that dog his due, so is he."

"It must be hard on you," I said, "keeping my secret."

Harold hesitated a moment before answering. "It's not easy. It's not pleasant. But it's becoming second nature."

I was a liar, and I'd made a liar of Harold.

"Sometimes," I said, watching the skinny old pigeon flap away in the leaden sky, "I hate myself."

"Why would you want to do that? There are plenty of people in this world who are ready to hate you just given the chance."

I laughed, but I wasn't really amused. "So, what you're saying is that if I don't love myself, nobody will?"

"Something like that." Harold looked out the window at the almost colorless urban landscape; his expression was unreadable.

"Harold?" I said after a while. "Do you remember the day we first met?"

"Of course," he replied. "You were wearing a floppy turtleneck tucked into high-waist jeans. It was an unfortunate sartorial choice."

"And you told me that you'd require a bowl of cream every evening, and regular brushing, and never to have to set foot in the suburbs."

Harold looked back to me. "And you've kept your word. And, I might add, your sense of style, though not fully developed, has improved. Why reminisce?"

"Do you ever," I said, "regret being stuck with me? It could be years and years more and—"

Harold laid one giant furry paw on my arm.

"Look," he said, "this conversation has taken a turn too grim for a sunny autumn day."

"It's a cloudy autumn day. It's starting to rain."

"Let's do something fun."

"Like what?" I asked glumly.

"Like . . ." Harold pretended to contemplate; of course, we both knew what he would suggest. "Let's take a walk to the fish market. You can buy me some big, fat shrimp. The air will do you good."

"I'll get my coat," I said.

15

It is a sad yet undeniable truth that in this world there exist those witches who draw great pleasure from the unhappiness and discomfort of others. When you encounter such a witch, and during the course of your lifetime you inevitably will, it is best to harden your spirit against him, or her, as the case may be. If ignoring the miserable being is not a viable option, you may then consider resorting to a course of cruel and systematic revenge.

"Don't look now, but we're being invaded."

I looked up from the large vellum account book opened on the counter. There they were, on the sidewalk just outside the store, the two most abominable witches in the city. I looked in panic to Harold.

"Is it too late to hide?"

"They've seen us. We'll have to make the best of it." Harold leapt to the top of a tall armoire; for cats, height is advantage. I stayed behind the counter, though no construction of mere wood and glass could protect me from *them*—

Inclementia and Temepstina, their poor, sad familiars in tow.

For a moment I studied the witches. Though I'd known them for years, their appearance still had the power to awe.

Inclementia Animoso was known as much for her absurdly long nails as she was for her absurdly nasty personality. The nails, which she swore were her own, were filed into points; these ten miniature rapiers were painted black and encrusted with what Inclementia claimed were precious gems. Harold had always maintained that the nails were as fake as the so-called gems; he pointed out that any large pharmacy carried all the supplies any woman could want for recreating Inclementia's fingertips—as if any woman in her right mind would want to.

Inclementia's familiar, a goat named Formosa, bore signs of her witch's nastiness; every time I saw Formosa there was a new scratch right down her nose. I could only hope that Formosa got her revenge when her witch was asleep, maybe by chomping on the upholstery.

If Inclementia had her signature nails, then Tempestina LaFrock had her trademark hair. She was quite vain about it, which, in addition to being abundant, was an unbecoming shade of silver. Tempestina wore her "crowning glory" in an elaborate updo, which, for certain social occasions, had been known to rise two full feet off her scalp.

Her familiar, a bright green parrot named Tom, had been known to retreat into his witch's updos for naps when the hour had grown late and Tempestina showed no sign of leaving the party. Rumor had it that Tom, exhausted by years of his witch's casual abuse, had taken to—er, defecating—in her coiffure. Harold swore he had it on good authority that this was true.

And now, these horrid creatures were standing right in front of me, mischief written all over their painted faces.

As if suspecting the unpleasantness that was to come,

Formosa swiftly took refuge behind a bin of velvet scraps. Tom flapped awkwardly, trying to extricate his talons from his witch's knotted hair, and when free, took off for the top branch of a coat rack.

Inclementia grinned; the papery skin around her eyes gathered into thousands of tiny wrinkles. "Dear Haven," she said, "have you gained weight? Your face looks positively fat."

Here's what I should have replied: "No, dear Inclementia, I haven't gained weight. Maybe your eyesight is failing. You know, you are getting up there in age."

Instead, I stood like a stone, fat cheeks burning.

"If you don't throw her out right now," Harold warned, "I am going to hiss in her pointy little rat face, no insult to my rat friends. And then I am going to spit in it. I might not be a llama, but I assure you, I can spit like the best of those smelly creatures."

"Don't!" I cried, but in my dismay I said the word aloud, for other witch ears to hear.

Inclementia raised her artfully drawn eyebrows. "Don't what, my dear?"

"Don't," I repeated, "ah . . . don't miss the beaded purses. They're from Germany."

Inclementia ignored my advice; instead, she turned to her cohort and laid a spidery hand on her arm. "So," she said, with an air of studied nonchalance, "when dear Howlite and Topaz are in town, we must have them over for a cocktail."

Both witches, as if on cue, looked slyly up at me. Oh, how they must have enjoyed the involuntary look of surprise on my face!

"But, surely, dear Haven," Tempestina said, her voice ripe with insincerity, "you know they're coming to the city. After all, you are their daughter and heir to the considerable Castle fame and, I daresay, fortune."

There was no point in pretending; there hadn't been for years. "My parents and I," I said, "are not close."

Tempestina looked to Inclementia. Cruelty buzzed between them as obviously as electricity in a cartoon.

"Ah," Tempestina said finally, "we understand."

No, I thought, you smug, horrible things, you don't understand. You don't understand a thing about me.

"Well," Inclementia said suddenly, tossing a silk scarf back into the bin from where she'd dragged it, "there's nothing here I want after all. Really, Haven, when is Fabula going to bring in some interesting new pieces. Everything in this place is so tired."

The implication was clear.

With a deliberate and destructive flourish—Tempestina knocked over a coat rack loaded with heavy wool capes—the two witches left Anastasia's Attic. Reluctantly, at least it seemed so to me, Formosa and Tom followed. I dashed from behind the counter and locked the door after them.

"Those two," Harold said darkly, "are a bad lot. They deserve each other. I wouldn't put it past them to—"

"Okay, okay!" I cried. Harold leapt down from the armoire. I collapsed onto a velvet ottoman. "You don't think . . . Oh, Harold, I can hardly say it!"

"You think your parents know you're the one responsible for banishing Jared and they're coming to denounce you to the coven."

I nodded. Harold rubbed against my leg, my ally.

"I wouldn't put it past them," he said. "They're morally bankrupt and they have absolutely no loyalty except to each other. But I just don't see what would be in it for them. Howlite and Topaz Castle never do anything unless there's a big payoff. Betraying their one and only daughter to her coven . . . Well, some might applaud their devotion to the rules of the craft, but I don't think that's enough of a perk for the Castles."

"Do you know," I said, "how sad it is not to be able to trust your parents?"

Harold looked at me with his big, round eyes. "I feel I should remind you that, being a cat, I don't have parents in the same sense that you do."

"Oh," I said, embarrassed, "of course. But can you imagine, Harold, if you were a witchy human, how bad it would feel to know you can't trust your parents, that maybe you never could? I'm almost thirty and I still feel bereft. I'm tired, Harold. I'm tired of feeling abandoned."

"Then don't feel it anymore. Just say, 'I'm over them.' If you'll forgive the unfortunate, but apt, reference, banish them from your life. What are they doing for you? Nothing."

That, I thought, is such a cat thing to say.

"You can't just throw people out of your life like, I don't know, like you can throw out a torn sweater. We're not talking about spring-cleaning, Harold. We're talking about my parents."

Harold's nose lifted in a feline expression of distaste. "Your parents are taking up space in your heart like a torn sweater takes up space in your dresser drawer. Toss the sweater and you have room for something whole, something you can actually use. Toss the parents and you have room for—"

"For what?" I prodded.

Again, Harold's impressive nose lifted.

"For love. Now, if you'll excuse me, I've succeeded in disgusting myself with all this talk of touchy-feely matters. I am going to take a much needed nap."

Harold paraded from the front room, tail held high. No one watching his haughty progress would ever suspect he had such a heart.

16

Never was a witch more tolerant, open-minded, and non-judgmental than this writer. However, even I must admit that there are certain behaviors to be considered indisputably reprehensible. When encountering such behaviors, never hesitate to roundly condemn the perpetrator or perpetrators. Never hesitate to believe that right, if not might, is on your side!

"I don't see why we had to come tonight," Harold said grumpily. We were at Talisman, the coven's primary social venue. Axel had pulled together a party for a friend visiting from Portugal. "I hate crowds and so do you."

I winced as feedback came screeching from the six-foot speaker to our left. "It was important to Jared," I said. And it was important to me to be as good a girlfriend as I could be—while I was still Jared's girlfriend.

Jared had gone off to get us drinks. Harold and I stood alone and surveyed the crowd. I knew everyone, to a greater or lesser degree, but I felt strangely out of place.

Watching Axel's friend shimmy past, clutching a skinny little witch to his chest in a parody of passion, I wondered how soon I could leave without being considered a wet blanket.

"You could at least try to have a good time," Harold suggested.

"Hmm," I said noncommittally. How could I have a good time when the thought of my parents descending on me, perhaps to expose me as the fraud I was, was eating me up inside? It felt as if every shred of self-confidence I possessed had fled, never to return, leaving in its wake only misery and dismay.

"You're being overly dramatic."

On some level I knew Harold was right. Still, misery, like love, couldn't be reasoned with.

Someone behind me in the shadows laughed loudly; witches turned to see where the laughter had come from and there I was. Suddenly, accidentally, I was the object of attention.

"They're not looking at you," Harold said. "Calm down."

But when we'd come in earlier, Jared and I, people had turned to look, and there had been no admiring glances, only puzzled ones; puzzled and disbelieving that Haven Castle, a witch so bland and boring, could be with Jared Cragmere, a witch so stunning and superior.

"You're being paranoid," Harold commented. He sounded bored. "Don't simply humans have a potion for that? Maybe you should see a therapist."

Before I could attempt a defense, I felt a stab of icy air on the back of my neck. I whirled around and was face to face with Tamara Decora, a powerful, arrogant witch with a suspected eating disorder.

"What does she want with you?" Harold said darkly.

"Hello," I said. My voice was unsteady.

"Aren't you the lucky little girl," Tamara drawled. Her familiar, a Chihuahua named Gertrude, crouched shivering in her woven handbag.

I attempted a social smile. "I don't understand."

Tamara's heavily made-up eyes narrowed. "Tell me, is he as good as everyone says he is?"

"Everyone?" I said stupidly.

Tamara shook her head; the snakes she'd woven into her hair hissed in accord. "You are a funny one, aren't you? I used to think you were playing at being innocent, but I see now that you really are innocent, or naive. I don't know which is worse."

Tamara sauntered off, snakes roiling.

"I haven't had a good snake dinner in a long time." Harold licked his lips loudly.

"Enjoy," I said, as Harold slunk off.

I felt horribly vulnerable standing alone in the pulsing dark, so I made my way to the bar, hoping to find Jared.

Instead, there sat Lumina Harbor and Belle Creek, two of the most popular, party-hopping witches in the city. Neither had ever paid much attention to me; then again, neither had ever been unpleasant to me.

Harold is right, I thought. I should at least try to enjoy myself.

I took a deep breath; deep breaths are supposed to give you courage. Maybe, I thought, I'll just say hello. Maybe they'll invite me to join their conversation.

But one deep breath can't undo a lifetime of habitual shyness. I stood right where I was, just out of sight but close enough to hear the conversation.

"So," Lumina was saying, as she stroked her familiar, a large hamster named Loki, "this simply human chick said to me, 'I thought witches were supposed to be, like, close to nature or something. I thought they, like, worshipped goddesses and ran around naked in the forest at night.'"

Belle put her hand to her chest in mock horror. Lola, her perpetual piglet familiar, squeaked. "No! What did you tell her?"

"Well," Lumina replied, "I told her that no witch would run around naked in the park, which is the closest thing there is to a forest around here, if she valued her life. I said to her, 'Do you know how many rapists and murderers there are in this city?'"

"So," Belle said, "what did she say then?"

Lumina rolled her eyes. "She asked me why I couldn't just 'zap'—that's the exact word she used—anyone who tried to attack me. What does she think I am, a Vegas performer with a sequined wand?"

Belle groaned. "I am so tired of being misrepresented."

"Let me tell you," Lumina went on, "sometimes I regret ever coming out. The questions! The stares when they think I'm not looking! What are they waiting for, red flames to shoot out of my eyeballs? And those stupid, simply human men! The only reason they want to sleep with me is because they think something outrageous will happen, which, of course, it will, but not in the way they're expecting."

Belle laid her slim hand on Lumina's arm. "I've always said it's best to stick with our own kind."

Lumina sighed. "I know. But I've already dated every worthwhile witch."

"And now that Jared Cragmere is taken . . ."

My heart leapt at the mention of Jared's name.

"Ugh!" Lumina made an ugly face. "Don't get me started! What is he doing with Haven Castle? She's such a nothing. He could do so much better."

"I know! He could be seeing you, or me."

Lumina and Belle broke into conspiratorial laughter.

I slipped away, hoping Lumina and Belle wouldn't see me and know that I'd overheard their cruel critique. But would they really have cared if they did know? Probably not.

Lumina was right. Compared with the other single witches in the coven, I was a nothing.

And then I saw Jared coming toward me from across the room, a glass in each hand, and for a second, I couldn't help but wonder if he'd been off with another woman.

"There you are!" I said, mustering a bright smile.

"I'm sorry." Jared handed me a glass of champagne. "I was waylaid by Lester Lustre; you know, he's got to be at least ninety. He's a nice old guy, very lonely, though. Boy does he love to talk."

I looked at Jared's clear, honest eyes and knew, most definitely, that he would never, ever cheat on me.

"You're too nice," I said. "You can't say no to people."

Something changed in Jared's eyes; they iced. "You can be sure," he said evenly, "I don't let anyone take real advantage of me."

I remembered then what Jared had said about being tougher than he looked. Jared, I realized, might be kind and easygoing, but he possessed a core of strength, something final and dangerous. I wondered: If he ever discovered the truth about me, would his hatred be unrelenting?

But I had no time to contemplate that frightening possibility because just then, like a sudden and unexpected flash of heat lightning, Angora slinked up, wearing a clingy, wraparound dress and, in spite of the season, open-toe, high-heeled sandals. At her side stood Spike, a glittering collar encircling his fat, bristling neck.

"Jared," Angora said.

Jared nodded. "Hello, Angora." Then he put his arm around my shoulders and squeezed affectionately. "You know Haven, of course."

Angora nodded in my general direction. Then, speaking distinctly to Jared, she said, "I'd like to come by your office some time this week. There's a story I want to talk to you about. Something big, something I think will interest you very much."

Jared nodded. "We're always open to our readers' ideas." It was a careful answer; Jared, it seemed, was a diplomat, as well as a gentleman.

Angora slinked away. That was too easy, I thought. No insults—no overt ones, anyway. And suddenly, I was convinced that the story Angora had to tell Jared was all about me. Somehow, Angora had beat Jared in the race to discover who'd banished him to the land of the Hebetatians.

The back of my neck felt sweaty; my stomach churned. Beyond Jared's shoulder I spotted Tempestina's horrid hair drawing near.

"Are you okay?" Jared asked. "You suddenly look pale."

"I'm fine," I lied, "just tired. The store was really busy today."

"Then let's get out of here. I'll get Mercury and meet you outside, okay?"

Jared went off; Harold suddenly reappeared as a heavy weight pressed against my calf. "Where have you been?" I demanded. "Feasting on snake?" I lifted him into my arms; he put his paws on my shoulder and settled against my chest.

"No, something much more appetizing. I've been chatting with a charming Siamese named Lulu. Horrid name, but what eyes, what form! And what a voice!"

"You're not going to leave me, are you?" I was only half joking. Familiars can't leave their witches, not easily, not under ordinary circumstances. Still, a witch could worry.

Harold nuzzled my face. "Of course not. Stop being so silly."

"Okay," I said, "I'll try."

Simply speak the following words to seal the metal com-
pound. If you follow these directions carefully, the bonds
will remain unbroken until the crack of Doom.

"I hope you don't mind, Haven. I just can't turn this guy
down."

"It's okay," I said, quenching my disappointment. "Have
a great time with—who is it tonight?"

Lia yawned heartily before answering. "The corporate
accountant. His name is Bert, or Bart, or maybe Bill. I can't
remember, but I'll find out soon enough."

After the call I stood with my hand on the receiver,
thinking about Lia's new flippant, cavalier manner. She'd
always been such a caring person, a person of real sub-
stance, but now? Now she was acting like the kind of person she'd always disdained.

And whose fault was it that Lia was treating men like
disposable objects?

It was mine.

I found Jared in the kitchen, wiping a counter with a

dishtowel. "I won't be going out with Lia tonight," I told him. "She's got another date."

Jared looked around to me. "She's awfully busy these days," he said carefully. "There's almost something strange about it . . ."

My stomach clenched. Had my spell worked so well that my own boyfriend was being seduced by my magically altered best friend?

"Are you attracted to her?" I asked, teasingly, as if I could never believe such a possibility.

Jared smiled. "No, I'm attracted to the most beautiful witch in this world and all others."

Jared's words were sincere, they always were, but they didn't comfort me. In fact, his very sincerity only highlighted my own duplicitous behavior. I felt wretched. Was there any truth between Jared and me? How could there be? Our entire relationship was based on a lie.

What, I wondered, would Jared think of me if I told him I was responsible for Lia's sudden and immense popularity?

He would be disappointed in me. He disapproved of romantic spells; he thought them all about manipulation, which, of course, they were. He would be disappointed in Lia, too. He would discount us both as shallow, and heartless, and self-centered.

"Lia's always been a guy magnet," I said with false cheerfulness. "You just haven't known her as long as I have, so it seems odd."

Jared shrugged. "Well, as long as she's happy. And as long as you don't mind her canceling on you at the last minute. Do you want to come along with Axel and me? We're going to play pool at some new place uptown."

I shook my head. "That would spoil guy night." Besides, I thought, I could use some time alone to have a full-blown, heart-pounding, palms-sweating anxiety attack.

Jared left about half an hour later. I stood at my bedroom window and watched him walk down the street, Mercury tucked under his arm. He passed only one person on his way to the corner, a middle-aged woman in a dark suit; she stopped and stared after him, much as I was doing.

As I stood there at the window in the clear dark of an autumn night, I wondered if I would always be watching him walk away.

18

The Journals of Angora Slate, The Month of October

I am in a foul mood.

That pesky landlord has threatened to evict me if I don't pay last month's rent, and I am finally forced to deal firmly with him. I have decided to cast a Moribund spell; it should render him deaf and dumb and largely paralyzed for at least six weeks, during which time I will hunt up what money I can. (The spell is a tricky one to cast properly. No matter. If it renders Mr. Riillo permanently disabled, the better for me!)

Spike has ruined another expensive sweater, the one I stole from the Armani boutique. And this time he didn't even bother to blame his destructive behavior on the rats. He is growing far too bold, that waddling pincushion.

But neither the landlord nor Spike is the real tragedy of my life. Today I learned for sure that—incomprehensible!—Jared Cragmere is dating—is in love with!—that little worm Haven Castle.

He must be mad.

I am far more worthy of Jared Cragmere's attention than that pathetic, untalented offspring of the Castles. (A delicious aside: What, I wonder, would La Topaz ever do if she knew her darling husband spent three days and nights in my bed last year when he was supposed to be in Frankfurt at a conference on ancient spell translation methods?)

Well, there's something gnawing at that little chicken, I can tell. Something's terrorizing her, and I will ferret out her dirty little secret. I have no doubt she's hiding something shameful, something that will sicken Jared.

And then I'll be there to comfort him . . .

Perfection requires perfection. Jared Cragmere should be with me. Jared Cragmere will be with me.

But first, a romp with the gorgeous tax attorney on the ninth floor. He's rejected my advances once too often; now, we'll see how he begs for me once I've cast my ever-reliable Compulsion spell!

Maybe he'll have some cash lying about . . .

19

Spread the mixture evenly across the marble slab and let dry for an hour or more, until what results is hard to the touch. Then crack off a piece and, after crumbling, sprinkle it atop the food of your enemy. Ingestion is guaranteed to produce instant paralysis of the limbs.

"It's like a giant litter box." Harold's nose twitched in disdain. "I don't see what you find so fascinating about the beach. And just look at that dog! He's making a complete and utter fool of himself."

Mercury was, indeed, enjoying himself immensely, running madly toward the water, then running madly back up to dry land; digging hundreds of little holes with his tiny front paws, then abandoning the holes to chase seagulls; greeting other dogs as dogs will, with wagging tail, yaps, and sniffs.

"Can't you even try to enjoy the experience?" I asked my large, furry familiar. He refused to put one paw off the blanket and found the caw of the seagulls repulsive. "Don't you like to try new things?"

Harold shook his front left paw; I supposed he suspected a grain of sand had been born there by the chill sea breeze. "No, and neither do you, so stop lecturing."

Harold was right. It had been Jared's idea to drive out to the beach. I hadn't responded with much enthusiasm.

"It's mid-October," I demurred. "Won't it be awfully cold?"

"We'll bundle up. Haven, the beach is beautiful this time of the year. You'll see."

It was beautiful, all subtle grays and blues, the heavy clouds full of odd, occasional light. Best, Jared and I were the only people in sight. It felt as if we were alone in the universe, alone at the rough, silvered edge of the world.

While I sat with Harold, Jared had walked down to the water. Now, he turned and waved for me to join him.

"I'll be back," I told Harold.

"Don't drown," he said dryly. "You know I can't swim."

I reached Jared and saw he was standing not at the edge of the autumn waves but in the dark water.

"I want to give you something," he said. "Come here."

Jared reached out for my hand; without hesitation, I took it. He positioned me just behind him; though the icy water lapped around my ankles, they remained miraculously dry. I looked down at Jared's jeans; they, too, were untouched.

And then I watched as he bent down and reached into a breaking wave—into it like it wasn't water but something more substantial, like a jelly—and gathered a handful of— water. Only when he turned and showed me what was in his hand I saw that it wasn't nothing, a wet palm, a trickle of water—it was something solid and translucent, something green and blue and white.

"A bit of the ocean to take home with you," he said.

I opened my hand, slowly, almost afraid, and Jared

placed the water—the solid water, not ice, something else— into it. It had weight; it was real.

"It's like a jewel," I said, stunned, "but better, more beautiful. I can see . . . I can see inside it and through it and . . . Oh, Jared! I could never do anything like this."

Jared enfolded me in his arms. "Then it's a good thing you have me, isn't it?"

Yes, I thought, as the low waves crashed around us, a very, very good thing.

When we got home later that day, tired, cold, but exhilarated, there was a plain white letter-sized envelope just inside the door to my apartment. It was addressed to Jared.

The envelope itself was innocuous, but suddenly, I felt afraid. It was bad news. I just knew it was bad news. "What is it?" I asked, as Jared tore open the envelope. "Who is it from?"

Jared didn't reply; he was reading a single piece of paper with hungry eyes. I clasped my hands nervously. The wait seemed interminable, though probably less than a minute had passed. Finally, he refolded the paper and put it back into the envelope. Only then did he look up at me.

"I'm sorry, Haven," he said, "I have to leave." He slipped the envelope into his jacket pocket. "It's from Axel. We might have found the culprit. There are some materials back at my apartment, some sources I need to check." Jared laughed. "Listen to me, I sound like a cop! I'm just excited. Do you understand?"

I nodded and tried to smile. "Of course."

Jared took me in his arms, then traced the line of my cheek with his finger. "We had a lovely day," he said, "didn't we?"

I nodded again, this time unable to speak. Jared kissed me on the forehead and was gone.

I stood there, just inside the door, for what seemed like a long time. Finally, I pulled the piece of the ocean from my pocket and stared down at it. Even in the dim evening light of my apartment it shone.

"Harold?" I said. "What do you think is going to happen?"

From where he sat, very still, by the hall closet, he said, "I don't know, exactly."

"Of course not," I said. My was voice dull. "But tell me, what do you feel is going to happen?"

Still, Harold moved not a muscle. "I fear," he said, "that this is the beginning of the end."

20

Remember, if you will, all those ancestors who met a fiery fate at the hands of false accusers, and tremble!

The phone rang at seven the next morning. I hadn't slept at all.

Harold poked me with one massive paw. "Are you going to answer it?" he asked. "You know it's him."

I continued to lie motionless, to stare at the ceiling. "I know," I said finally, as the phone rang for the fourth time.

"It won't be any easier to hear your doom on an answering machine."

So, I thought, Harold, too, was convinced the worst had happened. In the cold, dark, wee hours of the night Jared had learned that the woman he loved had betrayed him.

I reached over and snatched the receiver from the base.

"Jared," I said.

"Yes." He sounded weary.

Harold stepped over my leg so that he could watch my face. His eyes were worried.

"Did you—" I began.

"I did."

"Who is it?" There was a terrible buzzing in my head. I shot a look toward the bedroom door. I wondered how much time I had before the coven was tearing the whole nasty truth from me.

Jared sighed. "I want to keep you out of this as much as possible, Haven. It's been strain enough on you—"

"Just tell me," I blurted. It couldn't, I thought, be me. He wanted to keep me out of it. . . . Unless Jared was playing a cruel game, it couldn't be me. It couldn't be me.

"Okay, but keep this to yourself, at least for now, all right? I haven't quite decided how to handle things."

My hand was sweaty; my grip on the phone was starting to slip.

"Yes, all right, of course."

"It's hard to believe," Jared said, and there was sadness in his voice, "but it was Marta Herald who cast the spell that cost me a year of my life."

Marta Herald. Not Haven Castle. I was relieved. I was confused. I sat up and looked to Harold. "Not me," I said.

Harold stepped closer. "I don't understand. Ask for details."

"But, why?" I asked Jared. "Why did she do it?"

"I don't know. I hardly know her. Maybe she was mad at me, but for the life of me I can't guess what I might have done wrong. Maybe she intended something entirely different than banishment. All I know for sure is that there are clues that point to her particular practice."

"Oh," I said. I fell back onto the pillow.

"Tell him he's got it all wrong." Harold marched onto my chest; his four humungous paws would, I knew, leave four humungous bruises. "If you can't tell him the whole truth, at least try to convince him to reconsider the evidence."

I said nothing.

Jared yawned. "Look, I've got to get some sleep. Axel and I were at this all night. I'll call you later, okay?"

"Okay," I said.

Harold, with a look of deep disappointment, stepped off me.

"And Haven?" Jared said.

"Yes?"

"Thank you for everything. Thank you for loving me and supporting me in this. You're the best girlfriend, really."

"You're welcome," I whispered, and then he was gone.

I lay there utterly still, except for the mad pounding of my heart. It was the worst situation imaginable. If I didn't say something soon, an innocent witch would be accused of my crime, and even if she could prove her innocence, first she'd suffer needlessly.

"And when she does prove her innocence," Harold said, leaping heavily off the bed and heading for the bedroom door, "it will only make Jared that much more determined to find the real culprit. And when he does, he'll be that much more disgusted with her. I mean, of course, with you. I'd like my breakfast now."

21

Once you have gathered the ingredients for the Pine Barren Punch, be sure to wash all ingredients thoroughly in a solution of vinegar and distilled water. Failure to do so will result in severe gastric distress among the imbibers and, most probably, the miserable end of your dinner party.

"What do you know about Marta Herald?"

Harold had finished his enormous breakfast and was now engaged in his postprandial ablutions. "Probably not much more than you," he said. "She's always working. I don't think I've seen her at a gathering in the last six months."

Yes, Marta Herald was always working. She was a single parent; her fourteen-year-old son's father had taken off years before with no explanation or forwarding address.

I'd never heard anything remotely negative about Marta Herald. The few times I'd spoken with her she seemed generally pleasant, if a bit harried. Other than that, Marta seemed—unremarkable, as unremarkable as me.

"I do know one important thing," Harold added.

"What's that?" I asked.

"Marta, of all witches, doesn't deserve this fate. You need to tell Jared the truth, now, before it's too late."

I laughed bitterly. "Isn't it already too late?"

"Not for Marta."

Not for Marta.

But when Jared came over later that day, I revealed nothing. I just couldn't; I was terrified of every possible outcome.

"Do you want to get something to eat?" he asked. His eyes, I noted, were bright; he must have slept well.

"I'm not very hungry," I said. That, too, was a lie. I wasn't at all hungry. The very thought of food was revolting.

Jared suggested we put on some music and relax. Music? I thought. How about a dirge? How about a requiem?

"You choose something," I said. Jared did, a jazz CD he'd brought with him. I sat stiffly on a chair.

"Have you told anyone else?" I asked when Jared had settled on the couch; Mercury, his brown eyes alert, was on his lap. "About Marta."

"No," he said, "Axel insisted we review the evidence one more time, just to be sure. I know he's right, but I'm impatient to get this settled and behind me."

"Of course."

Jared looked at me quizzically. "Why are you sitting way over there? Come join me. I missed you last night."

Harold chose that moment to cough up a hairball at the door to the kitchen. I say he chose that moment because I believe he did. He knew that for the first time the thought of cuddling with Jared was terrifying to me. What right did I have to touch this man?

"I'll clean it up," Jared said.

"You know," I said, "I am hungry after all. Let's go out to eat."

Jared spent that night at his loft, working with Axel to confirm Marta Herald's guilt. For the second night in a row I didn't sleep. By morning my eyes were swollen and red.

"You should eat something."

It was noon and I hadn't heard from Jared. Harold, though disappointed in my cowardly behavior, was concerned.

"I ate yesterday," I told him.

"Almost twenty-four hours ago." Harold had spread himself on the windowsill, just above the steaming radiator. "Haven," he said, "this can't go on. You have to talk to Jared."

I left him to cook, as cats will, and ran water for a shower. I stood under the warm spray until my skin was wrinkled.

It was almost four o'clock before Jared came by, unannounced.

"You look glum," I said.

Jared walked into the apartment. His hands, I noted, were red with cold. "I am glum."

Mercury, attuned to his witch's mood, whined and settled against the wall.

"Why?" I said. My voice was a mere whisper.

"This morning I thought I knew who was responsible for banishing me. Now, I'm back to knowing nothing, not much, anyway."

I heard Harold leap heavily to the floor from his perch on the windowsill. I imagined smoke wafting from his belly.

"You mean . . ."

"I mean I was wrong. It wasn't Marta."

And in that instant I felt overcome with sleepiness. What would Jared think, I wondered crazily, if I excused myself to take a nap?

"And you don't know who is responsible?"

We were still standing in the foyer. Suddenly, Jared took

a step closer and looked at me with such intensity I felt he was trying to read my mind, my soul. I was afraid.

"No," he said, finally, decisively, "I don't know who is responsible."

Jared turned from me and went into the living room. He sat on the couch with a soft groan. I followed and sat next to him, not too far away, not too close.

"You must," I said tentatively, "be glad you rechecked your information before saying anything to the coven."

Jared dragged his cold-chapped hands through his hair. "Of course I'm glad. I don't know how Marta would have forgiven me."

"Maybe now," I said, then hesitated, trying to find the nerve to go on.

Harold appeared on the arm of the couch. "I don't suppose you'll listen if I tell you there's no chance—"

"Yes?" Jared asked.

I shrugged, as if I were about to voice a thought that had just occurred to me. "Well, I was going to say that maybe now is the time to just let this all go."

Jared's eyes pleaded with me to understand. "I can't let it go, Haven. I need to know who sent me away. I need to know why they brought me back."

I reached out and stroked his hair; it was so soft and thick. "Maybe," I said, "it was all just an accident, a stupid, foolish accident. What point is there in revenge?"

When Jared didn't reply I went on, fooled by his silence.

"Jared, it's eating you up inside, this pursuit, isn't it? You're obsessed with—"

Jared moved away from my touch. "I don't think I'm obsessed," he said simply. "There are plenty of other things in my life. I've got the magazine and I have friends and there's us. Unless you . . ."

"Unless I what?" I said, once again, afraid.

Jared took both my hands in his. "Unless you feel I'm ignoring you. Is that it, Haven, have I been neglectful?"

Why, oh why, I thought, did he have to be such a damn good boyfriend? "No, no, of course not!" I cried. "You're wonderful to me, Jared, you're kind and loving and just wonderful."

Jared pulled me against him; I buried my face in his chest and clung to him.

"When all this is over," he said, "you and I are going to England for a month. We're going to eat, drink, and be merry and not think about anything but us. How does that sound?"

Slowly, reluctantly, I raised my head and looked into Jared's lovely pale green eyes. "It sounds . . . fine."

Jared laughed. "Just fine? Haven, you really do need a vacation."

22

Never, upon pain of serious reprisal, reveal to those not members of the magical world a failure of spell or potion, a disaster of divination or charm, a miscarriage of incantation or balm.

"Sorry I'm late."

Lia walked into my apartment and sank immediately into an armchair. For someone supposedly having the time of her life, Lia looked terrible. There were dark circles under her eyes; her skin was dull; and when she took off her coat, I noticed that her blouse hung loosely off her shoulders.

"What's wrong?" I asked.

Without preamble, Lia said, "I need you to reverse the spell."

Harold was stretched out to the length of about a mile along the back of the couch. "This," he said, "is getting to be farcical."

"Why?" I asked. "I thought you wanted to be wanted."

Lia laughed bitterly. "I do," she said. "I just don't want

to be wanted like a deer wanted by a guy with a rifle. In other words, I'm tired of being hunted."

Delicately, Harold extended his front claws. "You got her into this," he said. "You're going to have to get her out. At least, you're going to have to try."

"Well," I said, ignoring my interfering familiar, "can't you just choose one or two guys you really like and tell the others to go away?"

Lia glanced warily over her shoulder, as if expecting to find a sexually starved man lurking at my apartment door. "I can't," she said urgently. "I'm overwhelmed by options. Every time I think I've narrowed it down to two or three fabulous guys, another four or five fabulous guys come along. Haven, you've got to help me! My social life is killing me."

"Be careful what you wish for." Harold rose; his back arched high into the air. "That old saw has some merit. Most of them do."

"Plus," Lia said suddenly, "there's something else."

"There always is," Harold said darkly.

"What else?" I asked.

Lia took a deep breath. "This one guy," she said, "told me he wants to kill himself."

Harold said a bad word.

I was stricken dumb.

"It's horrible, Haven." Tears formed in Lia's eyes. "I'm an awful human being! This poor guy says he's going to kill himself if I don't go out with him just one more time. I never intended to drive men to suicide! All I wanted was a few dates. But it's all become a giant mess."

A giant mess—that was putting it mildly. If that poor, lovesick guy killed himself, it would be on my head. I would, in effect, be guilty of murder.

I sank into a chair across from Lia. I was a menace to all men.

"What's wrong?" Lia demanded. "Don't tell me you can't reverse the spell! What kind of spell can't be reversed? What's going on, Haven?"

What was going on was that the last straw had been loaded onto the camel's back.

So, with an encouraging nod from Harold, who came to sit on my lap, I started from the beginning. I told Lia about casting the love spell on Jared and about it backfiring and causing him to disappear. I told her about how casting the attraction spell on her had unexpectedly brought Jared back. I told her about Jared's pursuit of the culprit, about his almost accusing the wrong person, and about how I'd kept my mouth shut even then.

When I finished telling the grim tale I felt strangely relieved, though nothing had been solved by my confession.

Lia whistled; I'd never known she could. "Suddenly," she said, "my own horrible situation doesn't seem so horrible. What are you going to do?"

An absurd little laugh escaped my lips. "I have no idea," I admitted. "One minute I think I should keep my mouth shut and hope no one discovers the truth, but how likely is that? The next minute, I think I should confess everything to Jared. Either way, I lose the man I love."

"You don't know that for sure," Lia said, but her tone betrayed her doubt.

For a few long minutes none of us spoke, not even Harold. The silence was welcome. I wished it might go on forever; I wished for stasis. For the rest of our lives the three of us would sit quietly in my living room, untouched by trouble or by witchcraft.

"So, are we on?"

Lia's sudden question startled me.

"She's insane." Harold jumped to the floor. "I've always suspected."

"You still want me to try to reverse the spell?" I asked.

"After what I just told you? I'm a terrible witch, Lia. Who knows what I'll do to you!"

"I'll take my chances," Lia replied steadily. "It's not raining men, Haven, it's pouring men, and I'm drowning. Eternal celibacy has got to be better than this."

Tears pricked my eyes. "Thank you," I said, "for believing in me."

Lia shrugged. "What choice do I have?"

I hefted myself from the chair and walked over to a small pine desk. In the top drawer I'd placed a piece of paper on which I'd copied out a complicated spell.

"Honestly," I told Lia, "I thought that someday you might get tired of being so popular, so I researched a reversal spell. I think—I'm pretty sure—I found one that will work. We can do it right now, if you want to."

Lia nodded. "Yes, I want to. But don't you need to light some candles?"

I grinned sheepishly. "Atmosphere, that's all."

"I," Harold announced, "will get the matches."

Later that afternoon, the phone rang. I was resting on the couch and didn't pick up, but I listened to Lia's message.

"Only three men followed me home earlier," she said excitedly. "I think the reverse spell is working! And I called that guy, the one who wanted to kill himself, and you know what? He said he lost interest in me! Isn't that wonderful?!"

"That's . . . great," I said to the answering machine.

Lia's voice went on. "I can't wait to spend a Saturday night alone at home! Thanks, Haven. Thanks for everything."

Later, I deleted the message. It wouldn't do for Jared to find it.

23

If you discover that foul play has been enacted against your person, proceed immediately to plan your revenge.

Around seven o'clock that evening I began to wonder what was keeping Jared; he was always so punctual.

At seven-thirty I peered out the bedroom window to see if he was climbing the steps to the building right then. He wasn't.

I checked the answering machine; there were no messages. I tested the phone cord; it was firmly plugged into both phone and jack.

Harold lay on the couch, one eye closed, the other watching my every move. But he offered no comment.

By eight-thirty I was sick with anxiety. I decided to eat something to quiet the rumbling in my stomach; I couldn't swallow.

A sneaking little suspicion, just the hint of one, began to tickle the corner of my mind, but I dismissed it with great effort.

Still, Harold lay motionless, watching. I didn't offer him dinner; he didn't ask for it.

At nine I decided that, in spite of all evidence to the contrary, Jared was a typical guy after all. He'd probably run into a buddy and, totally forgetting about the date with his girlfriend, was hanging out in some dive bar drinking beer and ogling women.

By nine-thirty there was still no call from Jared; I was absolutely frantic. I'd dismissed the notion of his having forgotten about me.

The sneaking little suspicion was now a huge suspicion; no longer at the corner of my mind but right smack in the center.

I looked down at Harold. "It never even occurred to me . . ."

"It's possible," Harold said, finally rising from his prone position. His voice was grim. "It's possible that by reversing the spell you put on Lia, the spell that seems to have brought Jared back from his unwilling exile, you might, in fact, have cast him away again."

"Why didn't you warn me!" I cried. "What am I going to do?"

Harold had the courtesy not to yawn, though I know he wanted to.

"First," he said, "my warnings usually fall on deaf ears. For better or worse, Haven, you're one of those witches who have to make her own mistakes. As to what you're going to do, I'd suggest you try to calm down."

"How can I be calm? This is a crisis, Harold, a crisis of major proportions!"

"We don't know that Jared—"

"We don't know anything, that's the problem!"

I grabbed a giant spell book from the messy pile on the coffee table. Then I froze. "I don't even know where to begin," I said helplessly.

"Try, Spell Reversals, Unforeseen Consequences of," Harold suggested wearily.

I did. Under the chapter heading I found the following entry.

> *Amateurs, in particular, are cautioned not to attempt spell reversals, especially reversals of spells that have gone spectacularly wrong, without the supervision of a witch of great experience.*

The massive tome fell to the floor. It hit my left foot; I was only vaguely aware of the pain.

"Haven," Harold suggested, "before you have a stroke, why don't you call Jared's apartment?"

Why, I wondered, hadn't I thought of that before?

Jared wasn't home. Listening to his obliviously happy voice on the answering machine and knowing he could be in terrible danger at that very moment was more than I could bear. I slammed the receiver back into the cradle.

"Do you know," Harold asked, "who he was seeing today? Was he meeting anyone for lunch?"

"I don't know," I admitted. My voice was trembling. "Wait, I'll call Axel. Maybe he knows something. Maybe Jared's with him now . . ."

Axel answered after five interminable rings.

"Axel, this is Haven."

"Hey, Haven," he said amiably, "how's it going?"

"Look, have you seen Jared?"

"Yeah," he said, over the beat of club music in the background, "we had coffee. Why?"

I looked at Harold; he was watching me closely. "Well," I said, "he was supposed to be here hours ago and he hasn't called and I'm, well, I'm getting a little worried."

"I wouldn't worry, Haven." I thought I heard Axel opening a bottle of wine. "Jared can take care of himself." And then he laughed. "Unless some idiot witch screwed up another spell and he's playing foosball on Mars."

I ended the call without a good-bye.

"That was rude," Harold said.

"You don't know what he said," I snapped.

And then there was a key in the door.

"I'm sorry I'm late," Jared said, slipping the key back into the pocket of his leather coat. "There was a disaster at the printer. I should have called but my cell phone died and—"

I threw myself into his arms and squeezed him tight.

Jared squeezed back. "Whoa, Haven," he said, "are you okay? Did something happen?"

My mouth was against the leather; I inhaled its smell, and his. Then I said, "It was me."

Jared placed a kiss on the top of my head. "What are you talking about?"

Sadly, I pulled away from Jared's embrace and wondered if I'd ever touch him again.

"Just listen to me," I implored. "Please."

Harold's voice came from behind me. "Courage, Haven."

"Okay. Sure." Jared looked confused. Mercury stood by his right leg, his staunch companion.

The confession would have to be a dash, not a saunter.

"I really liked you," I said, "and I thought you didn't even notice me and I knew it was wrong but I did it anyway. I put a love spell on you, but something went wrong and you disappeared. Every day you were gone I tried to find a spell to bring you back but nothing worked and Fabula was gone and I couldn't find her and I couldn't ask anyone else for help and—"

The look on Jared's face stopped me cold. His eyes were suddenly the color of certain ugly lizards.

"So," he demanded, "you let me waste twelve months of my life?"

I'd never seen him so angry. I didn't know what to say.

"Why didn't you go to the coven and tell them what happened? Why didn't you ask for their help?"

"I tried to contact Fabula," I said lamely. "I read through every spell book I could find. I—"

But Jared wouldn't let me finish. "And all this time since I've been back and we've been together you never said a word. You let me go on thinking that you loved me when all along you were just trying to save your own skin."

"But I do love you!" I cried. "I was just so afraid of losing you—"

Jared shook his head. He laughed in exasperation. Then he put his hands out before him as if to ward off any touch from me.

"That doesn't even make sense, Haven. Love isn't about lying. It's about trust. You should have trusted me enough—you should have respected me enough!—to tell me the truth right at the start. Yeah, I would have been mad, but I also would have respected your courage and your honesty."

Courage. Honesty. Two qualities I lacked in the extreme.

I took a step closer to Jared. Mercury let out an angry bark. I flinched and stepped back. The bark felt like a physical blow. Ever my champion, Harold fixed his tail in a downward arc, further fluffed his fur to emphasize his enormity, and galloped sideways toward Mercury. The dog was only saved from laceration by Jared's move to quickly scoop him off the floor.

"Why tell me this now, anyway?" Jared demanded. "What made you finally need to be honest with me?"

I felt weak with shame, but I'd gone too far to retreat. So I told him about the spell I'd cast for Lia, and how she'd finally begged me to reverse it. "And, then," I said, tears rolling down my face unheeded, "when you didn't come home tonight and I couldn't find you I thought . . . I thought that maybe I'd done it again, that I'd accidentally sent you away. I—"

Jared cut me off again. His tone was harsh. "And if you had sent me away again, would you have confessed? Or would you have let me waste another year of my life because you were too cowardly to admit you'd made a mistake?"

"Of course I would have confessed!" I cried. "Oh, Jared, I'm different now. I learned my lesson, I swear!"

Jared shook his head. "I wish I could believe you, Haven, but I just can't."

There was a moment of awful silence. And then Jared stalked toward the door. Once there he turned back to face me. His face was pale now; he looked sick.

"Here's the irony," he said, quietly. "I did notice you last year. I noticed you because you were different from all the others—at least I thought you were. Sweeter. Nicer. Unpretentious. And I was just about to ask you out when I found myself knee-deep in Hebetatian mud fields."

And then he was gone.

24

The Journals of Angora Slate, The Month of October

The next person I lay eyes on will pay the price of this foul mood.

I hope it is that pestilent landlord. He's threatened to evict me by the end of the week if I don't pay back rent. Evict me! Clearly, he doesn't know who he's up against. Still, the stress is wreaking havoc with my skin. I really must cast that Moribund spell!

But all is not grim. Yesterday I heard the most delightful news that makes the pesky landlord situation seem of no real importance.

Jared Cragmere and Haven Castle are no longer a couple.

Even now, just writing these words, a smile spreads across my face. I swear that when I heard the news (from that pathetic excuse for a man Boswell Van Der Minter; he actually seemed quite broken up about it!), I laughed for what seemed like hours. No one (not even Boswell) seems to know what caused the demise of that sickening romantic display, but I know as sure as if I'd heard it from Jared's own lovely lips.

The year with the Hebetatians rattled his brain, it must have, causing a severe lapse in judgment and, no doubt, a seriously diminished sex drive. (What man, simply human or witch, could get excited about that dishrag Haven Castle?)

But now, Jared, finally having come to his senses, will find me a most satisfactory romantic replacement. If need be, I will spell him, but I feel sure—absolutely sure—that my own native charms are more than sufficient to seduce him into my bed.

Damn that Spike! He's at the fridge again; he's already destroyed both vegetable bins, for which that worm of a landlord wants an extra fifty dollars to replace. Until the next report . . .

25

For severe and persistent pain, take three tablets, three times a day, with water. Should seizures occur, reduce the dosage to two tablets, two times a day. In the case of the extreme desire for self-laceration, discontinue use.

"Jared is avoiding me."

Lia put her coffee cup on the Formica-topped table. "That's understandable."

"I don't need you to judge me," I snapped. "I know what I did was despicable. I need you to help me."

"I'm sorry. I'll do what I can."

I'd met Lia for breakfast at Cuppa Joe. It was her idea. She was mad for their pancakes and sausage; food was the last thing on my mind.

The loss of Jared, every bit of him, inside and out, was unbearable. I ached, physically ached, for his touch. My stomach hurt; I couldn't stand straight. It felt as if I'd been hollowed out, like my spine was decaying, like I was breaking apart with every breath. And it was all my own doing. Jared hadn't destroyed me. I had.

I had no appetite. Sleep came unexpectedly and was short and wretched with dreams of Jared the last time I'd seen him, the night he walked out of my apartment and out of my life.

Conscious or unconscious, I was miserable.

I pushed away the plate of barely touched scrambled eggs. "I feel like I'm dying without him."

Lia patted my hand. "You're not dying."

"Maybe I am. People have died of a broken heart."

Harold was concealed in a large leather tote bag at my feet. Certain restaurants frown on cats sharing a meal with two-legged beings. "I won't let you die, Haven," he said from the depths. "In spite of the fact that you've stuffed me in a bag."

"I suppose this is a silly question," Lia said, nibbling a sticky bun she'd ordered on the side, "but have you considered putting a spell on Jared, something to force him to talk to you?"

Lia's words sent a wave of nausea through me.

"No," I said firmly, "I swore to myself not to use magic on him ever again, and I'm going to keep that promise. If I'm going to win Jared back, I'm going to do it honestly— no magical coercion."

Lia nodded. "Good. Are you going to eat that?"

I shook my head, and Lia dug into my neglected eggs.

"Aren't they cold by now?" I asked.

"Doesn't matter. I'm starving."

"Speaking of food," Harold said, "I will require an extra bowl of cream as an apology for this indignity."

"I don't know what to do," I admitted. "He won't return my calls or e-mails."

Lia finished chewing and eyed me. "You haven't been leaving creepy messages, have you? I mean, maybe he's not calling back because he's afraid of you."

"Of course not! All I say is, 'Jared, please let me apologize.' I don't even cry. I save that until I've hung up."

Lia drained her coffee and gestured to the waitress for more. "I think you should just show up at his door and force him to talk to you."

"I can't," I protested. "I don't have the nerve."

Lia rolled her eyes. Her recent experiences in the dating world had taught her to take life into her own hands and not let someone or something else—like magic—direct it.

"Okay, then," she said, "write him a note and slip it under his door. Trust me, an old-fashioned, hand-written apology can have a lot more power than some misspelled words on a screen."

"I use spell check."

"You know what I mean. So, he hasn't told the coven yet, you know, about you being the one?"

I shook my head. "I guess not. No angry crowd has appeared at my door in the dead of night ready to run me out of town."

Lia didn't say what I wanted her to say: that maybe Jared's silence was a good sign, that maybe he still cared about me just a little, enough to protect my reputation.

"Lia," Harold said evenly, "is your friend. She doesn't want to give you false hope."

My friend.

From the pocket of my sweater I pulled out the piece of the ocean Jared had given me.

"He did this," I said. "He made this. It's the ocean."

Lia put down her fork. "Wow. And I thought diamond earrings were impressive."

I put the gift back into my pocket, where it was safe.

"I have to get him back, Lia," I said tearfully. "I just have to."

Lia tossed some bills on the table. "Come on," she said, "Let's get you home or we'll never be allowed here again."

From under the table came a fed-up feline voice. "Fine by me," it said.

26

Once a decision has been made to take a particularly diffi-cult step, it should be acted upon as soon as possible to avoid the temptations of cowardice.

"I can't believe the elevator is broken. These lofts must cost a fortune; the least Maintenance could do is maintain!"

My heart beat madly. "What are you complaining . . . about?" I huffed. "I'm doing all the work."

Harold patted the back of my head with a giant paw. "I'm complaining on your behalf, of course."

"If you really . . . want to do something . . . for me," I gasped, "you can stop drinking a . . . second bowl of cream . . . before bed."

"Only five more steps to go."

Only five more steps and Harold and I would be on the landing just outside the door to Jared's loft.

"What if he's here?" I asked nervously.

"He's not. You watched him leave the building an hour ago. Unless there's a back way in, he's not in his loft and you know it. But if you hesitate any longer . . ."

Harold was right. There was little time to waste. On the landing I removed the backpack—and Harold—and tried to breathe normally. I looked at the bouquet of white lilies clutched in my left hand. Lilies are Jared's favorite flower. The note that I would leave with the bouquet was still in my coat pocket.

Somewhere in the building a pipe gurgled loudly and I jumped. Maybe, I thought, this was a bad idea. What if one of Jared's neighbors found me lurking outside his loft? What explanation could I give for my presence? I never should have listened to Lia!

"Do you ever just do something without worrying about it, too?" Harold asked rhetorically.

I placed the bouquet on the mat outside Jared's door. "I just want to look at the note one more time."

"You've already written and rewritten it at least twenty times. Stick it in the bouquet and let's get out of here."

Harold turned his back to me. I took the note from my pocket, unfolded it, and read. "I don't know," I murmured. "Maybe it's too abject; but then again, how can I be too abject? Maybe if I just—"

And then I heard voices, voices and footsteps. They came from a flight or two below and, as I listened, I realized they were growing more distinct.

"Run!" I hissed. But where? A few yards down the hall sat a group of about five metal garbage cans. "This way!"

Harold came thundering after me. I darted behind the center can and landed hard on my knees. Harold made a lump beside me.

"Haven?" he said. His voice was tight. "Why is the note still in your hand?"

Startled, I looked at the open piece of paper in my right hand, then down to Harold. The voices were very close now. One of them belonged to Jared.

"Do you think—"

Harold laid a restraining paw on my thigh. "There's not enough time. You'll just have to hope Jared figures out the flowers are from you."

I shifted just a bit and peered between garbage cans. A moment later, Jared came into view. With him was Angora Slate. Of course I hadn't recognized her voice; she'd deigned to speak in my presence only once or twice.

"Don't jump to conclusions," Harold said from his own vantage point. "She's probably just here to pitch that story idea she mentioned to Jared."

"Do you really believe that?"

Harold's silence was his answer.

And then Jared spotted the bouquet. He strode to the door and lifted the flowers to his nose. Angora stood beside him.

"Wow," Jared said, "these are beautiful. Strange, there's no card."

And at that instant I just knew what was going to happen. Harold knew, too. A low rumble started in his throat, and I sensed his body prepare for attack.

"Don't," I told him, imagining Jared and Angora finding me crouched miserably behind a garbage can, "it will only make things worse."

Harold reluctantly obeyed.

"I'm glad you like them," said Angora Slate to Jared Cragmere. "I was hoping you would."

27

In case of an infestation of disease-carrying creatures, the most effective treatment is not magical but rather professional fumigation.

"You're going to have to leave the house some time," Harold admonished one particularly chilly morning in November. I was prone in bed; he sat on the dresser, staring at me.

For days after the fiasco of the flowers I continued to stay holed up in my apartment. Halloween came and went; I didn't attend the coven's celebrations, and nobody called to ask why. I canceled two lunch dates with Lia. I failed to open the store.

Harold could scold all he wanted, but I just wasn't ready to face the world.

"You have a responsibility to Fabula," he said, "to open the store at least once this week."

Fabula. My friend and mentor. Harold was right. For her sake, at least, I would return to work, if not to life.

An hour later Harold and I were at Anastasia's Attic, the

space heater blasting at my feet behind the counter. Harold had settled on a gorgeous mink stole after consuming a cup of warm milk I'd brought in a thermos from home.

And while standing there in familiar surroundings, I realized that my life wasn't a complete disaster. Though I no longer had Jared, and nothing could make up for that loss, at least I had a job, and as a result of that job, a home. And on a freezing day in a city of thousands of homeless, a home was a thing for which to be grateful.

"I tried," I said to Harold, once the blood had returned to my extremities.

"You did," he affirmed.

"I can't make him talk to me."

"You can't."

"But—"

Harold shifted on his fur seat. "You need to be philosophical about this, Haven."

"I'm not in the mood for philosophy."

"What are you in the mood for? Self-pity?"

"Well, what if I am?" I asked. "What's so wrong with a little self-pity?"

"Nothing, if it really is a small dose, and if it's indulged in only once in a great while."

I wondered: Were all cats, even the nonmagical ones, smarter than their human companions?

"I hate to admit it," Harold said suddenly, "but I miss that little pug. He grew on me, a bit like a fungus; but you get used to things, and then they're gone and nothing feels the same."

No, nothing felt the same. I was about to sink into another fit of despondency—forgetting all about how lucky I was to have a job and home—when the absolute worst thing that could have happened, happened.

The door crashed open and in clumped Inclementia and Tempestina, Formosa and Tom in tow. The witches were bundled in various odd layers of cracked leather and rotted wool; their familiars, on the other hand, did not even sport scarves.

"Steady, old thing," Harold urged.

I don't know how I did it, really, but I forced a smile to my trembling lips.

Neither witch returned the greeting. Inclementia looked around the store as if it were full of fresh horse dung; Tempestina wiped her nose on the back of her tattered sleeve.

"You know," Inclementia said suddenly, grasping her companion's arm with her claw-like hand, "I saw Jared Cragmere just this morning and I must say he looks perfectly lovely, better than he's looked since he returned from those awful Hebetatians."

Tempestina nodded vigorously; the tiny wool cap that sat atop her enormous hair wiggled and threatened to fall to the ground.

"I know!" she shrieked. "Something—or someone!—is doing that boy a world of good!"

I gripped the edge of the counter.

Harold's eyes narrowed dangerously.

Then Inclementia looked to me as if noticing me for the first time. "Oh, I'm sorry, Haven," she whined, wrinkling her pointy nose. "Is it too weird to hear about Jared?"

Not for a minute did I believe she cared about my feelings. She and Tempestina had come to the store solely for the purpose of watching me squirm.

"No," I lied, with a bright and brittle smile, "it's fine. After all, we're members of the same coven."

"Well, then," she said, "you're not going to believe this, but Jared's given up the search for whomever sent him off to that horrible place!"

Inclementia shoved Formosa out of the way and leaned over the counter as if she were sharing a confidence with a friend. Her falseness sickened me; I took a step back. "Personally," she said, her red-rimmed eyes piercing mine, "I think it has to do with Angora. I think Jared's just in seventh heaven with her and doesn't care a wit about anything else."

Tempestina casually put a hand to her elaborate coif. I heard the rustle of wings from within; Tom must have retreated there for some warmth. "When you were with Jared he was really into the search, wasn't he?"

And Harold was in the air, a missile headed straight for the witches. He was a magnificent sight, hissing and screaming, claws extended, teeth bared. Inclementia let out a little shriek; Formosa bleated in consternation. Tempestina stumbled into a bin of cloth bags, while from his witch's hairdo Tom complained, "My heart, my heart, my kingdom for a heart."

At the very last moment Harold swerved and landed with a thud on the countertop.

"The store," I said firmly, "is closed."

A moment later the disgusting creatures were gone.

"Harold," I said steadily, "next time I want you to scratch their eyes out."

28

The Journals of Angora Slate, The Month of November

I have never been so furious, so absolutely livid—and, I must admit, so dumbfounded!—in my entire life.

Jared Cragmere—impossible!—is immune to my witchcraft. No man or woman, no witch or simply human has ever failed to succumb to my magical powers. Until now.

I must admit, Jared's indifference makes me want him even more fiercely . . .

Damn him!

If my native powers of seduction fail, and my witchcraft proves inadequate, what then will get Jared into my bed?

The truth.

For some unfathomable reason, Jared appreciates honesty. (Well, to each his own.) And more and more I am convinced—call it my superior instinct—that Haven Castle, that miserable little insect, is hiding a dread secret. Haven Castle, I am sure of it, is the one responsible for banishing Jared to that land of muck and mire. And if only I can prove it, if only I can deliver her into the avenging hands of the coven, Jared will be mine.

I must leave off here for now. An exceedingly irate investment banker is pounding on my door, ranting about my having stolen something valuable from his swanky penthouse when last I granted him my favors. The strangest thing—I think he's right. But was it the ancient Egyptian statuette that I snatched, or was it the lovely miniature grandfather clock?

No matter. He's not getting in and he's not getting his property back. And now, to let Spike handle my unwelcome guest . . .

29

On occasion, a witch might learn a valuable lesson from a nonmagical creature and even, though rarely, from a simply human.

"I'm seeing someone."

"I thought you wanted some Lia-time," I said, surprised. "You know, after the parade of men."

Lia and I were having coffee and muffins in my kitchen one gloomy Saturday morning. Well, Lia was eating the muffins; I was pushing crumbs around my plate. I tried to show interest in the conversation, but the truth was I was preoccupied by the sorry state of my own heart.

"I did want some Lia-time," she said. "But when Rob asked me out, I don't know, something made me say yes. And I'm glad I did. He's smart and funny and he loves P. G. Wodehouse just like I do and he's even sort of handsome. And he doesn't seem to mind that I don't have a body like Jennifer Lopez."

"That's nice," I said.

"And get this," she went on, reaching for her third muffin, "it seems that ever since he started at the firm two years ago he's wanted to ask me out."

I stared out the window; the sky was like brushed silver.

"Ask her why he didn't," Harold prompted from his seat on the third chair.

"Then why didn't he?" I asked.

Lia shrugged. "He's kind of shy, not in a weird way or anything, just normal shy. But here's the funny thing: Just when he'd worked up the nerve, flowers and candy and Tiffany boxes started appearing in my office almost daily. Naturally, he assumed I had a serious boyfriend, so he backed off."

"Sensible fellow," Harold remarked.

"Oh," I said.

"And then when the gifts stopped coming, well, he waited a bit before asking me out because he didn't want to be a rebound guy."

"I like this gentleman," Harold said. "You may tell Lia that I approve of him."

"Ah," I said.

Lia smiled. "But then he decided I was worth the risk. Can you imagine? All along there was this great guy right under my nose and I had no clue. If only I hadn't panicked and asked you to work that spell, I could have been with Rob all along."

"You are listening carefully, I hope."

I looked from the window to Harold, sitting so solidly, so reliably in his chair. I cut a small pat of butter and put it on the plate before him.

"See," Lia went on, more to herself than to me, "the trouble with witchcraft is that it's too easy to use as a fall-back. I should have trusted my own charms. I should have just let things happen naturally. Right?"

"Right," I said.

Suddenly, Lia reached for my hand. "Thanks, Haven,"

she said. I was surprised by the strength of her grip. "This whole experience has taught me a lot."

Lia left soon after; she was meeting Rob for lunch at a Jewish deli in midtown. Listlessly, I washed the cups and dishes and knives and spoons. Then I sat heavily again at the table. The whole day stretched before me, as bleak as the leaden sky.

"You could use some good news."

Ah, Harold.

"I know," I said. "Have any for me?"

"I do." I imagined a human grin on Harold's handsome feline face. "It's about your illustrious parents. They're not coming to the city. They never were. Inclementia and Tempestina were just being their nasty selves."

The day felt a teeny bit brighter. "But how do you know?"

Harold yawned before replying. "I have my sources. By the way, and you didn't hear it from me, Formosa and Tom have filed papers against their witches. In human parlance, they're demanding divorces, and I suspect they're going to get them."

"What are the grounds?" I asked.

"Intolerable cruelty, of course."

And for the first time in ages, I laughed.

30

Should your enemy suddenly appear at your door, there is one thing you absolutely must not do: Let her see your fear.

They say time heals all wounds. I don't know exactly who "they" are but "they" are wrong. I don't think time actually heals all wounds; it only causes a rough, itchy, ugly scab to form over the wound, a grim and constant reminder of the moment of infliction.

"You're rather morose today."

Harold was resting on a silk cushion after his substantial lunch of sardines and eggs.

Morose? No, I thought. I was bored.

I'd opened the store at ten, per usual. By two o'clock I'd sold only one item, a pale blue pillbox hat, to a simply human girl who'd eyed Harold with inordinate unease.

"Morose," I said, "isn't really the word."

"Then, melancholy? Pessimistic? Lugubrious?"

I shrugged. "Something like that."

"Well, Haven, our day is about to get even more bleak."

I whirled around from the beaded sweater I was refolding to see Angora Slate, the most beautiful witch in the city and Jared's new love, walking through the door of Anastasia's Attic. Spike waddled in just behind her.

"This place," said Harold, dryly, "is becoming a hangout for the lowest forms of life."

"Hello," I said politely to Angora. "Let me know if there's something I can help you with."

Harold grunted in disgust. What would he have liked me to say? "Die, you gravy-sucking witch?"

Angora didn't grant me a reply. Instead, she began to browse, slowly, deliberately, as if determined to examine every single item in the store, great or small.

After a full fifteen minutes my nerves were worn thin as filament. Harold, I noticed, had not taken his eyes off Spike, who seemed to be asleep against a stack of old gloves. Just when I thought I'd scream with frustration, Angora spoke.

"It's interesting," she said, then paused.

"Don't play her game," Harold warned.

"What's interesting?" I asked.

Again, Harold grunted in disgust.

Angora stroked the fur collar of her coat. "Well," she said, slowly, "I happened to be on Pinter Street the other day when the most extraordinary thing happened."

I thought: Pinter Street? Why does that sound familiar?

"Haven."

I looked over to Harold. His wide, unblinking eyes were on me now, not Spike.

"It's where you cast the spell on Jared. It's where he was just before he—disappeared."

I stared back at Harold. Of course, I hadn't really forgotten. Pinter Street.

I looked back to Angora. A slow grin spread across her perfect face.

"Yes," she drawled, "I thought so." Then she made a show of checking her watch. "How time flies," she said. "Well, you might want to make an appearance at Talisman tonight, around ten. I'm just dying to tell everyone what happened to me on Pinter Street. In fact, I suspect that you, Haven Castle, of all people, will be extremely interested in what I have to say."

Then Angora Slate looked me over from head to toe and back again. And with a dismissive little laugh, she left Anastasia's Attic; Spike rumbled behind.

The moment she was gone I dashed out from behind the counter and locked the door.

I stood perfectly still for what seemed like a long time. A hip young couple strolled past the store window, engrossed in conversation. A nun from the small Catholic school down the block came out of the bakery across the street carrying a white cake box. A private sanitation truck came to a screeching stop outside the tiny Italian restaurant next door.

Life, it seemed, was going on.

Other people's lives, anyway. My life, as I knew it, was about to end.

It was all too clear what was going to happen that night at ten o'clock. Angora Slate was going to publicly accuse me of spelling Jared Cragmere.

I had two choices: I could avoid the club and further seal my reputation as a coward and a fraud, or I could show up at Talisman and take responsibility, finally, for my misdeed.

Maybe, too, I would have the chance to apologize to Jared one last time.

I turned back to Harold.

"Are you asking me if you should go tonight?"

"No," I said. "Yes. I don't know."

Harold paused before answering. "I think," he said, "that you should. It won't necessarily be pleasant, but—"

"But what?"

"But I have a sense that it's important for you to be there. I'm not a seer, not in the real sense, but . . ."

"Okay," I said, "I'll go."

31

*There may be times in which even the most wise and expe-
rienced witch feels overwhelmed by circumstances beyond
his or her control. In these cases, it is best not to take hasty
action (for example, throwing oneself off a cliff) but rather
to submit to said circumstances. Remember: This, too, shall
pass.*

"Steady, Haven. You've made it this far; it's no time to
bolt."

Wasn't it? Harold and I had taken only a few steps into
Talisman before I began to feel sick.

The club had never felt so unwelcoming. The crush of
elaborately dressed coven members seemed menacing, a
mob ready to accuse an innocent of a horrible crime, a
crowd eager for a scapegoat to torture. I wouldn't have
been surprised to see flaming brands held aloft in grubby
hands.

"Overactive imagination," Harold said. "Flaming brands
would violate the fire code."

The red-velvet-covered walls seemed suited for the Marquis de Sade's prison cell; the black lights belonged in an opium den. Incense hung heavy in the air; it had never bothered me before, but now it stung and choked.

"Breathe shallowly," Harold advised.

Everyone, it seemed, had gathered to hear Angora's important news: Boswell Van Der Minter and Oscar, both perfectly groomed; the monstrous Inclementia and her evil sidekick Tempestina, their long-suffering familiars conspicuously absent; Lumina Harbor and Belle Creek, in full street style; Tamara Decora, her head now decorated with toads; and, interestingly, Marta Herald, the woman who had come dangerously close to being sacrificed in my stead. I felt a strong urge to throw myself at her feet and beg forgiveness, but a warning claw from Harold restrained me.

"Haven!" It was Axel; he was loping toward us, an open smile on his face.

"Hi," I said. What, I wondered, had Jared told his best friend about me?

"I've missed seeing you around."

"He means it," Harold told me.

"I've missed you, too," I said tearfully. I was glad when someone called to Axel and he loped off again.

"Do you see Jared?" I asked Harold, with hope, with dread.

But before he could reply, an excited murmur arose from the dark depths of the room. Harold leapt into my arms; I held him tight. Together, we turned to see Angora Slate standing—posing, really—just inside the door. She looked magnificent in a red couture confection with a train at least twenty feet long. Spike, lumped at her side, wore a red satin cape; how it wasn't already shredded I don't know.

Harold gripped me closer, in support. This was the moment I had been dreading for more than a year. Angora

Slate met my frightened eye with an utterly delighted grin. Then her eyes swept the rapt crowd; she opened her mouth and said, "Tonight—"

And then, there he was, between Angora and me, in full view of the entire crowd, alive and beautiful and standing where a split second before he hadn't been standing.

Jared Cragmere had transmigrated body and spirit from wherever he'd been to the floor of Talisman. And he'd brought Mercury along for the ride.

When the shock began to wear off there were cries of astonishment and murmurs of appreciation, even scattered applause. I could say nothing; I felt faint with awe. Jared Cragmere, the man I loved so utterly, was a rare witch, indeed.

Angora broke the spell; no one, not even Jared, was allowed to upstage her. With a loud rustle of her gown, she strode forward until she stood with him in the center of the blood-red room. Once again, she opened her mouth to speak; once again, Jared interrupted.

"Listen to me."

The crowd quieted. Spike bristled. Angora's hands clutched at her dress.

"I have proof," Jared said, "that for years Angora Slate has been using magic on both witches and simply humans." A few voices of protestation arose, but Jared, speaking more loudly, silenced them. "Specifically, she's been spelling men, women, and even the occasional underage victim in matters of the heart."

Jared paused. I felt rooted to the spot, my arms locked around Harold. Never, ever had I expected the night to take this turn.

Jared continued, "Now, as low as this practice is, it's not necessarily dangerous or deadly. But putting a Moribund spell on a simply human is."

Angora took a step and stumbled. A strange cry came from the depths of Spike's bulk.

"I have proof," Jared went on, "that she's spelled a certain Mr. Riillo, the landlord of her building. The spell didn't work quite as planned—or maybe it did. Mr. Riillo is at City Hospital in critical condition. His doctors fear he'll never walk again."

"He deserved it!" Angora's face was flushed, distorted by emotion. Several members of the crowd took a step back from her.

Jared remained utterly composed. "Why?" he asked. "Because he was trying to do his job by collecting the rent you failed to pay for the past six months?"

Angora had no answer. And then Perry Marble stepped forward from the crowd. He was a respected senior witch who rarely spoke, but when he did, everyone listened.

"This," he said in a sonorous voice, his dachshund, his familiar, sitting solemnly in the crook of his arm, "is serious, Angora. The good name of the coven is tarnished by your behavior. Worse, a man's life has been permanently damaged. What do you have to say for yourself?"

Angora stuck out her arm and pointed directly at me. "Haven did it!" she screamed, her eyes bulging with rage. "She's the one who made Jared disappear!"

There were puzzled murmurs and shocked exclamations. Several witches turned to look at me doubtfully. And then, in an instant, all gave way to laughter.

Harold, ever in control, allowed himself a small feline chuckle. And together we listened to the responses of our fellow witches.

"Please, Angora," Peony Netherland drawled, "a real witch knows when to admit defeat."

"I can't believe you've been lying about everything!" Caraway Granite whined plaintively. "Does this mean you didn't actually sleep with Brad Pitt and George Clooney? What about Jessica Simpson and Nick Lachey and Prince Edward?" Caraway stamped his expensively shod foot. "But what does it matter? Even if you did have sex with them all, it was spelled so it doesn't count!"

Angora shrieked; Spike bristled. "Why aren't you attacking her?" she cried, pointing once again at me. "It's Haven Castle who should be punished! It's Haven Castle who should be beaten and tortured and thrown out on her ass!"

Roger Legend hissed his disapproval as only he can; it has something to do with his forked tongue.

"Trying to divert attention from your own heinous crimes." Boswell shook his well-coiffed head. "It's just not the done thing, you know."

Angora yanked on her train; it caught against Spike's bristly back and tore. "I am Angora Slate! No one tells me what's done and what's not! I—"

Angora's desperate voice was drowned out by the sound of Flora Romane tossing her five-foot braids. They cracked like brutal whips before settling once again on her broad, Valkyrie-like back. "Forget going to bed with me again," she snapped.

And then Jared, my beautiful Jared, was at my side. He took my arm and whispered, "Come on, let's get out of here."

32

The most powerful and mysterious force of all, in this world and, I am told, in many others, is love.

I let us in to Anastasia's Attic. Before I could switch on a table lamp just inside the door Jared pulled me to him. We kissed for the first time in so long. It was Jared who finally pulled away. I put my hand to my head, dazed.

"Are you all right?" he asked, brushing my hair from my cheek.

"Yes, I think so." I looked up into his beautiful pale green eyes that were shining in the dark. "Is this real? Are you really here?"

Jared kissed me again. Oh, yes, it was real.

"I'd like to know what happened back there."

I looked to Harold; he and Mercury were sitting together on a tufted chair.

"I thought," I said, turning back to Jared, "that you were mad at me. I thought you hated me."

Jared switched on the table lamp and we moved farther

into the store. "I never hated you, Haven," he said. "But I was mad. For a while."

"Not anymore?"

"No, I finally realized it doesn't matter how we came together. I believe you love me."

"I do, I do love you, Jared, so much."

We hugged long and hard. Only Harold's pointed hacking made me pull away this time.

"Just swear, okay?" Jared requested. "Swear you'll never put another spell on me for as long as we live."

"Oh, Jared," I cried, "I swear! I'm so very sorry!"

"I know."

Then Jared stepped back from me. "Haven, I have to be completely honest with you."

I felt my stomach drop.

"How bad can it be?" Harold said, helpfully. "You've got him back, haven't you?"

"Okay," I whispered.

"Shortly before you confessed to me that night, I'd found something, a clue, never mind what, exactly. And it seemed to point to you as the one who'd banished me to the Hebetatians."

Then I remembered standing in the foyer of my apartment. I'd asked Jared if he knew who'd banished him. Before answering he'd looked at me with intense scrutiny, as if he were trying to read my mind.

"Oh," I said.

"But I just couldn't believe that you were responsible. I figured I'd misread the evidence. I forgot about it. Or I almost had when you confessed. And then I felt doubly betrayed, not only by you, but by my own feelings. I was so in love with you I didn't even trust my own skills. That made me angry. It's why it took me this long to come back."

"Oh," I said again. I was horrified I'd done so much damage to him, to us. "Jared?" I asked. "Will we ever be able to put this all behind us? Or will you always have a shred of a doubt about me?"

Jared put his hands on my shoulders. "Love," he said, "is absolute. It allows us to believe our loved ones are entirely trustworthy."

"All this talk of love is well and good, but I want to know the gory details of Angora's demise."

I laughed. "Harold," I said, "wants details."

"Harold," Jared said, "will hear them."

But first, there was something I had to know. "You and Angora. I heard—"

Jared winced. "I can imagine. But she never got what she wanted. I think it made her even more determined to prove it was you who spelled me. She suspected you. I don't know how, but eventually she found your trail. I suppose she thought exposing you would drive me into her arms."

I considered this for a moment. Finally, I said, "I don't understand. How did you know she intended to expose me tonight?"

"She hinted, broadly. But I found out for sure what she knew the same way I found out about her spelling her lovers and putting a Moribund spell on that poor man. Angora Slate keeps a journal, the old-fashioned kind, in longhand, no lock, no key. And she keeps it in her bedside table."

"But how—"

"She gave me a key to her apartment," Jared explained. "I read the journal and took photos of the incriminating pages."

"She trusted you with her key."

Jared's eyes darkened and I saw, again, a ruthless nature. "Her giving me the key had nothing to do with trust. It was just part of her campaign, along with all the tricks and spells, to get me into bed. I played along to a point so that I could learn how much she knew—and then, hopefully, use that information to protect you."

"By publicly exposing her." It was a fact, not a judgment, but Jared didn't hear it that way.

"Would you have preferred I resorted to blackmail?" he asked. "Which, of course, would have involved my admitting I knew you were the guilty party. Besides, Angora can't be trusted to stick to a bargain. She would have sold you out no matter what."

"I know that," I admitted. "It's just . . ."

For a moment Jared didn't reply. When he did his tone was milder. "If I could have saved you another way, I would have. Are you angry with me?"

I threw my arms around him. "Oh, of course I'm not angry with you! The whole thing is my fault! And I'm not sorry Angora was exposed, but . . ." I looked up to Jared's face. Oh, how I'd missed the way his beard began to darken by night! "How could she be so careless? Why wasn't the journal locked away?"

"Angora," Jared said, "is supremely arrogant. Arrogant people get sloppy when it comes to covering their crimes."

There was one more thing. "Those flowers," I said, "the lilies at your door? They were from me."

"I know. I mean, I didn't know at first. I believed they were from Angora, but then I started to wonder."

"I was hiding behind the garbage cans."

Jared laughed. "Poor Haven!"

I reached up and held Jared's face between my hands and wondered how I could ever let go.

"I know," he said, "I need a shave."

"You don't need anything. You're perfect."

Behind me I heard Harold sniff in contempt.

"No comments," I told him, "not now."

And then there was a stupendous rustling and a shower of glittering dust, and a case full of minaudières crashed to the floor.

33

Once in a great while there occurs a satisfactory, even happy, ending to a chapter of the life of a witch. Of course, there is always another chapter following, in which anything can—and often does—happen.

"I'm back!"

Jared coughed; I rubbed glitter dust from my eyes and saw that my long-lost friend and mentor, Fabula Luna, had chosen this auspicious moment to reappear. Venice, the magnificent white peacock that is her familiar, emerged from behind the voluminous folds of his witch's velvet robes and spread his tail in greeting.

Harold, never a fan of prey larger than himself, retreated with dignity behind a bust of Madame du Pompadour. Mercury followed.

"Fabula," I said.

Pink hair glimmering, Fabula rushed at me. "Haven, I've never seen you look more alive!" Only then, after crushing me to her, did she notice Jared.

"Oh, hello, darling boy!" she cried. "What are you doing here?"

Jared allowed himself to be smashed against Fabula's ample bosom. When he emerged, he said, "It's a long story, Fabula."

"You'll give me the short version."

So, we did.

"I tried and tried to reach you," I told her. "You must not have heard me."

Fabula laughed her tinkling laugh. "Oh, darling, I heard you. I just chose not to answer."

"But why?" I cried. "I needed you!"

"Darling, you only thought you needed me. But I knew better. I knew you could wade through this whole mess on your own. And look. You have!"

I thought of Lia's friendship and Jared's love and Harold's sound advice and said, "I didn't solve anything on my own. I had lots of help."

"Not magical help, darling."

I don't know what possessed me, but then I was saying, "Fabula, I need a month's paid vacation. Jared and I are going to England. He's going to show me where he was born, and we're going to eat, drink, and be merry."

I held my breath; Jared put his arm around my shoulder.

Finally, Fabula spoke. "You know," she said, as if the idea had just come to her, "I could use some time off. All this traveling is wearing me out. Darlings, this witch is not as young as she used to be."

"You mean . . ."

Fabula yawned widely. "Yes, of course, darling, go and be merry. And when you return we'll talk about a change to our little routine. Change, Haven, can be quite invigorating. Now, if you'll excuse us, Venice and I must go home and get some sleep."

They went out the way they'd come in, with a great, destructive flourish.

"You're far less messy when you do that," I told Jared. Then I noticed that Harold had emerged from behind Madame du Pompadour and was lazily batting at a pile of nasty somethings on the floor.

"What are those?" I demanded.

Harold looked up from his desultory game. "Really, Haven," he said, "scratching a witch's eyes out is a bit over the top. Still, I felt those two specimens needed some comeuppance . . ."

"You didn't."

"Oh, I did. These hideous things are Inclementia's acrylic nails. Well, they were her acrylic nails. I suppose they're mine now, though I have absolutely no use for them."

"I'm afraid," Jared said, "to ask what you did to Tempestina."

"The dog," Harold replied, "took care of Tempestina."

Mercury came trotting out from behind the Madame, a large gray wad of hair in his mouth.

Jared took my hand. "It's a good thing," he said, "that we're going off to Merrie Olde England. By the time we return maybe tempers will have cooled."

I looked up to Jared and felt, in that moment, like a very new Haven Castle. "You know," I said, "I don't care if tempers have cooled or not. Let them like me, let them hate me. I've got my own life now."

Harold wheezed. Mercury whined. Jared—well, you can imagine what Jared and I did.

Single White Witch

Carly Alexander

1

"Did you add murder to the list?" Judy cradled her paper coffee cup and leaned over the counter to check the notations I was making on a napkin. "It's definitely an effective way to deal with the boss."

Before I could answer, Landon wagged a thin coffee stirrer at her. "Annie can't kill him. Have you lost your mind, girl?"

Judy cocked her head so that a cluster of red curls fell over her eyes. "We all know I'm certifiable, but I thought we were working out of the box here, writing down all possibilities before we made value judgments."

"You're both right," I said. "Murder should be on the list if we're going to do a wide-open, stream of consciousness thing. And, no, I can't kill Simon. Much as I'd enjoy that in a *Celebrity Mole* sort of way." Death to Simon. While I'd be happy to avoid his smug, disapproving smirk, I had to admit that in some twisted way I would miss him, too. He had seen the potential in me, had taken a chance on a young writer, and had coughed up the budget to finance this three-month assignment in New York. Though death would definitely prevent him from walking into the Coffee Nook and delivering the inevitable news without any of the bravado of the Donald. *You're fired. Assignment ended. Pack your things, blow a kiss to Manhattan, and return to the dreary world of your childhood.*

I picked up a square of zucchini bread from the sample plate and thanked my lucky stars that my friends had come to the café to lend me moral support for what looked to be a difficult meeting with my boss. I wasn't sure that they understood the weight of today's deadline, but I also felt that it might be a bad omen to whine over the worst possible outcome. Negative wish fulfillment.

It had been Judy's idea to make up a list of ways to avoid the boss on this pivotal, end-of-project deadline day, and although I knew it was futile because you couldn't elude a man like Simon forever, I did appreciate the support. Judy was due at the city morgue and Landon was supposed to be finishing off a sculpture for a show at the New School, but here they were playing hooky and trying to buoy me up with kind platitudes and foamy cappuccinos. My friends were the best.

Outside the windows of the café, New Yorkers moved briskly in leather jackets and wool coats, eager to respond to the overnight dip in temperature and to put the hot, steamy summer behind them. A selection of comic monster tunes played amid the shush of the cappuccino machine. "Monster Mash" had just ended, and now Warren Zevon was howling over the "Werewolves of London." The café bar was strung with orange and gold paper leaves punctuated by accordion skeletons that danced in the air every time the door opened. At this time of year New Yorkers loved a good, spooky scare, even if it was the CVS plastic mask variety.

"Of course you can't kill Simon," Judy went on, "but don't rule out the possibility of accidental death. Wouldn't it be convenient if he were walking down the wrong street at the wrong time?" Red curls rolled over her black sweater as she tossed her head back to mull possible scenarios. "Passing under the piano that plummets three stories? Walking alongside the cab that accidentally jumps the curb? Partaking of the blowfish that absorbed just a trace of deadly poison?"

Landon leaned away from her. "Jooody," he intoned, "you need to step out of the coroner's office more often. I think you and your bud Dr. Chris are suffering major oxygen deprivation in there. Take a deep, cleansing breath. Fresh air in, deadly thoughts out."

"Can I help it if I have a knack for devising deadly scenarios? At least it works for me at the M.E.'s office." She curled her hands around her coffee. "Though Paulo has yet to reward my talent."

"Hey, you hang in there," I told her as I added "death by falling piano" to my list of ways of avoiding the boss. "A knack is a knack."

"Yes," Landon added, "and in your line of work, it's good to have a knack for nicking."

"Or while we're doing stream of consciousness, there's a nick nack, paddy whack, give the boss a bone." Judy screwed up her face, her green eyes glinting with satisfaction. "Now there's a possibility. Pump him up. Flatter him."

"Impossible. His skin is too tough for buttering."

"Tell him he's handsome. Mention something he's wearing, something about his eyes or his suave style."

That wouldn't be far from the truth. With thick, brown hair and eyes so dark they seemed encrypted with dark mysteries, Simon cut a striking silhouette. Even in his usual Armani suit, the man exuded a certain fluid power, unlike some of the three-piece men I'd encountered who resembled lumpy scarecrows stuffed into pin-striped wool and easy-press collars.

"You've met Simon," I said. "He's gorgeous, but he knows it."

Landon rubbed the creases in his forehead. "Why is it that the cute ones get the ego to match? It's like they're born with the combo pack."

I nodded. "Supersized at birth."

"Supersized?" Judy howled, almost in sync with Warren Zevon, then covered her mouth with her hands. "Oh, Annie, does that come with fries?"

"It comes with all the fixings," Landon insisted. "Some people are simply born with the silver spoon. The double-shot venti."

Judy shook her head. "While the rest of us are stuck in the deli line waiting for a cup of watery regular."

"Don't sell yourself short, sister," I teased Judy, who wasn't beautiful by Malibu Barbie, supermodel standards, but had so much more to offer. If I had learned anything during this assignment in New York, it was that physical beauty wore thin after the second or third roll in the sheets. Oh, there's that initial thrill at winding your hips around Michelangelo's David, until he tosses you off to answer his cell phone or lets you in on how he's been dropping Viagra to go all night (which, really, is such an unnatural state. Why can't men realize that too much of a good thing is not a good thing at all?). But back to Judy, who obviously needed a little boost. "People would kill for your hair," I told her. Those fiery red curls prompted some women to actually stare in envy. "And your smile."

"A product of TMJ," she said. "If I had the money to get my jaw fixed, you'd realize I'm not smiling at all. This is my way of gritting my teeth. My perpetual snarl."

I squinted at her. "Then you give good growl."

"Hear me roar."

"And while you're handing out the compliments, Annie . . ." Landon batted his eyelashes at me. "Are you going to tell me that bald men are sexy?"

"Nothing so mundane," I said. "But truly, a thatch of hair would only mask the exquisite shape of your head."

He smacked my hand playfully. "Get out! But first, tell me more. It sounds so good coming from the author of the *Single White Witch* column. I mean, you're the expert, with your 'Worthy Man' campaign going strong."

"I'm supposed to be." But I was also supposed to have culminated my search for a "Worthy Man" by today, and although I had stayed on deadline with my column over the past few months, I had failed in my ultimate goal: finding a worthy human man.

Oh, I'd met many a man, but somehow I'd attracted men of the worth*less* persuasion, and I didn't have the time to examine what that revealed about me or why I had so much appeal for the bad boys of New York.

Today was my final deadline, and I had nothing to show for it. I'd kept up the search and chronicled it in my columns over the past few months, but Simon wasn't one to give credit for trying; he was a results man, and I cringed at the thought of facing him.

"I can't believe my time is up. When I started this assignment, it seemed like I had all the time in the world." I leaned down and rested my face in my hands, barely staring at the black hair falling around my fingers. "Three months, and I still haven't found a worthy man."

"Hang in there," Judy told me. "You can't expect to find a mate within a certain time frame, and don't try to make us feel sorry for you. Some of us have been on the lookout all our lives with no success at all. Falling in love isn't meant to be a short-term job goal; it's a lifelong pursuit."

She didn't realize that my boss had given me a very specific deadline for the "falling." None of my New York friends knew all the details regarding my assignment, and they thought the name of my column—*Single White Witch*—was just a clever way to snag the "goth girl" market. They had read a few of my columns but didn't subscribe to *Ephemera Online*, which was fine with me. I preferred to supply certain information on a "need-to-know" basis.

Landon rolled a round paper coaster down the bar toward my coffee cup and missed. "Ach, a gutter ball . . . and I can't believe we're having this conversation again. Why are we talking about this? You just tell Simon that some things cannot be rushed. You'll meet your man in good time." He swirled his hands around, as if tracing planets in distant galaxies. "When various elements and aspects in the universe fall in alignment, so will your love life."

"Easy for you to say." I slid his coaster back to him. "You met your soul mate in the Sandbox."

That would be a club called the Sandbox, where patrons take off their shoes and cavort in heated sand. Hell on a pedicure, but Landon loved getting closer to the "elements" in an earth, wind, water, and fire sort of way. A metal sculptor, he was content to flip down his visor and groove to the flame of his blowtorch for days at a time. Which was just fine by his partner, Jeremy, who worked as an editor at a downtown publishing house. Jeremy's job was a fairly routine ten to seven, and he loved to come home and find Landon welding madly to his muses. Landon had never been deadline oriented, which was probably to be expected of an artist who disappeared in a Long Island City loft for weeks at a time, then emerged to report that he's taking a break because he's reached an impasse on a piece. When I'm stuck for a story idea, I imagine Landon's blue eyes glowing with raw inspiration under his safety goggles, blowtorch roaring as he flits around his studio like a firefly.

Pressing a coffee stirrer against my lower lip, I soaked up the café scene one last time: the orange paper skeleton dancing over my friends' coffee cups on the bar, Judy checking her watch with resignation that she would have to head off to work, and Landon flipping through the comic section of a discarded newspaper. My Manhattan friends; my favorite savory café; this cantankerous, pulsating city—these were things I would miss, and dearly.

"Annie-bananee, how's this for a horoscope?" Landon lifted the newspaper. "You're a Scorpio, right? 'The stars are turning your way as Venus pushes in.'"

"Really?" I croaked. Normally I wasn't a fan of the cheesy two-line horoscopes in newspapers, but here was a ray of hope, albeit melodramatic. "Isn't Venus the goddess of love?" I snatched the paper from Landon. "'Don't worry about the romantic roadblock you're facing,'" I read on. "'You're destined to find love in the most unlikely places.'"

"Well, that's ripe with possibilities," Judy said. "You've just got to hit some unlikely places. Bowling alleys, Off-Track Betting pits . . ."

"You could take a field trip down to the DMV and wait in line for a few hours," Landon suggested. "Or maybe there's a Star Trek convention in town?"

"Thanks, guys." I pressed a crease into the newspaper and stared out at the busy street, feeling my enthusiasm dip at the prospects of the day ahead. If Simon had his way, I might not even *be* in New York City this afternoon. No Trekkies for me; I'd be beamed up to another astral plane. Yep. And there he was now.

"*What?*" Landon asked, pressing toward me. "What is it? You look like you just got a terminal prognosis."

Amazing how insightful the boy could be having known me for barely three months. I would have spared him a smile if I'd been able to pull my eyes away from the man moving swiftly along the café window, and now passing through the door.

Simon McAllistair looked as thin and buoyant as the skeletons dancing under the air vents. Walking death.

I gripped the edge of the bar and shot a desperate look at Judy and Landon. "It's Simon . . . he's here."

"Don't sound so shocked," Landon teased. "You were expecting him, right?"

"On time, as usual," Judy said, checking her watch. "And I really need to get to work, or Paulo will bite my head off." She squeezed the nubby sleeve of my Lauren tweed jacket. "You hang tough, honey. I want the whole recap after work."

I nodded and swallowed hard, hoping I'd still be alive on planet Earth this evening.

Judy swung around toward Simon as she shrugged her coat over her shoulders. "Well, hello. Remember me? We're the friends, just on our way out."

"I can stay," Landon said blankly, and though I would have loved to have him here for diffusion, he melted at the scathing look from Judy. "But actually, I should go." He wrapped his muffler around his neck and picked up his coffee cup. "We'll catch you later, Annie."

I waggled my fingers, watching longingly as they disappeared out the door.

"Annie Quicksilver . . ." Simon's voice was laden with disappointment. "I had such high hopes for you." His British lilt and smoothly styled suit reminded me of an operative from a James Bond movie. "Let's not waste time." He unbuttoned his jacket and took over Judy's stool at the bar. "Are you ready to concede that your assignment here was unsuccessful?"

It was going to be over, just like that?

I blinked, suddenly remembering the leather portfolio resting by my feet. "I beg to differ." It wasn't over yet. Not if I could help it. "I've accomplished a lot here." I reached down for my portfolio and propped it on the bar. "Maybe we should start by going over some of my columns."

He rolled his eyes and sighed. "Somehow I knew this meeting with you wasn't going to be short and sweet."

I slid the zucchini bread closer to him. "You want short and sweet, try a piece with a small latte."

"Ms. Anastasia Quicksilver, why must you make this so difficult?"

Because I'm not an expendable person, I thought, unzipping the portfolio with some satisfaction. Annie Quicksilver would not fade away . . . .

At least, not without a fight.

2

Simon ordered himself an espresso and placed a crisp twenty on the bar. "Honestly, I don't know why you would want to stay in this godforsaken land. The traffic is horrendous, the residents quite loud and opinionated, and the cuisine seems to suffer an identity crisis. Italian or Greek? Thai or French? Afghan or Russian? Such a mishmash of cultures and fashions, I don't know how the locals tolerate the uncertainty."

"Some people like to make choices."

"Tedious, don't you think?"

"I'm pro-choice," I joked, realizing it was probably wasted on my audience. "That is, I like making choices. I think decision making is good for the soul."

Simon shook his head disparagingly. "You have come a long way from your roots. I dread to think of your readjustment back in Ephemera; however, that's a matter for later discussion."

Not if I could help it. I didn't want to go back, but I had decided to take a professional tact and support my case with my work.

He slipped two dollars into the tip box and tucked away the rest of the change. "Now, then, shall we review your progress here? Or should I say, lack thereof?"

"Try to be fair about this. I know I didn't meet the ultimate deadline, but it's not for lack of trying. I put myself out there and got results. Maybe not the end result we were looking for, but you've got to give me credit for finding some men. Many men."

"Ah, yes. If only quantity could replace quality," he said with a fake sigh.

I pulled a fat folder out of my leather bag—printouts of my *Single White Witch* columns. "It's all been documented in my columns, Simon. And from the volume of e-mails I've received, it's clear that the column has hit a vein. People relate to the search for love, the quest to find a man who isn't misrepresenting himself."

"That's *your* pop-psychology interpretation," he said quickly. "In my view, people want to read about sex, and they're pleased to know that someone out there is having a far worse go of the relationship game than they are. Readers are simply staring at the train wreck that has become your life."

Though his words stung, I reminded myself that Simon was notorious for his acerbic criticisms of all the writers on staff at *Ephemera Online*. Besides, I'd had the satisfaction of receiving reader responses to my columns, genuine thanks and cheers from people relieved to know that someone else had traveled the same bumpy road. "Look, you're the boss," I shot at Simon, "and if you don't place a value on reader feedback, that's your prerogative. But personally, I think reader opinion matters, and if those heartfelt messages of regret and hope are all I get out of this assignment, it's still worth it."

"You do have a way of candy-coating things," he said. "And a happy ending for all."

"Not necessarily." I handed him the first column I'd written at the beginning of my assignment here. "Read on, MacDuff. Bad things do happen to good people."

He glanced at the page, then back at me. "I'm far too old to read any story that begins with 'once upon a time.'"

"You published it," I pointed out, "I think you can manage a quick review of it."

He took the paper from me. "Ah, yes, the magic kingdom fable. Amusing how, when all else fails, you wax allegorical. Is that what they tell you in Journalism 101?"

"Just read it," I said, and to my surprise and embarrassment, he did. Aloud.

LOVE, AMERICAN STYLE

Once upon a time on an island of towering dreams there landed a young maiden with hair the color of obsidian and eyes full of insight and curiosity. This maiden, Annie, had been sent by her kingdom with a single quest: to find one noble knight, one earthly man deserving of her love and affection.

In those first sunny, long days, the maiden crisscrossed the isle of Manhattan in pursuit of the noble knight. She quickly befriended many of the good citizens and local merchants and was invited to local rituals: picnics in Central Park, softball games, cocktail parties at cavernous museums, and a spectacular summer tradition—the gathering of people on rooftops to watch colors explode in the night sky. The July 4th celebration was a festive culmination of Maiden Annie's first week on the isle of towering castles, and much to her surprise, she left the party that night with an intriguing gentleman by the name of Denver. An old-fashioned romantic, Denver insisted that he win her heart before he pushed his way into her bed.

Annie was charmed as Denver showed her the sights: There were kisses atop the Empire State Building, blue martinis at Nobu, and midnight carriage rides through Central Park. He asked her opinion on the various settings of diamond rings at Tiffany's and told her to go ahead and register at Bloomingdale's. Marriage was imminent; Annie's quest was culminating in a spectacular finale.

He paused, not a moment too soon, as the story had sent me spiraling back to that time—to the newness of Manhattan; my own blithe, vulnerable spirit; the magical emotions that eddy around two people who are attracted to each other.

Denver had embodied my childhood dreams—a successful, handsome man of wealth. I had fallen for his proposal, headfirst.

"Let me ask you this," Simon said thoughtfully. "Did you love him?"

I burst out laughing, surprised that Simon would ask such a question and uneasy over the answer, over the fact that, at the time, I didn't have a handle on my feelings.

"Not that love is a requirement for your assignment," he said, "it's just that, you seemed so distraught when it didn't work out. Was that because he tricked you? Because you had invested so much in him? Was it disappointment or devastation?"

"I'd have to think about that one," I said, running my finger along the seam of my coffee cup. I could trace the demise of my relationship with Denver down to one night, one moment when I got a glimpse of his true nature.

Which would be a cross between warthog and big fat liar.

It was the middle of July, and we were spending the weekend in the Hamptons, staying with Denver's friends in a rose-covered cottage on a quiet lane. That particular night we went to a wild, loud party at a brown-shingled estate on Dune Road. The house wasn't much to speak of, but it faced the ocean and the grounds had a swimming pool and a garden that branched out into a network of tiny paths leading to private guest houses. "It's a party campus," one of the guests had remarked. "We're all registered for summer session. I'm majoring in Tropical Martini 101!"

I found it funny the first time he'd said it; the third time, Denver and I moved on to the other side of the pool. Inland the air was still and thick with humidity, but a steady breeze blew off the ocean, making it bearable to dance and eat and chat with other guests. It was dark and the sky was speckled with stars when Denver pulled me out onto the patio to dance; I swung my hips, playing out a seductive scenario, wondering if I could stir something up. Despite sessions of heavy petting and my own rapturous moments brought on by Denver's masterful fingers and tongue, we had yet to seal our relationship with sexual intercourse, and frankly, Denver's chaste "after we're married" vow was driving me a little crazy. I was a girl with hormones, and I wanted this man, all of him, now.

Our host had mentioned that a few of the guest houses were empty, which shrieked "opportunity" to me. Feeling like a harem girl, I circled my man, took him by the hand, and led him off down a garden path. The guest house we found was far from the ocean, but it had a private atrium in the center with a fountain and a hot tub. Denver went into the kitchen in search of drinks. When he returned, I sat with my feet in the bubbling hot tub, my clothes tossed on a chair and a fluffy white towel wrapped around me. The blue lights from the Jacuzzi were the only illumination and they cast a gentle glow over my body. The flowing element of water combined with the blue of good fortune and inspiration . . . seduction was inevitable.

"I found champagne," he announced, hoisting the bottle, "and you've found a towel but . . . lost your clothes."

"I thought we could relax in the hot tub," I said, lifting my chin.

"A great idea," he said, slipping off his designer loafers. At least Denver didn't have any hangups about getting naked. A minute later, he was swinging into the hot tub, filling champagne glasses. I kept my towel on as I watched him move through the water, his muscles tight, flexing slightly, his body so perfectly proportioned. Was it any wonder I was dying to make love with this man?

"To our life together," he said, clinking my glass. "To our bond through eternity."

"You're so romantic," I said, taking a sip.

"We'll have a dozen babies," he went on, "beautiful, dark-haired toddlers. Little girls who all look like you."

I nearly sprayed champagne in his face. "Let's not rush ahead." Not that I had any objection to children, eventually, but back in Ephemera there was such a huge emphasis on progeny that it sucked the romance out of a relationship. I preferred the prevailing American man attitude, the "let's make love and party" song over the "time to research local schools and apply for a mortgage" dirge.

"You're right." He put his glass on the tiles beside me and reached for the top of my towel. "Why think of the future when the present moment is so delicious." His fingertips ran along the top of the towel, titillating as they slipped under the fabric and pulled gently. My breasts burst out, and he clasped them as he hungrily dropped kisses along my neckline. "Very delicious," he murmured as his hands covered my skin.

I shoved the towel back and opened my legs to him so that he could move close—dangerously close.

"We have to be careful," he whispered. "Can't let go till we're married."

"Mmm-hmm . . ." I lied as I ran my hands over his

shoulders and through his thick hair. With the stone-hard evidence of his excitement pressing against me, I knew he wanted me, and I saw no point in waiting for a formal decree of our union. I wriggled my hips slightly, loving the feel of him between my legs, his strength against my soft resistance. Passion swept through me like the rising tides in the Atlantic beyond us, swelling and lapping and slapping over the sides. I was well on my way, but this time I wanted to take him with me. In me. I moved his hands up to my shoulders and slid into the water, wrapping my legs around his waist.

He moaned. "I'm not going to be able to stand this." He held me close, pressing his hardness into me as I rode him slightly. "You're too beautiful, too sexy, too much." Steam rose around us, bubbles popping, spiking the air with the clean tang of chlorine. The heat simmered us into a piping hot brew, too much to resist.

"I can't take it," he muttered abruptly. Suddenly, he was unhooking my hands and legs. "Quick . . . turn around." I was extracted and spun in the water, so that I was facing our half-full champagne glasses at the side of the tub. Before I could react he had his arms around me and was pressing against me, nudging rhythmically into my lower back. No entry, but from his rushed breathing I knew it didn't matter for him. Denver was finally approaching the mountaintop, and I clasped my arms over his, determined to view from the summit.

I smiled as he squeezed me tight. Sweet ecstasy.

Then came a bellow unlike any I'd heard on the planet. It was more like a doleful groan, followed by a watery snort.

Not a human snort.

Panic shot through me as Denver's arms felt suddenly bony and cloying. Glancing down, I gasped and pushed away, flailing against the black hooves, the furry joints, the pathetic wail of the animal behind me. To my horror, I realized that Denver wasn't a man at all but a shape-shifting warlock.

Half-man, half-warthog. A cursed warlock . . . the worst kind.

3

"I should have known," I told Simon. "How stupid was I to think a human man would just want to get married out of love?"

"So you did love him?" Simon probed.

"Did I?" Was it possible? My relationship with Denver had left me so soured that I found it hard to appreciate the high points of our relationship. I sucked in a breath and gripped the edge of the coffee bar, trying to distance myself from the memory. "It wasn't love. How can you love someone who's hiding their true nature from you?"

Simon shrugged. "Let me remind you, our project was never about finding love, as you well know. On the other hand, your 'quest,' as you so aptly put it, did center on finding a worthy human man, which excludes Denver, the naughty, nefarious warlock, from the competition."

"Thank my lucky stars. The last thing I want is to be bonded with a warlock, a marauding, self-centered master of deception." Oh, I knew that breed well; I grew up with them, dodged their pranks in grammar school, fought them off as a teenager, and steered clear of them as an adult.

Although society and my witch lineage pointed me toward a warlock match, those primordial satyrs were one of the reasons I was here searching for a human man. Denver's demonic deception was a prime example of the treachery I had been trying to escape most of my life.

"Let's not overexaggerate," Simon said. "Not all warlocks are evil."

"Right, the dead ones are harmless."

"Ouch." Something flickered in his eyes—a glimmer of humor?—but a second later it faded to the usual opaque darkness.

"Wait a second . . . you're a warlock yourself," I said, folding my arms.

"I'd prefer to keep our private business private." He turned to see if anyone was listening, but the café was sparsely populated now and the hangers on who lingered were either absorbed in newspapers or blabbering into cell phones. "And you forget, my mother was human."

I didn't recall that about Simon, but I didn't want to let on. "Oh, right. A bad choice on her part."

"She seemed fairly content with her lot, but let's get back on track as I'm a bit short on time. So you landed in New York and immediately fell for the trickery of a warlock masquerading as something he was not," Simon said. "Boohoo for you."

I winced, annoyed with Simon and with myself for falling for Denver's facade. "I'm not looking for a pity party, but you've got to admit, it's a despicable quality you warlocks possess."

That was the thing I hated most about warlocks—the deception. As the premier shape-shifters, they could cast themselves into a beautiful facade: graceful features, pumped up muscles, thick hair, and opalescent eyes. However, once they reached the moment of climax, their true nature was revealed. Thus, poor witches had to cope with husbands who transformed from gods to goblins before their very eyes. Let me tell you, it certainly darkens the glow of a magic moment. That's why warlocks are so caught up in the marriage thing; they possess a strong compulsion to mate and produce offspring. So they trap cute young things into a lifetime slaving over bubbling hot cauldrons, and in Ephemera, marriage seals the deal for them, since divorce is not an option. (Ludicrous, I know, but I didn't make the rules; I'm just bound by them.)

"Let me ask you something." I squinted at Simon. "When you reach that magic moment, do you turn into a reptile? A warty green frog? Or a snake? Wait . . . I'd say your true nature has to be something that crawls through the dirt, low to the ground. An insect? A furry centipede?"

"Once again, you're forgetting that I'm half mortal, which means I can't hide behind an assumed image like full-blooded warlocks." He held out an arm, gesturing down to the toes of his smooth leather shoes. "This is my true nature. Lovely, don't you think?"

"In a narcissistic sort of way." I tucked the column about Denver into my portfolio and pulled out the next one—a more upbeat account of a relationship entitled RUNNING IN FLIP-FLOPS. "Do you remember Vladimir, the shoe designer?" I waved the column in front of Simon. "Readers really adored him."

"Yes, I'm sure they did," he said as he stole a glance at the Coffee Nook's pizza plate clock. "Unfortunately, there really isn't time for all this, as I'm due for a meeting with the Magickal Council and you, my dear, have a hefty satchel of writing samples there, a body of work that will take days to examine."

"Okay . . ." I sucked in a breath tentatively. I could smell a brush-off as well as the next girl, but what exactly did it mean? Was I condemned without a thorough hearing, or given the green light for a stay on Earth? "So what are you saying, Simon? Am I staying on here . . . a regular contributor to *Ephemera Online*?" How blissful to be allowed to remain in New York, keep my friends, continue my job . . .

"Let's not jump ahead of ourselves," he said with a sour expression. "In fact, you are one of the matters I need to discuss with the Council."

"Moi?" I croaked. "I haven't done anything to draw unnecessary attention to myself, haven't revealed any secrets or cast sacred spells . . ." Granted, Simon had pulled a lot of strings to get my visa for a stay in New York, but I'd been on my best behavior, really and truly. "If they wanted to reprimand someone, they should take a look at Denver's activities on this astral plane."

"My responsibility is the Council's verdict on you," Simon said, and once again I wished that the Council's rules were more flexible. Despite the fact that there were dozens of astral planes to explore, a witch needed permission from the Magickal Council to stay for more than a week. The Council was cautious about disrupting other worlds, and the general sentiment seemed to be that witches should be thrilled with their lot in Ephemera.

And most witches did live in bliss. Ephemera was a matriarchal society where women ruled. Not a bad place to thrive, but standards were high, especially in domestic areas where I fell short; unlike my mother, a domestic goddess, maternal angel, artist of home and hearth. I don't think my mother was at all unhappy with her life in Ephemera. She married my father when she was twenty-three, and they went on to have nineteen children together. Yep, nineteen. That would be because the culture in Ephemera is a little different from that on Earth. Witches grow into a very active cycle called erotica, in which they become quite sexually active, while warlocks are motivated to mate for life and spawn numerous offspring. Males are the nesters, pushing for a wife who can provide a beautiful home, steady meals, and a long line of downy witch babies. This was the cheerful pattern of Ephemera, a lifestyle that worked for most witches.

But not for me.

"I wish the Council would loosen up on their immigration laws," I said, worrying at the prospect of a long line of shrieking babies.

"It's a question of clearances and quotas," Simon explained, "and there'll be some questions about why you missed your ultimate deadline."

That damned deadline was such a bitter pill. I swallowed hard. "Do you think they'll give me an extension?"

"For the long term, I doubt it," he went on, "but in the meantime, we must extend your visa, at least for a few weeks, until we have a chance to review the body of work you've accomplished here. That and the fact that I'll never find a replacement for you before Halloween."

True to legend, Halloween was the most celebrated holiday in Ephemera. Think Christmas times ten, take away Claus, add bonfires and sex.

"You're saying that I'm still on assignment here?" I asked hopefully, glad for the reprieve, albeit brief.

"You're good to go till November first, but we'll need to meet over the next week to continue your review, and I'll approach the Council on your behalf. Sadly, I don't know where we could possibly place you after this. As you know, there are assignments in various other astral planes, but considering your limited success here . . ."

I'll stay here! I'll stay here! I wanted to chant, but I didn't want to push Simon beyond his level of tolerance.

He swung off the stool and buttoned his coat. "I'll be in touch regarding our next meeting. Till then, remember the rules: low profile, high intellect, and all that rubbish."

Feeling oddly grateful, I nodded rapidly, my portfolio

pressed to my chest as he strode out the door, leaving a cool breeze that set the paper skeletons dancing again.

A reprieve.

And for my first act as a free woman I headed crosstown toward Sixth Avenue and the largest department store in the world. Cooler weather was setting in and I needed a coat. And while I was there, maybe some worthy man would stroll in looking for winter gear, too.

Hey, in New York City, you never know.

4

Call me crazy, but the turn of events that morning woke me up to the fact that our time on this planet, or any planet if you're looking at astronomical itineraries, is short, so we need to soak it up while we can. I paused over a grate to absorb the roar of the subway. I chased a man down the street to hand him a dollar bill he had dropped. I even stopped at a vendor's cart and imbibed in a hot dog, dubbed "dirty water dog" by Judy. If playing time was short, I wanted to be sure I was in the game.

New York City held so many attractions for me, but dirty water dogs were near the top of the list, along with Thai food, fast food, Krispy Kreme, Starbucks, and all the trendy bars where you could eat hors d'oeuvres for dinner. Domestication was highly touted in Ephemera, but here in New York I could grab a yogurt for lunch and eat out every night and nobody even cared.

As I popped the last of the hot dog into my mouth and wiped mustard from my lips, I remembered the disappointing day of my Domestic Cooking final exam. I was twelve years old. I hadn't really been paying attention all year, but I wanted to pass that class and get it over with.

Professor Pinwort waited with folded arms as I circled a platter of beef, summoning a spell.

Poof! It was a stir-fry of beef medallions with pearl onions, bright bell peppers over white rice.

Professor Pinwort lifted one brow skeptically, waiting as I attacked a rubbery blob of chicken breast.

A stab of my powers and—poof!—it was lemon chicken with broccoli and risotto.

Next was the ultimate challenge—a log of pork roast. Pork, the tasteless meat. I zapped it into a marinated roast rolled in sesame seeds, served with garlic mashed potatoes and green beans.

As I bowed to old Pinwort and waited for the tasting, I remember feeling a wave of relief, so glad that I wouldn't have to repeat a domestication class over the summer.

That was right around the time the professor began to gag. Something had gone wrong, some error in my calculations or chemical balances or metaphysical exchanges. Unfortunately, all three dishes were inedible.

I failed the class, but worse was the realization that I would never succeed as a domesticated witch. I think my mother was disappointed, but I knew she would get over it. After all, she had eleven other daughters.

By noon I had landed in a cushy warm black suede jacket with a fake fur collar that brought out the light in my jet-black eyes. I had also found a stunning pair of red gloves, traded in a special coupon for a little canvas bag with purple witches on it, and talked with Judy and Landon, who'd agreed to meet me for dinner at Plaid Thai.

Afloat on a wave of accomplishment, I allowed myself a slow cruise through the shoe department, avoiding the clodhopping boots and orthopedic canoes and lingering near the designer heels with skinny straps; the pumps crafted of velvety soft, gem-colored suedes; and the mules studded with winking rhinestones.

These whimsical, impractical shoes reminded me of Vladimir, my Vlad, who believed that a woman's feet were the wings of goddesses, and that shoes were the regal crowns meant to adorn them.

Plopping into a chair in the shoe section, I reached into my portfolio for the Vlad story.

RUNNING IN FLIP-FLOPS

Vlad had come to New York City from one of those small, newly independent Russian nations in Eastern Europe, and from our first meeting it was clear this was a man with two things on his mind: shoes, and the glorious pair of feet that would wear them.

There is a square, submerged plaza dropped into the corner of 49th and Seventh Avenue. The stairs lead down to a restaurant and the subway station, but the street level is gated off with a clear Plexiglas rail through which you can see the feet of hundreds of New Yorkers passing by. One summer afternoon as I paced in search of a blind date Judy had set up for me, my feet were fortunate to catch Vladimir Pitka's attention.

"One thing I like to say to you, you should never, never run in flip-flops."

Although the "never, never" sounded more like "neighbor, neighbor," I totally got him.

"Tell me about it." I shucked off one flip-flop and lifted my foot, flexing my manicured toes. "They always rub me the wrong way, right between my biggest toes."

"Oh, what a pity," he said, his hands spread in an expression of sorrow. "A crying shame."

In my opinion, foot discomfort didn't merit that level of remorse; however, I appreciated this man's sincerity and his ability to sit still and observe for hours in a city where most people were swept up in the mad rush of pounding feet. "Come, sit with me," he said. "Rest your feet." We sat on the steps for hours. I talked while Vlad sketched shoes. When my date didn't show we shared a sandwich and a Snapple, then parted cheerfully.

The next day, I couldn't help myself. I took the number one train to 49th and there was Vlad, observing footware, sketching designs from his dreams.

I recognized the artistry in Vlad's work. With some convincing, he let me show his designs to Judy, who has a friend at Nine West. The friend was encouraging, but pointed out that the designs had to go beyond sketches. Vlad needed to create three-dimensional models of his shoes. Models that could make the rounds at Dolce & Gabbana and Manolo Blahnik and Jimmy Choo.

Overnight, Vlad's studio apartment became a design center, all lights pointing on his work space. Over the next few weeks, using my size seven feet as a model, Vlad created spectacular paper shoes: sweeping arched high heels trimmed with frivolous feathers; strappy sandals of the goddesses; glass-heeled gems worthy of the Waterford Crystal Collection; glittering, classic ruby slippers. Stunningly beautiful shoes, all crafted of paper.

He was an artist, and I was his muse.

With each design I felt us draw closer, as he discovered things about me that I didn't even know myself—

*the sexy rise of my arch; the perfect proportion of my
toes; the vulnerable pressure point just behind my big
toe.*

I stopped reading. Going on would be too painful, especially since I still blamed myself for the demise of our relationship. My fault. Well, not completely. I'd been trying to
help, but sometimes the best of intentions kick you in the
shin.

My brilliant idea was to get Vlad's shoe collection some
exposure—a little buzz—before he took it to the design
studios. So one night, when Vlad and I had planned to
meet at the New School for the opening of an art exhibit
for which Landon got us tickets, I slipped my feet into a
pair of paper shoes—the black-and-white zebra print heels
trimmed in feathers. Perfect! I grabbed my bag and was
off.

My first mistake was taking the subway. Grime and
paper do not mix.

Then, as I climbed the subway stairs, my feet were as-
saulted by a mild river of rainwater cascading down. Rain.

I should have known better. Even all these months later, I
still felt bad about Vlad.

Back in the shoe department, the Macy's clerk pulled me
out of my miserable reverie. "May I help you with something?" he asked politely.

I held up a pair of gray leather spiky-heeled pumps, and
as he disappeared to find my size, I tucked away my Vlad
story with one last glance.

> *Three words of advice:*
> *RAIN MELTS PAPER.*
> *Vladimir never spoke to me again. Hard to believe
> that a relationship can snap over a pair of paper shoes.*

I thought I would be his savior, his Joan of Arc. The arch of my foot was his inspiration.

Lesson learned: There are plenty of feet in New York City.

Next time it rains, I'm wearing flip-flops.

5

"Love the shoes," Judy said that night as the waitresses placed platters of steaming pad thai and pineapple rice and Pad Ee Euiw on the lazy Susan at the center of our table. "They remind me of the little shoes sculpted by that Russian guy you used to date."

Judy had held my hand through the whole Vlad meltdown, which turned out to be a bonding experience for us. When it was all over, I let her read my article, RUNNING IN FLIP-FLOPS, and when she grinned and called it "cathartic," I realized how much we had in common, that the whole witch–human conflict was entirely overrated. Judy and I were sisters in the heartbreak vortex of this astral plane.

"Funny, I was just thinking about Vlad today." I held my feet out the side of the booth to show off my new low-heeled mules, black with white piping. I admit, slip-on shoes are not the most practical item when you're hoofing it through a Manhattan autumn, but it's hard to restrict yourself to functional shoes when you once reigned as the foot goddess.

"Ah, yes, the shoemeister," Landon said. "How is he doing?"

"I wouldn't know. He refused to speak to me after the melting shoe incident."

"I hear he landed a job designing for Ventani," Judy offered. "My friends at Nine West see him all the time. Apparently, the foot models love him."

"I'll bet. At least he landed on his feet," I said. "No pun intended."

"Or at least he's among friendly feet," Landon added.

"Don't you hate those ugly, nasty breakups?" Jeremy said. "When you're just ready to tear each other's eyeballs out?"

Landon tipped peanut sauce onto his plate. "Is there any other kind?"

I turned the lazy Susan so I could reach the pad thai, a rich mix of shrimp and pork and chicken and bean curd and crushed peanuts. Whoever thought that so many flavors would taste right together? I thought of all the characters in the Annie Quicksilver dating pool, all the guys I had written about over the past few months. They'd made my assignment quite tasty, though none of them was suitable for an entrée. "You know, all things considered, it's a wonder that any two people ever hook up for good. When you think of all the factors at play—personality, looks, interests, views—how can anyone find the perfect match?"

Jeremy shook his head disapprovingly. "Annie, nothing is ever perfect. Show me a perfect match and I'll show you pretension and repression."

"Right," Landon agreed, "so maybe you should change the name of your campaign. Instead of the *Worthy Man*, how about, the *Suitable Man*? The *Tolerable Man*? *Mr. Possibility . . .*"

"*Mr. Delusions of Adequacy*," Jeremy added with grin.

"Wait! Hold on!" Judy said over a mouthful of sticky rice. "That's what I've been dying to tell you: I've got a guy for you—a worthy man."

I bit my lower lip. "Thanks for trying, Jude, but we've been down that road before." A few thousand times. Good friend that she was, Judy was clueless on how to match up personalities.

"Dead end," Landon chimed in. "Icks-nay on the et-up-say."

"Ind-may your own eezewax-bay," Judy told him.

Jeremy held up his beer bottle and sighed. "I wish I had an aptitude for foreign languages."

Landon picked up a skewer of beef saté. "Didn't you spend a year in Germany?"

"Well, sure, but between the skiing and castle tours all I really had to learn was how to count in German so that I could order beers for my friends."

"Doesn't anybody care about my worthy man?" Judy glanced around the table. "Annie? You mentioned that your deadline was extended. You never know what might develop between now and Halloween."

I ran a thumb over the label on my Thai beer. "Honestly, if I haven't found him in three months, I'm thinking it's not going to happen anytime soon. After my meeting with Simon, I've been thinking. I'm going to push for an indefinite extension based on the merit of my column. If I can just get him to rethink the concept of *The Worthy Man*—think of it more as a process, as a lifetime pursuit than an end result."

"The process . . ." Landon nodded sagely. "I totally get it. My work is all about the process."

"Forget the process." Judy spread her hands wide, nearly clearing our table of beer bottles and glasses. "I've got a worthy man for you. This is not your average, ordinary setup. This is a really great guy. I know because I work with him. You've met him, Annie. I'm talking about Dr. Chris."

I gulped down a swallow of beer. Dr. Chris Moreland was adorable. He was also Judy's best friend at work.

"A doctor!" Jeremy's eyes went wide. "Not bad for starters."

"Get those visions of *ER* right out of your head, honey. He's a doctor of the dead," Landon pointed out.

Jeremy shrugged. "So? Think of the upside. At least he won't be on call, running out on you during dinner parties and movies."

"I can't go out with Dr. Chris," I said. "He's your best bud at work. You know him too well. He's like a brother."

"Exactly!" Judy nodded, pleased with herself. "We know he's trustworthy, and kind, and reliable."

"Are we talking about a date, or a personal banker?" Jeremy asked.

I scraped at the label on a beer bottle. "It would feel too weird, considering how close you are to him. In fact, I've always said that you two should get closer. Why don't you go out with him, Jude?"

"I keep telling you, that's not going to happen." Judy's curls bobbed as she shook her head. "It's totally platonic between us."

Landon grinned. "Why don't you just put him on the lazy Susan at the center of the table and we'll all take turns?"

"But I just can't," I said.

"But you have to," Judy insisted. "He's meeting us at eight."

"Tonight?" I crunched into a spring roll, wishing Judy hadn't taken such liberties. Tall and athletic, with a short brush cut and an adorable smile emphasized by braces, Dr. Chris really was a cutie, but in the few times I'd met him, I'd developed a sibling instinct toward him.

"I told him we'd get a table at the Cosmo-A-Go-Go," Judy went on.

Jeremy checked his watch. "To be honest, I am so not up for clubbing tonight."

"I know." Landon rubbed the creases in his forehead. "I think I left my blowtorch on."

"You did not!" Judy accused.

He shrugged. "But I need to get home. Jeremy has work tomorrow, and I'm close to finishing two pieces for the exhibit."

"You can't stay out a few hours later to help our friend keep her job?" Judy accused.

"Whoa, there, Lone Ranger." I hated to see my friends argue. "If the guys need to go, it's okay. We'll hook up with Dr. Chris on our own, right?"

To be honest, I was peaking now, aglow from beer and the reprieve from Simon, a little tired from sweating out the morning, and perfectly content to whomp it up with Thai food and witty conversation, then call it a night. A setup was the last thing I wanted, but I knew that Judy had gone to all this trouble out of the goodness of her heart, out of friendship and girlfriend love. How could I crush Judy's plans?

"Hey, how's it going?" Dr. Chris surprised us by having a table secured, courtesy of Mercedes, our favorite Go-Go waitress, who had casually draped herself onto the vinyl seat.

"Chris, you're early." Judy leaned over the table and gave him a friendly nudge on the shoulder. "Were you waiting long? I hope not. I told you eight, you ninny."

"I finished up early," he said, "and Mercedes has been keeping me company."

Mercedes cocked her head toward Judy and me, her

bright blue rectangular glasses catching the light. "Hey, gals. Who's up for a grapefruit martini?"

"We definitely need a round," I said, thinking I'd need a little bolstering for this last-minute date.

"I'd better stick with beer," Dr. Chris said, standing up courteously. "Sam Adams, please."

"Aw, Chris, I pegged you as a brewsky man," Mercedes teased him as she slid out, revealing blue suede platform boots that matched her glasses. A Mercedes trademark—coordinated eyeware and shoes. She was a big girl, almost six feet, I think, and she seemed to enjoy turning heads when she entered a room. She rose beside me, whispering in my ear, "Looks like you've got a hottie on your hands."

I just grinned, hoping Dr. Chris didn't hear her. No reason to be so calculating, though her assessment was correct. Dr. Chris *was* looking a lot better than I had remembered, but then the cold fluorescence of the city morgue left everybody looking a little green. Dr. Chris may not have practiced medicine, but the man possessed enough bedside manner to seduce half the girls at Cosmo-A-Go-Go—sparkling green eyes, broader shoulders than I'd remembered, and that smile all a-sparkle with braces. I was dating the cutest boy on campus.

We shook hands, as if ready for a consult, and slid into the booth.

"Okay, you two," Judy said, leaning over the table with an expectant smile. "I just want to say, I don't know why I didn't think of putting together my two best friends in the world before this." Her eyes were wide and gushing love in the dim light. I caught myself squirming and crossed my legs, uncomfortable at Judy's high expectations. "I'm just going over to the bar, so . . . you guys can talk, okay?"

I grabbed Judy's hand. "Don't be silly. Stay!"

"I'll just sit and talk to Fletch." She was already heading

off, walking authoritatively into the blur of the crowd, leaving us stranded on our own urban island. I wanted to join her, wanted to talk with Fletch, the father of three who had been tending bar here since this place was called Finnegans or Flannigans or something like that in the seventies.

"Judy's great," Dr. Chris said, smoothing down his necktie, making me wonder how he managed that perfect balance between comfort and professionalism in a shirt and tie.

"Judy's amazing," I agreed. "I can't tell you how many times she's saved my life since I got here, but I guess you know her better. How long have you two worked together?"

"It's been three years now. She was here when I joined the coroner's office. I keep telling her to go back to school for more training. With talent like hers . . ."

In this light, I noticed a small scar on his head, nearly hidden by his bristled hair—a tiny V-shaped crease. When I asked him about it, he laughed and told me how he and his brother had raced on sleds down the hill behind their grandfather's house. It was a great hill, except that a road cut across the bottom of it. Chris had to ditch his sled one day when a truck was coming, and he ended up rolling into a stone. "The worst part," he admitted, "was that my little brother won the race that day."

We laughed, and I told him one of my most embarrassing childhood stories of how I hot-glued a birdhouse onto my skirt during a craft class at school. "It was pretty awkward walking around that afternoon with a birdhouse in my lap," I said.

As we talked, I studied Dr. Chris and tried to step out of myself and see the big picture, the rounded-out profile of my attractive, bright, polite date of the moment. I noticed little lines near the edges of his eyes—laugh lines—and Dr. Chris had dimples. Clearly, this was a man who spent a good part of his days and nights with a smile on his face. Very un-goth of him in a rather gruesome profession, but Judy claimed that he loved his work, enjoyed the challenge, respected the dead, and admonished the living to enjoy life.

A Worthy Man?

I'll say!

Interested in me?

Let's just say that so far he had eluded the Annie Quicksilver charms, and I'm not talking witches' spells. Dr. Chris had come to the Go-Go tonight as a favor to a friend, a promise to Judy. And despite Judy's obvious, doting glances our way, nothing much was happening in the way of romance. Dr. Chris might be a genius in the lab, but sexual chemistry is a brew beyond concoction.

I thought of Landon's comment about changing the name of my column. Maybe he was right. Actually, if I even have a column after the end of this month, maybe I should go with something less committal.

MR. POSSIBILITY

You take the quizzes in all your favorite magazines, checking off the answers without thinking twice. Yes, he's gorgeous. Polite, check. Considerate, kind, responsible, on time. Check, check, check, check.

According to every survey, you have met the ideal man, that god among men, that idol among women.

But now that you've got him, you're not quite sure you want him, not even sure what to do with him. Unfortunately, this is a huge problem.

You've landed the perfect man, but in your arms he will only be Mr. Possibility. You see the potential here. You understand why other women watch him as he crosses the bar. You would love to love this man.

But you don't.

And who can say why not? When all of the obvious factors fall into line, why isn't there a mutual attraction? Where are the sparks, the heat, the fire, the passion?

The man sitting across from you could easily become your best friend, but the idea of pulling him into the janitor's closet and peeling off his Dockers seems . . . undignified.

Across the table, Dr. Chris glanced up as Mercedes appeared with our drinks.

"Fletch says these are paid for," she said, placing a pint of beer in front of Dr. Chris. "Judy's running a tab."

"She didn't have to do that." Dr. Chris shot a look over at the bar and I followed his glance.

Judy sat on a stool, facing us, as if she were watching us on DVD. She lifted her glass in a toast, her lips wide in a smile.

"Wow," he murmured, "no pressure."

I took a deep drink of my grapefruit martini—liquid courage. "Chris, I have to be honest—"

He cut me off, "I know, this is awkward. It's late, we're both tired, and Judy is watching us with eyes as wide as those of a barnyard owl."

I laughed. Dr. Chris had a way with play-by-play. Not exactly what I'd been thinking, but since he was opting out of the evening, I figured the end result would be the same. "Do you want to be the one to break her heart," I asked, "or should I?"

"She'll be okay if we're just postponing." He took a sip of his beer, considering. "Let's go keep her company while we finish our drinks. I'll call you tomorrow to set something up."

I sensed that his promise to call was just another favor for Judy, but it was hard to differentiate with all this "niceness" in the air.

"Sounds like a plan." I licked a bit of sugar from the rim, then lifted my glass. "Here's to Judy, a good friend."

"A great friend." He took a sip, then headed toward the bar.

I followed him toward the bar, admittedly checking out the movement of his pants over his rear end. Pants a little baggy, but very nice.

Oooh, why couldn't he be my guy?

6

When I retrieved my voice mail the next day there was a message from Simon summoning me to the Wild Boar Tavern in the Village that afternoon. It unnerved me a little, as I was more accustomed to meeting Simon once or twice a month to discuss my column. Why did he need to see me immediately? Was it something to do with the Magickal Council?

I tried to call him but got his voice mail. Darn, I'd have to meet him. Turning on the shower jets full-blast, I tried to look on the bright side. At least I could give him MR. POSSIBILITY, the latest installment of my column that I'd worked on late into the night. For once, I would be ahead of deadline.

Down in the Village I passed a human-sized, inflated canvas ghost, advertising the SCARIEST PRICES! at a store on MacDougal and was reminded of how much Americans loved celebrating Halloween—almost as much as witches. Most witches are in it for the wild and crazy sex, whereas humans seem to go for the adrenaline-pumping scare factor and the prospect of dressing up as someone else for one night. In both cultures, it was a night of abandon, a chance to escape the ordinary for one night. Nearly every shop I passed was decorated, strung with orange lights or glowing jack-o'-lanterns. Purplish black cats screeched from the awning of a pet store, their glass eyes glowing green. Rubber bats bobbed in the wind alongside plastic skeletons. One storefront display featured mock tombstones with inscriptions such as IDA LIVED and JACK SPLAT and MS. EERIE. While I love the way Americans mock death in their celebration of Halloween, I'm not thrilled with the depiction of witches as puckered, wart-faced women in need of rhinoplasty. And really, to give us green or purple faces? I can only imagine that a warlock had a hand in that design.

A chill wind scattered some leaves past my black jeans. It was far too cold for my short-waisted, black-and-white plaid blazer with the low-cut fake fur collar. I was fighting off shivers, but I'd picked it up at yesterday's sale and couldn't wait to wear it, especially if my time in New York was limited. Sadly, it would be useless in Ephemera, as fabric couldn't survive the fade to another astral plane.

At first glance I didn't recognize Simon. What was the likelihood that the dark-haired guy in the black shearling coat was my boss, the man who never stepped out of a business suit? I circled, taking in the streaky jeans, the casually slung striped scarf, so incongruous with the dark hair and piercing eyes that were signature Simon.

"I didn't think it was you." I took the stool beside him and slapped my portfolio onto the bar. "Trying a new look?"

He straightened his shoulders, as if testing the feel of the cozy jacket. "It seems I've been spending far too much time with my friend Giorgio."

I blinked. "As in . . . Armani?" Usually warlocks didn't have a clue about how to dress on Earth. "That's a fairly handy friend to have. Maybe I can introduce him to my buds, Dolce and Gabbana." I was joking, but he stared at me as if he weren't quite sure.

"Shall we get on with the evaluation?" Despite his casual attire, he was all business. "In my meeting with the Magickal Council yesterday they agreed to the November first extension. They've already begun reviewing your work, though I must warn you, the members of the Council are more concerned with the protection and sanctity of our society than with flimsy entertainment."

So my column was flimsy entertainment? In the same league as a lingerie commercial? I pushed past the "flimsy" barb and quickly extracted my latest work from the portfolio. "Before I throw myself at the mercy of the Council, let me give you this, my next column," I said, handing him MR. POSSIBILITY. "It was inspired by my date last night. He's a great guy. If you stick to the facts, Dr. Chris is probably a very worthy man, which got me thinking . . ."

He clenched his teeth. "Thinking again? That's a frightening development."

"It occurred to me that maybe I've been putting too much weight on the love/chemistry thing." I pictured Dr. Chris—the tiny laugh lines and the way his eyes sparkled wide in a wacky scientist sort of way. "Dr. Chris seems to possess all the qualities any woman would want. He's attractive, considerate, bright, and upbeat. The man even has a sense of humor."

"And a doctor, no less. A worthy package on the surface; however, you of all people should be cognizant that facades can be deceiving. After one date, how can you be sure the man isn't an imposter? Some sort of social deviant who preys on unsuspecting young women?"

I couldn't tell if he was being cynical or cautious on my behalf. His eyes were lowered, reading my new column as he snorted. Yep, it was cynicism.

"Dr. Chris comes with a solid recommendation," I told him. "My friend Judy has worked with him for years. She says he's the best part of the office. And what? What is it you object to?"

"Be honest. Did women really watch him walk across the room?"

"Well . . . yeah."

"That's hard to believe."

I raked a lock of hair out of my eyes, trying to focus. "That's off the point. The real revelation I had last night was that I've been unrealistic in my own requirements for *The Worthy Man*. Even though I kept saying I was searching for someone suitable, I think I've been holding out for more, looking for the magic that makes you want to shrivel up and die a little in his arms because you're so incredibly excited just to be with him. That amazing love depicted in movies. The equation in which one plus one equals one instead of two. Simon, I think I've been waiting to fall in love, and since that hasn't happened, I've found fault with every guy I've met."

"You must admit, these men had legitimate flaws."

"Of course they did; it's the beauty of being human. But it's not their fault. And with Dr. Chris, I don't know . . . I guess my idea is that I should jump into this relationship and give it a chance. Let the chemistry develop between us. Go for it now and let love grow."

"Seems to me you've already tried that tact." Simon's mouth was twisted in a bemused knot. "As I recall, you covered the loveless relationship when you wrote the column called MR. GOOD IN BED."

I rolled my eyes. "Why do I feel as if we're speaking different languages? Oh, that's right, you're a man."

"Flattery will get you nowhere. I don't see why this doctor fellow is any different from your bed buddy."

"This is way different. Dr. Chris is about starting with a friendship and moving toward a physical relationship. My bed buddy was all about sex."

MR. GOOD IN BED . . . I'll never forget describing my relationship with that man to Judy. What was his name . . . Derek? Or was it Devon? Anyway, I had told Judy about the feelings of liberation, the wonder of not having to deal with this man in public, no pressure to meet his friends, no need to make conversation. The relationship encompassed just our weekly date, usually at his apartment.

"Oh!" Judy smacked her forehead as if she needed to knock the answer out of her head. "I get it! You've got a sex buddy."

Just like that, my relationship in a nutshell. Honestly, I found it hard to cozy up to such a pert expression, like those snack cakes called Hostess Twinkies, as blithe as a Jiffy Lube Express or a Big Mac. I didn't like my relationships boiled down to two words with all the pep and mobility of a finger puppet.

But as I analyzed the relationship, I saw the true nature of it—a raw, healthy, carnal workout. Putting it in my column was the best way I knew to articulate my feelings.

MR. GOOD IN BED

For most women there comes a time when you've hit an emotional plateau on the landscape of relationships—a pervasive ennui that taints your desire to "date," despite those stinging hormones that cry out to find a coupling. At this juncture, you need a break from your search for serious contenders. You don't have the energy to get yourself out there right now. You're too jaded to recognize Mr. Right even if he were to buy you a Manhattan and nibble your cherry. And yet, you feel the need to fill that void in your life, make a physical connection, have great, mind-blowing sex.

Ladies, I give you the sex buddy.

Now, before you hold up your hands and protest that you're searching for meaningful relationships, that you can't be comfortable with someone who doesn't care about you, that you only enjoy sex when you're in love with the person, take a moment to consider the prospect without the judgmental baggage society loads on your shoulders. What's wrong with the occasional meeting between friends who have only one thing in common?

I have a theater friend—female—who attends Broadway musicals with me. Afterward, we go out for a late dinner to discuss our take on the show. Then we descend into the Times Square subway station and don't see each other until another show opens.

There's Madeleine who cuts my hair every six weeks, and truly, the only thing we know we have in common is hair. The people in your book club have very little in common with you. Men have their golfing partners, whom they meet without guilt once or twice a month.

Does this help you think of your bed buddy without guilt or anxiety?

And while there is no emotional attachment to your buddy, there is something highly romantic about scheduled pleasure. His key waits under the mat in the early predawn hours. You let yourself into his apartment, close the door behind you, then proceed as your eyes adjust to the darkness.

You know the way. You've been down this hallway before, dropping shoes onto the carpet, slipping off your skirt and jacket as you walk to the pleasures that await between the sheets.

Sex for the sake of sex. Nothing wrong with that, except that it pulled me away from my quest: the search for a worthy man. Mr. Good in Bed was worthy in one or two categories, but he lacked when it came to social grace and intellect. Translation: It's nice to have someone you can enjoy outside the bedroom, too.

Which brought me back to Dr. Chris, who was scoring high marks outside the bedroom. "Here's the thing about Dr. Chris," I told Simon. "Our relationship isn't starting with the need to have sex. It's beginning as a friendship. MR. POSSIBILITY is about the notion that a relationship can grow, that we can start off as friends, and as our involvement deepens, so does the chemistry, the romantic bond, and the physical attraction."

"Highly unlikely," Simon said flatly.

"Just like that? Can't you give the guy a chance?"

"Admittedly, I'm skeptical that anything lasting would develop between you two in the next week. Remember, your deadline has already been extended. I suggest you focus on ways to ease your transition back to life in Ephemera."

Ephemera! My jaw dropped. "Tell me you're kidding. I can't go back there, not to that mind-numbing routine, tamping down swelling hormones and fighting off desperate warlocks, working toward a perfect home in a perfect community, glazing cookies and tying ribbons on gift baskets. I don't want to be a Stepford witch."

"Boredom is a small price to pay for such prosperity, and many witches are quite content, even happy with their domestic bliss."

Domestic bliss . . . a suitable description for the daily existence in Ephemera, a place where you can transfigure your body into any shape, conjure any material object you desire, abolish darkness, and soak in the light.

Many people loved that existence; I was one of the few who questioned the bliss. Without darkness, I found the light relentless. Without flaws, witches were boring. Without obstacles, the day passed too smoothly—a long, sweet yawn.

"Domestic bliss is not for me," I said. "I find it smothering."

"Don't you miss being able to whip up any material item you desire with a spell?" he asked.

"I'd rather shop a sale at Bergdorf's."

"I'm afraid those shopping days are waning, as is your developing relationship with this Mr. Possibility. The Council would like you to curtail your romantic activities until they can make a determination."

"What?" Suddenly my Irish coffee was thick as mud. "That's not fair, and they gave me an extension. If I can't use this time to complete my mission, what else am I supposed to do?"

"Trick or treat?" His brows rose, then fell somberly. "No, I suppose not. Sorry, Annie, but the Council doesn't want you to create any new messes. Can't have you leaving behind a string of broken hearts."

"If that's not the lamest excuse! They weren't concerned about broken hearts when I first took this assignment. Why don't you tell them to take their broken hearts and shove them where—"

"Don't shoot the messenger, Ms. Quicksilver."

"But I need to find a worthy man! Simon, help me out here. How else can I help myself?"

"I'm afraid I can't answer that." Simon pursed his lips together, looking contrite.

And that worried me. I had never known Simon to be contrite, never seen his sympathetic side. This could mean but one thing: He knew I was sunk and felt sorry for me.

Poor, pitiful me. I was sinking fast.

1

With my options disappearing, it was time for desperate measures—Aunt Gladys.

One of my earliest childhood memories was of Aunt Gladys secreting me away in the folds of her red gown and ushering me out of the garden where classes were being conducted on Divinities and Spells. I couldn't have been more than five or six, but I had heard that Aunt Gladys was the black sheep of the family, the fallen daughter who wanted to leave Ephemera for another astral plane. As a kid I didn't quite get what all that meant, but as far as I was concerned, any witch who would get me out of Divinities for a dip in the lake had her priorities in order. Aunt Gladys was my guardian goddess.

Over the years, Aunt Gladys had rescued me a time or two. There was that teen prank when the slacker girls had all banded together to cast a spell on the homecoming witch. It was supposed to be a harmless spell, of course, but it went astray, probably because one of the girls substituted her own hair for the hair of a bat. Anyway, we didn't mean the donkey ears to be permanent, but we had no idea how to correct the spell. If it weren't for Aunt Gladys, we would have had to appear before the Magickal Council.

And I'll never forget how she had stood up to my father and frightened him to his senses before he signed his quill to a contract of marriage for me. Imagine me married off to a mottled old warlock at eighteen . . . repulsive.

So it made sense to call on Aunt Gladys now, hoping for some solid advice on how to get an extended visa from the Council. Aunt Gladys was an expert on bending the rules, and she had experience, having emmigrated from Ephemera. Besides, she was geographically desirable. After she'd married a mortal years ago, Aunt Gladys had settled in New York City, where she managed a costume design studio in the garment district. After my discouraging meeting with Simon I called her; she told me to come right over.

I'd been to her studio on West Twentieth a few times, as Aunt Gladys had been a sort of mentor to me since I came to New York. I took the stairs up to the studio, a large, high-ceilinged space that currently resembled a giant marionette theater. A gang of larger-than-life skulls hung from the ceiling, their ethereal black capes a stark contrast to the sickly glow-in-the-dark properties of their huge heads. Strains of classical music plunked through the air, filling the studio with a calm energy. Over in the sitting area someone was doing a fitting, and seamstresses surrounded a petite woman in a red gown that was a cross between a Southern belle and a whorehouse lampshade. Two other workers furiously guided fabric through chomping sewing machines. When I asked for Gladys, one of the women pointed toward the floating skulls.

I entered the field of skulls, finally spotting one with legs. "Aunt Gladys?"

"Annie? My little malachite minion!"

I stepped around a bobbing skull. "What show are you designing these guys for—*Night of the Living Dead, the Musical*?"

"They're for the Village Halloween Parade, of course."

Of course. I had heard the buzz over the small parade that ran through Greenwich Village, though I didn't get the fuss about the locals transforming themselves in comical, ghoulish costumes. When men and women dyed their hair blue or green or orange and wore chains and leather and spikes and torn denim on a daily basis, what was the big deal about wearing an odd costume for one night?

"There we go." Aunt Gladys lowered herself from the cranium of a giant skull and stood tall again, an elegant, statuesque beauty in yards and yards of black velvet. "Can't have him cracking his noggin before the big parade. And look at you, my star sapphire! I've enjoyed your last few columns, though I must say that the one about the sex buddy was my favorite."

My staunchest fan. "I'm glad you're still following the column. According to Simon, it might end after Halloween."

"Disgraceful, those Council elders. They wouldn't know titillation if it popped up and hit them in the face." She stepped around another dangling skull and headed toward the workstation. "But we'll figure something out for you. If you don't mind me stitching while we talk, you can bring me up to speed."

"Let me help you with something," I said as I followed her over to a rack of threads in a broad spectrum of colors.

She pointed to one section of a divided tray that contained a spool of silver. "These snaps need to be sewn into the back of the skeleton capes," she said. "Two snaps in each, over the X marked with chalk. Tedious, I know, but necessary to keep the puppeteer concealed."

I followed her over to a row of capes. "Sometimes tedious is a nice distraction," I said, "unless, of course, you're facing a lifetime of it in Ephemera."

"Ah, yes, the community dedicated to the arts of domestication." She took a threaded needle from the cushioned part of her apron as she settled onto a stool. "You know, some witches do love it there. They're comforted by the ritual, the sameness of each day. They enjoy the liberty of having a wealth of material possessions at their fingertips."

"It may serve some people well, but not us, Aunt Gladys."

"Yes, we're the oddballs, you and I, the rare, black diamonds. I do count my lucky stars everyday that I met my Carlo and found a happily ever after on this earthly plane."

"That's one of the things I wanted to ask you about," I said, poking the needle through the snap but jabbing one finger. "Ouch! I was wondering about how you got that permanent visa from the Magickal Council."

"Well, marriage, of course. Although the Council doesn't generally approve of a mixed marriage, they still consider the bond sacred. Even a marriage between a mortal and a witch."

It made sense. Of course, the Council would extend the sanctity of wedlock to Earth. On Ephemera, marriage was sacred, with no tolerance for divorce. This was the reason so many warlocks put on a fake facade to woo their young witches; once the marriage vows were taken, a poor witch was stuck with her warlock for life. So in Ephemera, you've got hideous-natured warlocks shape-shifting to find a bride among young witches who experience a spike in hormones— or whore-moans, as I used to think they were called. Let me tell you, I was relieved to arrive on Earth and find those hormones somewhat tempered. (Though, in many cases, they were running rampant through some human men I'd dated.)

"Marriage is still the easiest way to beat immigration law," Gladys went on. "Fortunately, in my case, it was a love match, too. My Carlo. I don't know how, but I found the kindest, funniest man on Earth. A true worthy man, but you can't have him."

"Like I'd ever have a chance," I said. "He's too crazy in love with you." I knotted the black thread, then cut off the needle. "Actually, I've been thinking that *The Worthy Man* isn't going to be my ticket out of Ephemera. I sort of missed my deadline, and now the Council is probably going to revoke my visa. My boss seems to think it's all a lost cause, so I need another plan, a way to stay on Earth. I know other people have made it here without work visas. Like . . . the hostess at Manchuria. Did you know she's a witch?"

"The blonde with the pierced brow and the attitude?" Gladys winced. "How do you know?"

"I saw her use witchcraft in the ladies' room. She opened up the sky just to fix a run in her pantyhose."

"What a waste of craft! And pantyhose are so yesterday. No wonder my fingertips burn whenever I have drinks there."

"But I want to know, how did she get the green light to stay here? Or that vapid warlock Denver. How did he get a visa?"

"The shape-shifter you wrote of in your first column?" She shook out the black fabric. "Clearly, the warlock Denver is a political pick. What can I tell you? Someone from his coven must know someone on the Council."

"Exactly. So why don't we have an 'in' on the Council? Don't we know anyone?"

"Believe me, I've been down that avenue." She lifted the needle and smiled knowingly. "Marriage, my little malachite; it's the only answer."

"It's definitely an out," I agreed, muttering, "just haven't found the guy to marry, yet."

"Of course you haven't, giving yourself only a few months. That was a ridiculous assignment from day one.

But don't you know a man who'll marry you, in name only, for the time being? I know the Council doesn't allow divorce, but once you've immigrated here, you're beyond the long arm of the witches' law. Haven't you any friends?"

"Sure, I've got friends. Jude and Landon are great, but—"

"And the Jude isn't Jude Law, I take it?"

"Jude is a girl. And Landon, well, he's sort of taken, sort of not interested in females."

She screwed up her mouth slightly. "Then you don't want to torture him with this red tape. I wonder if Carlo has a friend . . . ?"

Carlo was a fiftyish man who worked in the garment district, loading and unloading, pushing racks of clothes through streets choked with traffic. The few times I'd met him he'd seemed very nice, but when I tried to imagine what his single friends would be like, I kept coming up with Tony, the deli guy who always, everyday, asked me if I wanted sugar in my tea, and when I said no, he always, everyday, barked out, "That's right! You're sweet enough, doll!" Doll. Could I marry a man like that to stay on the earthly plane? I was trying to weigh how much I loved Manhattan and my friends when Aunt Gladys threw in a new twist.

"What about using witchcraft?"

Witchcraft was standard practice in Ephemera; witches used it every day to create the things they wanted and needed such as clothes and houses and furniture, but it was forbidden here on Earth, and every time a witch here practiced her craft, a distinct wave of energy rose into the atmosphere, sort of like the light that would rise from a rooftop hatch at night. I had been warned that the shaft of energy could make things go haywire, foiling air traffic communications, setting off alarms, and causing power surges. And besides the trouble on Earth, a skybeam of that magnitude was like a beacon of alarm to the Council, who could then pinpoint the witch's astrolocation and punish accordingly.

Aunt Gladys went on, "Have you tried using a spell or incantation to get your way?"

I bit my lower lip. "Well . . . that would be against the rules."

"Oh, yes, of course. Forget I said that. But what about your friends? Perhaps they could bend things a bit for you, this Junie and Lambchop you mention?"

"Judy and Landon. They're mortals. I don't think they realize I'm a witch. Of course, they know the name of my column, but Landon once told me it was a clever gimmick. They never made the connection."

"Really? How utterly cosmopolitan of you! Can I tell you how proud I am of you, blazing your own trail here with a pair of unpredictable mortals? Give us a hug!"

I fell into her cloak, embraced by the delicious scents of Aunt Gladys. And I do mean delicious. Today, she simmered like a savory stew, a mixture of sage and garlic with a hint of something tangy and exotic. "Mmm . . . nice brew you're wearing."

She rolled her eyes. "The curry, every time I eat Indian I wear it for days. But who can resist tandoori chicken?"

I nodded, thinking wistfully of how much I would miss all the exotic, mishmashed, nouveau New York cuisines. Not that witches don't eat, but outside of ritual debaucheries there's lots of emphasis on health and not so much interest in trying something new. Think wheat bread with sugar-free grape jelly.

"But back to this business of spells," Aunt Gladys said, lowering her voice slightly. "Do you mean to tell me you haven't performed any witchcraft since you arrived here? Not even a teensy-weensy spell?"

"Well . . ." I winced, realizing how petty this would sound. "I would never cast a love spell on a man or anything major to meddle with someone's fate. But there was this spread in the Sunday *Times* magazine—fall fashions?"

She groaned. "Yes, yes, phenomenal, wasn't it?"

"And I was obsessed with the Ralph Lauren collection. These blazers and jeans and skinny skirts. And they had bedding to match . . ."

"Yes, yes!"

"It wasn't out in stores yet, and I couldn't resist. One day I was desperate to wear that blazer, and I cast a spell and wound up with a closet full of Ralph Lauren."

"Divine, my ruby carnelian! You haven't lost your touch if you were able to recreate the House of Ralph."

"My friend Judy couldn't believe her eyes. I made up some line about getting free samples from an old boyfriend, not that it made any sense."

"And this is the friend who doesn't know you're a witch?"

"Honestly, I think it's the last thing she'd suspect. She's a good friend, and friends see the best in you."

Gladys stopped stitching to study me. "You've learned a lot in your brief time here. I do hope you'll be able to stay."

"So do I." Though the prospects were bleak.

"Just find a husband," she said, as if getting married were as easy as finding a cup of Starbucks coffee on the Upper East Side. "I'm sure there's a kind young man here in New York who would humor you?"

"Have you really been reading my column?" I said as my Gucci bag began to quiver on the floor.

"Looks like your vibrator is calling," my aunt quipped.

As I picked up the cell, she added, "Maybe it's Mr. Worthy phoning you to propose on the spot."

I checked the caller ID: Dr. Chris.

Kismet? Destiny? Was Mr. Worthy on the line?

I could only hope.

8

Dr. & Mrs. Christopher Moreland.

Chris and Annie request the honor of your presence at their wedding . . .

Yes, I'm a doctor's wife.

Although I knew this was all supposed to be a setup marriage (*if* Dr. Chris would even go for it), I couldn't stop my mind from wandering down that rose-trellised, highly romantic wedding lane. I pictured Dr. Chris in a gray tux, myself in an off-the-shoulder gown with delicate beadwork along the bodice, the pristine white of the gown a stark contrast to my dark hair and eyes. And there was Judy in a satin bridesmaid gown in burgundy—no, that might clash with the orange in her hair. A rich, dark emerald green . . . or maybe a royal purple . . .

It was totally crazy, these wedding hormones that ran through a woman's body in this earthly plane. Did female humans get a higher dose of Romantica in place of the Erotica hormone female witches possessed? Truly, in all my life in Ephemera, I had never once thought of the braided frosting piping on a three-tiered wedding cake, satin bridesmaid gowns, or the way light filtered through the stained glass windows of a church.

A church—now there's a rich irony. Contrary to popular beliefs, witches do not shrivel and melt in holy places. In fact, we revere sacred ground and would be quite comfortable abiding by the rules there, believing that in the end we are all worshipping and beseeching the same life force. However, this philosophy is not too popular among the sects that have tried to drown, torture, or burn some of our membership in the past.

But this wedding hysteria was premature; as of yet, I had no groom. . . .

Though Dr. Chris was looking better and better, especially under the warm glow of the low-hanging rose lamp in one of the booths at Cosmo-A-Go-Go. There was a friendly openness to his face and an athletic stance in the way he hunkered over—as if he were the perennial friend of the older brother who always won the backyard hockey game but lost the girl because he spent so much time playing hockey in the freezing rain.

I smoothed down my Ralph Lauren cashmere sweater as I followed Mercedes to the table, admittedly nervous. How should I start? Would "Marry me, please!" be too pushy? Yes, it was over-the-top. I decided to open with a compliment.

"You're looking scrumptious tonight," I said merrily, only realizing from the lost expression on his face that my words sounded vapid and blood-hungry. "Not that I'd eat you or anything," I said, making it even worse. I tried to cover with a laugh, flipping open the menu. "You know how it is when you're starving and all you can think about is food?"

"Tell me about it," Mercedes said flatly as she pushed her mottled brown glasses onto her head. Tonight she was sporting leopard-print mules with demure bows on the toes." I haven't eaten anything but vegetables since Tuesday. It's that new Fiber Force diet."

"I've read about that," Dr. Chris said. "Does it really leave you feeling full?"

Mercedes shook her head. "I feel like I haven't eaten since Christmas, but according to the book, the miracle juices of broccoli and turnips should be kicking in. Any minute now." She checked her watch. "I'm still waiting, but call me skeptical. What can I get you?"

"Let's have a rush order of appetizers so Annie doesn't waste away to nothing," Dr. Chris said. "And, Mercedes, you're welcome to join us."

"Don't tempt me."

I chose stuffed mushroom caps; he picked buffalo wings. You have to love a guy with enough confidence to order wings on a date, that pesky snack food that slobbers red sauce onto your lips and cheeks and winds stringy meat through your teeth. And there was Dr. Chris, with braces on his teeth and ordering wings. Brave man.

"I love wings, but they're so messy," I told him as Mercedes headed off with our order.

"Not a worry." He shrugged. "We'll get you cleaned up." He shot me a shy look. "So tell me, Annie, why haven't I ever run across your column? Judy says it's very entertaining."

"It's published in an online newsletter," I answered, omitting the fact that only witches could subscribe. "It's one of those paid subscriber deals, but Judy has seen the hard copy on a few of my pieces."

"She says you're a talented writer worth keeping an eye on," he said. "I'd love to read a few of your columns. Judy has recounted a few highlights for me. The story about the paper shoe designer, in which you try to wear his designs to an art gallery but get caught in the rain."

I nodded. "People seemed to enjoy the comedic aspects of that one."

"When Judy tells the story, it's very funny. What else did she mention? There's the evening with the cowboy you met at that western dance place. What was the title of that one?"

"SPUR OF THE MOMENT," I said cautiously as Mercedes arrived with our drinks.

Dr. Chris thanked her for the beer, barely missing a beat in the conversation. "Judy told me all about LIVING SINGLE, when you studied all the year-old marriage licenses at City Hall and discovered that two thirds of all married couples had fled the city. And a column called CHOPAHOLICS, when you dated that chef who was obsessed with carving ice and butter sculptures."

"Wow, Dr. Chris." I twirled the cherry in my whiskey sour. "You're good at this. You seem to know me better than I do."

"It's Judy," he said. "She's the real expert. And another one . . ." He laughed. "Called ARE YOU GETTING THE VIBE? when you lost your vibrator and had to retrace your steps that day to see where it fell out."

"Oh, she told you about that one . . ." I forced a smile. Somehow, it didn't seem like the most graceful introduction to Dr. Chris, but he seemed so genuinely amused that I let it go. "So this is what you two talk about down at the medical examiner's office? Chopaholic chefs and missing vibrators?"

"Can you blame us?" His eyes sparkled. "Actually, I enjoy my job. Not that I can admit that to most people I meet. They'd think I'm some morbid freak. But you know how it is, how Judy and I enjoy piecing together the evidence, trying to fill out the picture in our minds. It's not nearly as glamorous as those TV shows crack it up to be, but it keeps us occupied."

Our appetizers arrived, and as we ate the conversation turned to more mundane subjects like city government, stand-up comedians we didn't get, and cooler weather. As we talked I kept imagining Chris's necktie turning into an ascot, the braces fading from his shiny teeth, and his ring finger sparkling with a gold band.

"So Judy tells me you've only been here a few months," Chris said. "What part of the country are you from? I'm usually good with accents, but I can't identify yours."

I bit my lower lip, feeling a twinge of guilt. *It's because I'm a witch, Dr. Chris, a witch from the land of Ephemera. But don't let that turn you off, because, you see, I plan to marry you. . . .*

"Annie?" He leaned across the table, his eyes earnestly searching my face. "You okay?"

"Fine! I'm just fine," I lied, thinking that I'd better step away before I bore down on Dr. Chris like a freight train. "If you'll excuse me—" I folded my napkin and slid along the banquette. "I'll be right back," I promised.

Just as soon as I brainwash myself in the ladies' room.

9

"Just stop making wedding plans," I muttered to myself as I breezed into the ladies' room. "Forget the wedding and focus on the man." A woman came out of a stall and squinted at me. Probably wondering whom I was talking to.

And stop talking to yourself, I added silently, smiling at the curious woman. It wasn't till I was sitting down on the toilet with the door closed that I noticed the little book—a spiral-bound address book with a pink psychedelic cover and a tiny graphic of a girl talking on her cell phone.

"Did somebody leave an address book in here?" I called out to the other ladies, whom I could hear washing and chatting near the sinks.

"It's not mine," one woman called.

"I saw it, too. I think it's been here a while," someone else said.

I opened the cover. BRIDGET'S PHONE DIARY was written on the first page in flowery script. Apparently, Bridget didn't think to leave a phone number.

Under *A*, where I expected to find Anderson and Alberston,

maybe Andrew or Alan, Bridget had written ANIMAL EXHIBI-
TIONIST and ABSOLUTE ASSHOLE and AMAZING APARTMENT and
ANTS IN HIS PANTS. All of these entries were followed by short
explanations and a phone number, sometimes two. Raising
an eyebrow, I tried to decipher the handwriting.

*AMAZING APARTMENT: Keary isn't a bad guy. A lit-
tle too vanilla with no nuts. But his apartment makes the
boredom fade. Great place for a party if you can swing it.*

Not your standard phone book.

Intrigued, I flipped ahead. Under *K* I found KNOCKOUT
KISSER and KILLER EYES. Under *O* there was only OH, OR-
LANDO!

Feeling rather impressed with the clientele at Cosmo-A-
Go-Go, I grabbed the book and barreled out to the sinks. "I
guess I'll give this lost address book to the manager," I told
the woman reapplying her lipstick in the mirror. "I'm sure
Bridget will miss it."

"Yeah," she said, sparing me that brief, concerned glance
of a New Yorker who is worried because they've been engaged by a stranger. In New York, the only people who talk
to strangers are the deranged, the hookers, and the tourists.
Well, I guess I fit two out of three.

After lipstick girl left I was about to drop Bridget's handy-
dandy book into my purse but decided to check under *M* in
the hopes that MARRIAGEABLE PROSPECT or MARRYING KIND
or some equally convenient description might be there.

No such luck. Though I did find MISERABLE MASOCHIST.
Now, there's something that's good to know before you in-
vest your emotions in a guy.

Back in the dining room I noticed a bunch of people at
our table.

Not just any old people, but my friends, Judy and Landon
and Jeremy. "We were just leaving," Judy said, trying to slide
out of the booth. "Really, we came for dinner; we didn't

know you'd be here. Small world. Stopped by the table to say hi, but we'll go somewhere else."

"Why are you being so neurotic?" Landon asked Judy. "Annie and Chris don't mind if we stay. Chris invited us to join them."

"I did," Dr. Chris said, turning to me, "if it's okay with you, Annie."

"Sure," I said, automatically motioning Judy to slide back in. As I sat down beside her and considered the situation, I felt even better about the fact that Dr. Chris wanted my friends to join us. He wanted to hang with my friends; how perfect was that? A long-term relationship with a guy who fit right into my social life . . .

"We were just talking about ordering some entrées we can share," Jeremy said, perusing the menu. "A crab quesadilla would be nice—ask them to split it five ways, please. Let's get a teriyaki steak. And how about a gourmet veggie thin-crust pizza?"

As the guys discussed food with our waitress, I turned to Judy, keeping my voice low. "You will never believe what I found in the ladies' room."

Judy winced. "I'm not sure I want to hear this."

"It's a phone diary, sort of. Numbers of all these guys, and they're rated, sort of. She gives them all nicknames." I flashed it toward her under the table so the guys wouldn't see.

Judy squinted at me. "Sounds adolescent, sort of. Why don't you give it to the waitress? I'm sure they have a Lost and Found."

"I'm keeping it," I hissed. "This is a little gold mine."

"Don't tell me you're going to call some stranger in there."

"Why not? These men are pre-screened. Bridget has dated them and lived to tell the tale."

"We hope." Judy lowered her chin, her eyes intent.

"How do we know her body isn't stuffed into the trash can in the ladies' room?"

"What's this about a body?" Dr. Chris jumped in.

Under the table I slapped the diary closed and eased it toward my bag. "Just Judy with an overactive imagination. You need to leave your work at the morgue, Jude."

"Oh, it's in the air with Halloween so close. The ghoulishness, the walking dead," Jeremy said. "Some of our neighbors in Queens have gone wild with decorations. Tombstones on their lawns, orange lights, and those inflated ghosts and Frankensteins. I find it festive, but some people go overboard. Like the effigy hanging from the porch two doors down from us."

"I thought they made some creative choices, dressing the dummy in a denim jacket as opposed to the traditional flannel shirt and overalls," Landon said. "Besides, it scares the dog-walkers away from our side of the block."

"Halloween is so much more fun in the suburbs," Judy said. "I miss trick-or-treaters."

"But you'll see your fair share of costumes at the New School party next week," Landon said. "And we'll be able to see the parade from the rooftop there. You're all coming, aren't you?" He had managed to get us invites to a fundraiser at the New School that promised a great view of the Halloween festivities in the streets of Greenwich Village. Landon waggled his fingers at Mercedes, who was passing by with a tray of drinks. "You're coming, right?" When she shrugged, he turned to Dr. Chris. "Can you join us? They put on a fabulous costume party every year."

"Oh, is it a costume party?" I asked. "I wasn't really planning to dress up."

"Costume is not mandatory," Jeremy said.

"But really," Landon interrupted, "on Halloween, it's all about the costume. It's the only time all year when it's okay to pretend to be someone you're not."

"But it requires so much effort." Jeremy glazed over. "I'm not sure I'll be up for it this year."

Landon dismissed him. "You always say that, and then, come October thirtieth, you're rushing all over town looking for some bizarre accessory like cat-eye glasses or green felt boots."

"I don't do that." Jeremy smiled sheepishly. "Do I do that?"

Just then two servers appeared with plates and platters of food. My laid-back friends were instantly alert, sampling and distributing, making sure everyone got their fair share.

"I have always loved Halloween," Judy said as diced vegetables tumbled from her slice of pizza to the tablecloth. "Every year, my sister and I started digging through the old costume bag in September. Charlotte always spent her allowance on a new costume, but I was happy to recycle what we had. Cinderella or Catwoman or some generic fairy princess."

As I cut into a rare square of steak my heart warmed to the image of a skinny, young Judy in a Catwoman bodysuit or a thick, black Snow White wig with a fat headband. This dress-up ritual of humans could be odd; when witches did rituals, we usually *shed* our clothes.

Judy sighed and popped a mushroom into her mouth. "It was so much fun to be someone else, someone pretty, even if it was just for one night." From the wistful look in her eyes, I felt I was there with her, a gawky kid who felt sure that a rhinestone crown had the power to transform her into an enchanted princess.

"I'm sure you were always beautiful, Jude," Chris said, "even without the costume."

She glanced at him shyly. "You didn't see me in high school."

"*Before* her nose job," Landon added. Judy smacked his arm. "Ouch! Just kidding, of course. Our little Judy is too granola to be a surgical swan."

"I can't imagine that you'd want to change any of your features," Dr. Chris said, his eyes intent on Judy.

She rolled her eyes, and for a second it looked like she was beginning to blush. "Oh, I don't know, we all have our hangups, but that was the beauty of Halloween: instant transformation. A night spent as someone else."

"I can relate," Dr. Chris said. "I spent quite a few years chasing the superhero image. Batman and Superman. I was Luke Skywalker when all the other kids had scarier Darth Vader costumes. They were all way cooler than me, but I didn't want to go to the dark side. I just had this hero thing, I guess."

Landon cupped his hands to his mouth, his voice reverberating. "Luke, I am your father."

Jeremy and I laughed, but Judy just smiled at Dr. Chris, one of those slow smiles of dawning recognition. "That is so sweet," she said.

"And so obvious," Dr. Chris admitted. "Hero complex? It's no wonder that I went on to become a doctor."

I folded my napkin. Dr. Chris's hero complex wasn't the only thing that was obvious. As I watched the way he and Judy interacted, I couldn't help but notice the bond between them. Judy always said he was like a brother to her, but I sensed something more here—a definite attraction lingered under the surface.

"But you followed a different track than most, Chris," Judy said, supportive as always. "You specialized in forensic pathology."

"And the rest is history," Landon said dramatically.

"But I don't know this history." Jeremy cocked his head, studying Dr. Chris. "Truthfully, I'd like to know how you started on the med school path and ended up in the medical examiner's office." He seemed genuinely interested, and I was glad for the diversion in the conversation, which gave me a chance to sink down in my seat and soak up the flying vibes.

And the mini-bolts were flying so fast I was surprised that our entire table wasn't emitting auroras to rival the northern lights.

Judy and Chris . . . I had made the connection before, but Judy denied interest so vehemently that I had believed her (fool that I am).

So where did this leave me?

The most obvious answer was that I had a job to do here; it was my duty as a friend to see that Dr. Chris and Judy found each other. And I needed to play matchmaker fast, as my chances of staying around weren't so good, especially now that I'd lost Dr. Chris as a candidate for husband.

I let out a quiet breath as visions of wedding cake danced out of reach, planting a last cancan kick to my chest. I wasn't going to meet my ultimate goal here. What was that saying?

Always a bridesmaid, never an emancipated witch.

10

When I got home that night, there was a message from Simon. Probably because I'd turned my cell phone off at the Go-Go, and thus had ignored his three calls.

"I distinctly remember asking you to curtail your romantic activities," he said crisply in the message. "And yet, you defy Council orders and pursue a human man, actually go on a date in public?"

"How do you know?" I asked aloud. Had he been stalking me? Despite the various spells we witches practiced, none of them entailed psychic or X-ray vision.

"I'm warning you to maintain a low profile. Spend this final week on a farewell column for *Ephemera Online*."

It was too depressing. I reached into the back of the fridge and snapped off a square of my secret Godiva stash—dark chocolate with raspberry filling. When all else fails, there is always chocolate.

"I shouldn't have to remind you that the Council is not going to be pleased with your recent behavior," Simon's message went on, "and I'll be forced to report you if you persist, Ms. Quicksilver."

Ooh, snippy.

I closed my eyes and visualized Simon and the Council floating away on a river of dark chocolate, up a creek without a paddle . . .

Later, as I sank into the cushy comforter on my bed, a puffy purple satin quilt with square patches of lavender, orange, and red, I felt my eyes misting over at the thought of the inevitable. I stared out at the floodlit apex of the Empire State Building—orange and purple for Halloween—and I wondered if it was worth going on. Why was I fighting so hard for something that was clearly beyond my grasp?

I wasn't going to find a worthy man, at least not a man for me, and though I was thrilled for Judy and Dr. Chris, I couldn't stop myself from a moment of extreme remorse for myself. Love was out of the question, as was the notion of staying here in New York. Simon was right; I would be sent back to Ephemera to lead the life of a good, domesticated witch. Hardly the guest of honor in a pity party by some standards, but for me that life was deadly.

My bedroom was dark, lit only by the waning moon and the glow of the city. I slid off the bed, stretched across the Chinese carpet like a cat, then perched on my knees at the windowsill to stare out at the tall apartment buildings facing mine across the avenue. Some of the windows had no blinds, and over the months I had tuned into various people moving through their lives—a woman tending her plants, a gay couple who danced under a small glitter ball hanging in their living room, a room I imagined belonging to an elderly person that was lit by the changing bluish glow of a television screen through the night. Tonight, the plant lady had her lights on, a soft, rosy glow. In an upper-floor apartment I noticed a new unshuttered entry, a woman typing on a computer that faced out the window. Her face was lit by the monitor, as if she were a glimmering underwater mermaid, and I wondered if she could be a writer like me. Or working with numbers? Or maybe just sending e-mails to her friends?

I squinted, trying to read her features, to glimpse her life. Was she happy? Was she struggling? Was she fighting her way to achieve an impossible dream, as I was?

She was too far away to get a good look, but I sensed a certain calm about her that I didn't possess. This was a woman who would stay on track, slow and steady, working her way toward a goal.

I envied her. Once upon a time I took an assignment, determined to hold tight to my heart's desire. I was enthusiastic and bullheaded and strong. I still possessed some of that strength, but I wasn't stupid. After weeks of jumping over obstacles, I had to acknowledge that this road was ending. A dead end.

At least I could hold tight to the knowledge that Judy would hook up with her happily ever after. Maybe that vicarious joy would get me through the tedium of witches' play in Ephemera.

I sucked in a deep, wimpery breath and rested my head against the windowsill. There were so many things about New York that I would miss—the bagels, the subways, the swell of noise. I had enjoyed my independence here and had embraced this city where nothing was surprising and anything seemed possible. But most of all, I would miss Judy and Landon and Jeremy. It was going to be a long lifetime of winters without my friends.

When the phone rang the next morning I rolled over in bed, determined to ignore it. But don't you hate caller ID? I couldn't blow off Aunt Gladys.

"You've got a lot of nerve waking a girl during her last week of earthly sleep."

"Nonsense, my rosie moonstone. I thought you'd found a worthy man?"

"I did, but he's secretly in love with my best friend."

"That does muddy the brew, but not to worry. Carlo has found a potential husband for you. Now I want you to keep an open mind. Should I tell you his best features or his worst?"

"Unless you can tell me he's marrying me in the next few days, I don't want to hear anything."

"Well, that's the thing. It's all possible. Bruce wants you to meet his mother, of course. They live in Queens. Sounds royal, eh?"

"He lives with his mother?"

"Open mind, open mind. And please, no cracks about his weight."

"I would never be so cruel . . ."

"He says it's a thyroid condition, but really beneath that tonnage is a heart of gold . . . somewhere. Listen to me, he's alive and he's very sweet and he's male, and at this point you can't expect much more."

"I've lowered my expectations," I said. "As of now, they're in the basement. Really, Aunt Gladys, I've realized there isn't time for me. I was hoping to patch up something for my friend Judy before I'm plucked from here. So tell Bruce I appreciate his heroism but—"

"Just meet him, will you?"

"The Council wants me to keep a low profile—no more dates."

"Phooey on them. You've got another week, right? Just meet him. How about at your Halloween party? I've just made him a fabulous costume."

"It's not my party. I don't even know how to get him an invitation."

"Trust me, no one is going to say no to a three-hundred pound man dressed as a sumo wrestler."

I covered my face with my hands, trying to escape the vision of a burly, bare-skinned sumo proposing to me. Not that it would attract undue attention in New York, but Simon would be furious, nonetheless. He'd spit fire from his fingertips, zap me back to Ephemera, probably post me in a job as a live-in nanny to five pyromaniac warlock boys.

Oh, well, if I was going back to Ephemera anyway . . .

"Tell Bruce I'll meet him at the party . . ." I gave her the details.

As I swung myself out of bed and ended the call, I wondered if Simon had the ability to tap my line. How else could he know everything I was up to lately?

He was expecting me to write one more edition of *Single White Witch,* though I was forbidden to do research. Like that made sense.

I went to the kitchen counter and flipped open BRIDGET'S PHONE DIARY. I did have a few more days, right? Why sit around and waste an alphabet of opportunity? I let my fingers scrabble through the pages and randomly opened to book to *P.*

Hmm . . . should I start with PERFECT GENT, POWERMEISTER, or PRESCRIPTION FOR FUN?

11

That day began my worst week on the planet.

It wasn't so much the disappointment of not finding a Worthy Man for myself as the relentless, pounding rejection that greeted me with each phone call I made to the men in Bridget's little book.

By Tuesday, I had stopped calling contenders, but I did keep dragging myself to appointments I'd already set up. I was able to confirm that ABSOLUTE ASSHOLE deserved his name, that JUNGLE JIM should have stayed in the Amazon rain forest, that PERFECT GENT had to be pushing ninety, and that HUNKOMANIA should have been called CHUNK NO-BRAINIA for his largess of body and smallness of intellect.

By Wednesday, I was getting so many weird return calls that I turned off my cell phone.

By Thursday, I was ready to torch BRIDGET'S PHONE DIARY. Who was this woman, and why had I thought I would benefit from her pool of male resources? Not that she didn't try to warn me with her quirky nicknames and brief critiques of these men. Oh, Bridget had been blunt, but did I heed her warning?

Add to that Landon's reimmersion into his metalworks sculpting and Judy's sudden unavailability, and I was feeling fairly miserable and lonely.

Thursday afternoon I turned into the Cosmo-A-Go-Go and marched straight up to the bar. Over the past few days I had stopped into the Go-Go between disastrous dates looking for a little moral support and some serious reality checks, which Fletch and Mercedes had delivered on all counts. Right now I contemplated leaving the book where I'd found it in the ladies' room. It seemed like an easy way to be rid of it, but the notion lacked social consciousness, since some other man-hungry chick could easily pick it up and make the same mistake I'd made. I wanted to stop the madness and destroy the book, like a bad chain letter, before it could do further damage.

"How was your date at the zoo?" Mercedes asked, placing a tray on the bar.

"Two words: elephant poo."

I slapped my purse onto the bar, took a seat, and lifted the heel of my left shoe; formerly a Cabernet red Dolce & Gabbana pump with a majestic high arch, it now suffered from a dull, mustard-like glaze. My poor shoes. I wanted to cry.

"I think my shoes are ruined. Actually, it's just the left one. Do you think the smell will come out?"

Mercedes shook her head. "I don't know about that, but I hear it makes great fertilizer."

I tipped my shoe up, and Mercedes and I both winced at the muck on the bottom.

"It's alive!" she said, fleeing to a spot behind the bar.

Pointing my shoe toward Mercedes, I let out another shriek, which bubbled up into hysterical laughter as I thought back to the paper shoes I'd ruined in the rain. "I guess I'm just hard on footwear," I said, wiping back a tear. "I need shoes of armor, or ruby slippers."

"What was that?" Mercedes asked.

"Oh, I'm just mourning my shoes and wondering why I bother with these guys."

"You know . . ." Mercedes leaned closer over the bar. "I've been wanting to ask you about that. You date more than anyone I know. Not that I've ever seen you hook up with anyone, but the fact that you find these guys is amazing."

I frowned. After more than a dozen "dates" over the past three days, I was ready to call it quits with "these guys."

"Sorry if I hit a sore spot."

"No, it's okay. I'm just . . . oh, I don't know." I took BRIDGET'S PHONE DIARY out of my purse and plunked it on the bar. "This is the reason I've been dating twenty-four/seven lately. It's some chick's little black book, and not a very good one."

She pulled the book in front of her and began to leaf through it. "This is how you meet men?"

"Just in the past few days, and believe me, it doesn't work. I don't know this Bridget, but I'd be willing to bet she unearthed these guys at a meeting of the local chapter of Losers Anonymous."

Her eyelids lowered behind the rhinestone frames. "Did you meet MUSEUM MOGUL?"

"Yes, and he's a pompous ass, though the Japanese Garden at the Metropolitan Museum of Art is definitely worth a visit."

She nodded. "And this is for your job, right? That column you write."

"Yes, though I'm afraid that's ending. I'm going to have to leave New York." I rested my elbows on the bar and leaned my chin against my fists. "I'm going to miss this place." I had never confided quite so much in Mercedes, but she seemed willing to listen.

She flipped to another page and muttered, "Tough break."

Now I knew why I had spared Mercedes my problems.

"Can I get you something?" Fletch asked as he returned to the bar.

"Just a diet soda. I've got another meeting with 'LECTRIC LUKE in an hour."

"Still dating all those fellas? Looking for Mr. Right?" Fletch asked as he squeezed a lemon into my drink.

"A worthy man," I said. "Though at this point I'd call the dates informational interviews."

"OH, ORLANDO!" Mercedes read from the book. "Is this Orlando Bloom?"

"I wish."

"If only I were twenty years younger." Fletch wiped the bar with a soft white cloth. "I'd have been in the running."

"Are you kidding?" Mercedes slid the book off the bar and turned away. "Major delusions of adequacy."

"I was a looker then," he called after her.

"In my book you're still a looker," I told Fletch, "but you're taken."

He winked at me. "That's more like it."

"Mercedes?" I called after her. "I'm going to need that book back." Her interest in it worried me. Was she memorizing phone numbers?

She turned back toward us, her usual deadpan expression, and slid the book toward me. "Take it. I was just trying to see if any of my customers were in there." She lifted her tray of drinks. "By the way, Fletch, I didn't see you listed under the *F*s."

He grinned. "Nobody said the book was an antique."

I dropped the poisonous missive in my purse and tried to think of a clever way to cancel the rest of my meetings.

"A worthy man," Fletch repeated as he polished the bar. "Hate to say it, but I don't know that you'll find one at the Go-Go. Not in all of New York. Hate to condemn a whole species, but men are pigs." He cocked his head and sniffed. "And what's that smell?"

12

As expected, my date with 'LECTRIC LUKE was less than electrifying; he thought I'd be impressed sitting beside him at a Broadway matinee and watching him push buttons and move levers on the light board. Big yawn. Wake me when the house lights come up.

When I got home I tossed my elephant-poo shoes down the chute to the incinerator, along with Bridget's little phone book. It may seem excessive to destroy a good pair of shoes, but I wouldn't be able to use them in Ephemera, and I could hardly pass them on.

With an odd sense of satisfaction I washed my hands with lavender-scented soap, then changed into jeans and a sweater. I had finally tracked down Judy, and she was meeting me here with plans to take in a movie. She thought it was going to be a typical girls' night out, but I had a hidden agenda: the Dr. Chris pitch. Somehow, the thought of matchmaking gave me a lift. This was going to be the bright spot of my week—maybe even the finale of my trip to Earth.

When Judy arrived she seemed distracted. She didn't even unbutton her plaid duster but grabbed a magazine and sat down carefully in the red suede chair of the living room that Simon had allowed me to furnish with fun art deco pieces. "What are we doing, a movie?" she asked as she flipped past Brad Pitt's face without the tiniest ogle.

"Sure," I said cheerfully, "I thought we'd see *Bewitched*." I was always curious about the PR we got in this astral plane. "And hey, you'll be happy to know that I tossed away the phone diary I found in the ladies' room."

"Oh, really?" She didn't flinch; she didn't really seem to care.

"Remember the one you were so worried about? The little book I found at the Go-Go?" She blinked, her face blank. "Judy, are you okay?"

"Fine, I'm fine. I've just been . . . really busy."

"At work?"

"That, and . . . other things."

She glanced away, unable to look at me.

I hated beating around the bush. "Listen, I should probably be more delicate about saying this, but you know delicacy is not my style. The truth is, I know you're attracted to someone I've been seeing, and I totally understand."

She froze, a deer in the headlights. "You do? You know? Oh, Annie, I've felt so guilty ever since he approached me. You know I would never go after someone you're interested in, but I hope you understand, it was more his doing."

"I more than understand, and don't you dare feel guilty," I told her emphatically. "I think it's good that you're together. It's great. Whoopee! You two are perfect for each other."

"Do you really think so?" she asked. "I'm so crazy about him, but he seems out of my league."

"Are you kidding me? You two are perfect together!"

"Really?" She smiled giddily. "How do you know?"

"Jooodee, it's so obvious. Is that why you haven't been around? You've been seeing him."

Her eyes glazed happily. "All the time."

I clapped my hands together. It was too easy! "We need to celebrate! Let's go catch a movie, then I'll buy you dinner." I ushered her out the door, thrilled with the turn of events. Judy had been secretly seeing Dr. Chris! I should have guessed that something was up.

I nearly danced her into the elevator. My life here was about to end, but Judy was getting the happy ending she deserved, and I wanted to soak up the vicarious thrill. Although Judy still seemed distant and a little disconnected, at least now I knew where her head was. Okay, maybe it hurt that she was separating from me emotionally, but in the long run it was better that she move on and involve herself with Dr. Chris.

As we stood in line at the box office, I told myself again that Judy's withdrawal was a good thing. I didn't want her missing me when I was gone, did I?

I swallowed hard over a knot in my throat. Well, maybe just a little . . .

We bought our tickets and moved toward the door, but suddenly someone stepped in our way.

"Ms. Quicksilver." Simon squinted at me, his lips pressed together in a sour expression. "Sorry to interrupt, but we need to talk." The anger burning in his eyes indicated that he wasn't *that* sorry. He was probably just being polite for Judy's benefit.

"Oh." I paused. Having broken so many of Simon's rules over the past few days—meddling and matchmaking, dating and maintaining my search for a worthy man—I wasn't sure which violation angered him most, but I didn't want to tip my hand. I turned to Judy. "This will just take a minute, if you—"

"Actually, it may take a while," Simon interrupted, yanking one ticket from my hand and giving it to Judy. "Go ahead. You don't want to miss the coming attractions." He shooed her away, and Judy receded obediently, leaving Simon to tower over me, his arms crossed, anger flaring. "Where have you been? Where is your cell phone?"

I lifted it out of my purse. "Right here."

He yanked it out of my hand and pressed the ON button, rolling his eyes over the cheerful jingle that sounded as the phone turned on. He checked the phone display, then held it in front of my face. "Thirty-two messages, thirteen of which are from me. How do you expect your boss to reach you when you don't turn on your cell phone? Check your voice mail."

"Like I need to hear thirteen irate messages from my boss?" I checked my watch. "By my calculations, I have a little more than one day left on this planet, and I'm trying to make the most of it. I don't need grief from you."

"You see, that's where you're mistaken. You do need me. Right now I may be the only person who can save your life here."

"The last time we talked you didn't have any solutions," I said. "And the last message I collected from you was just a pompous order to cease and desist. I couldn't just stop living, Simon. I may be fading from this astral plane, but I've got to make the most of it while I still can."

"Don't you get it?" He stepped toward me. "I'm trying to help you. I've spoken to the Council twice on your behalf, trying to get you a waiver . . ."

A waiver? My heart danced hopefully in my chest. It was the first I'd heard of this.

"But every time they consider your case, there's some new development here that weighs against you." Simon frowned. "They know that you were pursuing a man after you'd been warned to stop. I almost got them to forgive that violation, and then in comes the report of a voluminous phone book of dates."

"Phone book?" I chirped, wondering how Simon knew

about that. Maybe he'd been watching me, had staked out my apartment or shadowed me around town.

"A different man every hour?" he went on. "Really, Annie, have you no conscience?"

"I was just trying to pursue every option." My voice was suddenly hoarse with emotion. Had I blown it again? "Why didn't you tell me you were appealing to the Council?"

"Annie, I did mention it. Don't you remember?"

"Well . . ." Of course, he had said it, but I didn't take him seriously and I didn't have much faith in his negotiation skills. A miscalculation on my part. A big one. "I've been trying to bail myself out the only way I know how, Simon."

His dark eyes were sad. "A botched effort, I'm afraid."

"What can I do now? How can I let the Council know that I'm serious about staying here . . . that I deserve to stay here?"

"If you want them to believe you're earnest in your desire to stay, you must stop intervening with others. I suggest you return to your apartment and lock yourself inside. Do not see anyone, do not call anyone, do not take any calls, save for mine."

I shook my head, my eyes stinging with rising tears. "I can't do that. I've only got one day left, and there's a huge party . . . my last chance to see my friends, to make sure Judy and Dr. Chris work things out and—"

"Listen to yourself a moment." His jaw clenched in anger. "You ask my advice, then respond with adolescent angst? *I've got to see my friends!*" he mimicked.

At that moment I hated Simon more than ever.

My hands balled into fists, and I had a deep desire to conjure a spell or two—a web of taffy or a mouthful of marbles—harmless witchcraft, just enough to prod his ego, but I knew it would be lost on Simon.

I let my fingers relax and took a deep breath. "After all

your time in this astral plane, all your dealings with humans, you still don't get it, do you?"

He squinted, struggling to change gears. "I beg your pardon?"

"Doesn't the Council find it surprising that you've remained aloft from the humans here? That you keep yourself separate and apart and uncaring? That, after all this time, all the missions you've overseen here, you haven't developed compassion?"

He detached, his eyes settling into a glazed look. "I am not the one whose future is at stake."

"No, that would be me, and let's just say that after tomorrow I'll be fading fast." I lifted my chin, aware that my voice was quivering, but I wasn't going to let that stop me now. "And since I'm a goner, I'm going to spend my last day being in touch with mortals and trying, at least *trying* to do the right thing by them."

"Yes, I imagine you will, and that's a pity."

I wanted to yell that he was totally missing the point; that he was heartless and uncaring, and that after all these months, he didn't understand what I was about, what mattered to me. But what was the point of arguing when it wouldn't affect any positive changes?

"Yes, well, poor, pitiful me, going back to Ephemera." I looked down at my movie ticket. "The movie's going to start. Guess I'll see you in the next plane." I took a last look at my boss, and then headed into the dark theater, willing myself not to look back. I would have loved to curse him, glare at him, blame him, but as I opened the door and stepped into the dark theater, I realized the truth: I had no one to blame for my failure.

No one but myself.

13

An eerie hush squeezed the night air, as if the city were en-capsulated in a huge balloon and some celestial giant was sucking on the end. Or maybe that was my own fear throw-ing a vacuum on the night, fear that I was running out of time and wouldn't be able to soak up enough memories on this, my last night on this planet.

Sixth Avenue was closed to traffic, blocked with chipped blue barricades and a line of cops who murmured quietly to each other, distant and unconcerned, passing the time. I rec-ognized a few conventional costumes—a mad scientist, a mad cow, a mad president—but most people were in drag, dipped in shining face paint and adorned with sculpted hair and feathers. I was amazed at how quietly these spangled, painted, contorted-looking humans shifted and receded through the streets, as if cast about by an invisible tide.

Was it the pull of the moon?

Though the moon wasn't full, its light permeated the darkness, seeping out from behind the canopy of buildings. I tried to focus on the distant clatter; the rhythmic drumbeat echoed through the streets like trash trucks slamming repeatedly. Ahead of me, Judy didn't seem to notice any of this, but pushed past pedestrians, a woman on a mission.

"Are we in a Tarzan movie?" I said aloud, trying to loosen things up.

"That's the parade," Judy explained as she sidestepped a man in an elaborate head-on-a-platter costume. "You'll hear a constant rumble of drums tonight. Sort of catchy."

"So this is Halloween in the Village." I gazed around, soaking it up. "A mystical experience. What's your hurry?"

"You know . . . he's going to be there." Judy pressed a green hand to her green chin. "I have to see him."

After working with him all day? I hitched up the spatulas hanging from my belt so that I could walk faster. "That's quite an attachment."

"I am devoted to him," Judy said emphatically. "I can't stop thinking about him."

"That's great!" I was thrilled for her, though she didn't seem quite as happy herself, the way she forged ahead as if hell-bent on a dark path. It wasn't like Judy, who usually stopped to seize the moment. I could only guess that she was tired . . . or maybe the green face paint was getting to her.

Masquerading as Elphaba from *Wicked*, she wore a standard dark frock with a tall, pointy hat and spectacularly green makeup on her face and hands. With the wig of long black hair covering her red curls, she was nearly unrecognizable, and although the contrived witch image here on Earth had grated on my nerves at times, my heart melted over Judy's desire to be a misunderstood witch who's willing to take on Oz in defense of creatures who are different. That was Judy—so determined to represent right that she didn't mind spending the evening in unfashionably green skin.

By contrast, I felt a tad cheesy in my Grecian gown, my belt strewn with spatulas, a feather duster, and a mini-plunger. I'd thought the domestic goddess guise clever, but now I realized that the lack of crazy makeup and wig and flashing electronic lights suggested boredom to everyone I passed. No risk, no rave.

We passed through a revolving door into one of the New School buildings. I was surprised to see the university with a life of its own, people streaming into the auditorium, bounding into stairwells, waiting for elevators. Classes were in session tonight. Of course, Halloween was not a national holiday, but I couldn't imagine concentrating amidst the beating drums, the surreal disguises, and the mysterious atmosphere of this night.

Taped music echoed through the party room, a very simple rehearsal studio, large but charmless, save for the costumed crowd and the paper lanterns that had been set up for the event. Judy and I hustled off the elevator, trying to avoid getting hooked on the fake barbed wire one guest had coiled around his black-and-white striped prison attire. We waded into the scattered crowd cautiously.

"Where is he? How will I ever find him?" she muttered to me, staring at a thoroughly wrapped mummy. "With everyone in costume? It's overwhelming."

"Not to worry. Let's go right to the bar," I said, trying to steer clear of a towering, hairless man dressed as a monk. I passed a man dressed in a long blond wig with a spangled dress. "Nice Madonna," I said.

"Actually, I'm Donatella Versace, but thanks for noticin', Lady Liberty."

On the way to the caterer's tables we passed a butterfly, a devil, a harlequin, and a bare-chested man who appeared to be showering in the tub apparatus wrapped around him.

"Hey, can you pass the soap?" I teased him. "Leave some hot water for me."

He turned to me, a deadpan expression on his face. "I've heard them all, believe me."

I thought about chatting up some of the other patrons waiting in line, but Judy was so engrossed in her search for Dr. Chris that she was no fun. "Where is he?" she asked, gazing at the revelers like a lost child.

"Easy, Elphie," I said, feeling a little sorry for her, "he'll be here. I'm supposed to be finding a man named Bruce dressed as a sumo wrestler, and do I look worried?" Not that I held out any hope for the man Aunt Gladys had set me up with, but I did need to make an effort to at least find him and introduce myself.

"It's about time you two made it," came Landon's familiar voice at my elbow.

I turned and saw two Neanderthal women in cartoonish, one-shoulder, fur tunics. Landon had a red bouffant hairdo, whereas Jeremy sported a jet-black pageboy. "Guys?" I giggled. "Love the wigs."

Landon's face went pink, an unflattering contrast to his red wig. "Jeremy made me wear this. I know, Wilma Flintstone and Betty Rubble, very TV Land, Nick at Night retro—"

"But Hanna-Barbera is coming back in vogue," Jeremy insisted.

"What do you think, Jude?" I squeezed her skinny green hand, but she pulled it away from me. "Judy?"

She moved across the room, as if summoned by an invisible beacon that drew her through the crowd and out the door to the rooftop.

"What's her deal?" Jeremy asked.

"She's been so worried that she wouldn't be able to find Dr. Chris in costume," I said, motioning the guys forward. Slightly baffled, we followed her into the night punctuated by banging drums and shrieks from the revelers four stories below us. Most people had congregated near the low balcony wall so that they could watch the parade below, but Judy found her man chatting with someone just outside the door. "See? She found him," I said with relief as Judy threw her arms wide and embraced someone in a wolf mask. "Now, maybe she'll be able to relax and have some fun."

"Hold on a second," Landon said, "that's not Dr. Chris."

"What do you mean?" I watched as Judy reached her arms around his neck and planted a big wet one on the lips beneath the cutaway mask. His head and face were obscured by a pointy-eared headpiece and furry mask, but from the way Judy was kissing him, it had to be Dr. Chris. "Oh, it's got to be him. She's crazy about him."

"Maybe it's a sheep in wolf's clothing," Jeremy teased.

Landon puffed up indignantly under his red wig. "I'm telling you, that's not Chris. We saw him out in the hall wearing a ten-cent Dracula costume. The black eyeliner, widow's peak, fake blood, silly fangs."

"That's right." Jeremy's black wig tilted as he shook his head. "Chris is Dracula. So, then, who's that kissing Judy?"

"Could she have made a mistake?" Landon asked.

"And she's making out with the wrong man?" Jeremy pressed a hand over his mouth. "Wouldn't she realize her mistake? I mean, there's kissing technique alone, shape of the lips and chin, sound of his voice and . . . Wait! He's taking off his mask!"

The three of us swooned forward in unison as Judy's guy pulled the mask from his cheekbones and lifted . . .

The furry hood peeled off his head and fell over his back as he ran a hand through his flattened hair, primping.

"Oh, no!" I gasped, taking in his regal brow ridge, thick blond hair—the whole gorgeous package of the warlock Denver. "What's she doing with *Denver*?"

"That's Denver? The guy who skunked you?" Landon tapped a finger on his chin, assessing. "Cute. What a pity he's so vile."

Yes, Denver was vile, despicable . . . and at the moment, he was spooning my best friend.

14

"She said she was seeing Dr. Chris . . ." I babbled, "that she was falling in love with him." Or had she? My mind edged back over the details, though it was impossible to remember. There was no way she had mentioned Denver, as the sound of his name would have made my head explode. Had she mentioned Dr. Chris by name, or was there just some vague reference to someone I had been seeing?

"This is so not like Judy," Jeremy remarked. "She would never be in love with two men at one time. Actually, I've never seen her show affection in public that way. Either she's in love, or she's lost her mind. Or maybe it's Halloween madness?"

Landon shot me a look of concern. "Judy's version of Halloween madness would be indulging in a Snickers bar. This is not our Judy."

He was right. This woman who hung from Denver, tossing her head back and giggling, was so unlike our friend. And I had a feeling I knew why.

Landon and I rushed forward, confronting Judy and Denver.

"You . . ." I met Denver head-on, restraining myself as a cool wind gusted by.

"Who are you?" Landon asked Judy. "And what have you done with my friend?"

She laughed in his face. "Oh, you're so funny." As she waved Landon off and leaned her head against Denver, I noticed that the light was gone from her eyes. She was walking and talking like Judy, but she was dead inside.

Because of Denver. Damn him, he'd used magick on her. No wonder she'd been so distant lately.

I pointed a finger at him, restraining myself from shooting sparks. "We need to talk, Denver. Just you and I, if you'll excuse us for a second, Judy."

Denver's lips curled into that evil smile I hated. "We can talk in front of Judy."

"I don't think so," I said, "unless you'd like me to explain about your alter ego."

"I'll be right back," he told Judy, gently pushing her away and joining me a few feet away at the brick wall. I could see Landon questioning Judy, trying to talk some sense into her, but he didn't have a chance, not while she was under Denver's spell.

"What do you think you're doing, using magick on a mortal?" I railed at him.

"Who are you, Glinda, the Good Witch? Can you honestly say you've never cast a spell on Earth?"

I reached out and sank my fingers into the fur at his chest. "There's quite a difference between a little spell to heal a paper cut and the magick that bends someone's will."

"It didn't take much bending," he said, combing his fingers through the thick, blond hair at his brow. "She was quite attracted to me."

"Only because she doesn't know your true nature. And attraction is one thing; blind, submissive devotion is slavery, Denver, and you know the Magickal Council will jail you for this. Now reverse the spell and free her."

"I don't think so. It's not about her; it's about me. I want to stay here, in a place where the women value marriage and eternal romance—"

"And warlock slavers? Pretenders?"

"Don't we all make the best of our features to win a mate?"

"This is not about accentuating the positive, Denver. What you did . . . what you're doing here to Judy is fraud. You know the Council is going to boot you off the planet when they hear about this."

"Not after I'm married. We all know the Council would never act to break up a sacred pact—even one involving a mortal."

"You can't do that," I sputtered. "You can't marry a human without Council permission."

"Oh, really?" He shrugged. "Didn't you get the memo, honey? It's better to ask for forgiveness than permission."

"You know it's wrong, Denver. You've got to reverse the magick. Now."

He shrugged. "No can do."

"Denver . . ." I snarled through gritted teeth. "Take the spell off, now."

"Sorry, babe, but she's my passport to permanent residence here."

"Not after I alert the Council," I said.

"Annie, really, I thought you were smarter than this. By the time you get word to the Council, it will be a done deal. Judy and I will be married."

Could he move that fast? I wondered how I could get to the Council quickly. There was Simon, of course, who might not answer my call. Besides, he had told me to stop meddling in earthly matters. But this was different—a question of compromising Ephemera, violating Council rules, enslaving mortals. . . . Still, I would need to get Simon to take my call, and he considered himself finished with me. And my time here on Earth was ticking out.

And how quickly could Denver force Judy to the altar? I searched her, trying to assess; poor Judy, decked out in green paint and a pointy black hat. She was so entranced, nothing would surprise me.

"I'm going to stop you," I told him. "You can make it easy and reverse the spell right now, or you can make it hard . . . in which case, you'll find yourself fading to dust by the time I'm done with you."

"I'm quivering in my hooves," he said flippantly. He checked his feet, lifting one boot. "Oh, right. I've got boots in this astral plane. And—how could I forget?—you have no power over me, you little witch. A single witch can't put a dent in a warlock's spell."

He was right about that. I would need more power and experience than I possessed. "Denver, for once in your existence, have a moral conscience," I said, trying to appeal to the minuscule nugget of character buried deep within his beastly being. "Please, I'm begging you, just be a gentleman about this and do the right thing."

"You're out of luck on this one." He shook his head. "I won't do it, and you can't make me, so step off, okay?" He moved away from me, extending a furry arm toward Judy. "Okay." He grinned as she toddled into his arms. "Did you miss me?" he crooned.

Judy giggled, "Desperately."

As he picked her up and swung her around, Landon and Jeremy joined me.

"An appalling display," Jeremy said. "I can't bear to watch people in love."

"It's not really love," I said, unsure how to explain the effects of Denver's magick on Judy. "It's more like obsession."

"I never thought I'd see Judy behave this way." Landon touched his chin. "Do you think she'll snap out of it?"

"Not fast enough," Jeremy said, nodding toward the door. "Here comes Dr. Dracula."

The wind lifted his cape behind him as Dr. Chris crossed the threshold and headed toward us. His eyes swept the rooftop, right over Judy and Denver, then back to us. "Hey, guys," he said, looking me up and down. "Domestic goddess, right? Very clever. Where's Judy?"

So he didn't notice, didn't realize she was a few feet away kissing some other guy . . .

"She was just here," Landon said quickly, "but she wanted a better view of the parade . . . downstairs . . . on the street."

"Right," I said quickly, "I was just going to head down to look for her." I pointed toward the door. "Want to come?" I don't know exactly why, but I felt the need to protect Dr. Chris from the sight of Judy with another man—especially one as wicked as Denver.

He lifted the edge of his cape to his chin. "I'd be delighted," he said in a bloated Transylvanian accent.

As we headed inside, Landon stepped up beside me and squeezed my arm. "What the hell are we doing? Are we going to leave Judy here . . . with *him*?"

I glanced back, wincing at the sight of Denver wiggling his furry tail for Judy. "Short of knocking her unconscious and dragging her out, I don't know how to get her away from him. But I may have a way to snap Judy out of this."

"Something illegal?" He squinted at me. "Do tell. Are we talking drugs, therapy, airborne pilates?"

"Actually, none of those, but if all else fails, I'll keep the therapy in mind. Your job is to keep Judy here. Promise me you won't let her leave this party, and definitely don't let her leave with Denver."

"I'm on it," he said. "If all else fails, I'll have Betty Rubble turn on the charm."

As Dr. Dracula and I left the building, we passed a cluster of guests on their way in, which included a large man dressed as a sumo wrestler. Could it be Bruce? I paused a moment to stare at the rubber bald head and large, plastic buttocks.

"Wow." Not my type, but Uncle Carlo's friend had a solid build—a brick wall. I watched as the elevator closed on him, thinking that I'd catch him on the rebound.

15

I sent Dr. Chris on a wild-goose chase, telling him to walk
down the parade route to Fourteenth Street while I headed
uptown looking for Judy. I felt bad about tricking him, but
I figured that the alternative—a confrontation with the
spellbound Judy—would be worse right now.

Then I headed uptown, hoping to find Aunt Gladys in
her studio on Twentieth Street. Something Denver said had
tipped me off, when he pointed out that a single witch didn't
have power over him. I couldn't foil him alone, but with
Aunt Gladys's help, who knew?

I found her in a tent set up in the street outside her building, where seamstresses rushed around helping people shed
their costumes at the end of the parade route. "Costume
reclamation," she called it. Some of the pieces used in
Broadway shows were worth a fortune.

"I know you're busy, but I really need your help." I explained about the magick Denver had performed on my
friend, and the dire consequences for Judy—a lifetime of
abuse from a two-faced warlock.

"Say no more, my golden sunstone. Desperate times call for desperate measures. Come along."

I followed her out of the tent, in the door, and up the steep stairs to the wide-open studio, where a young woman was running sheets of fabric through a sewing machine. Aunt Gladys rushed her along, and she finished up and ran the costume downstairs to the tent.

"Let's see . . ." My aunt gently placed a fat book on her worktable; the book emitted a cloud of dust that curled back around itself in a puff of smoke. The blue smoke darkened to purple, then began to glow red, then a fiery orange.

I felt my jaw drop at the distantly familiar sight. "The *Master Craft* book? How did you get a copy here on Earth?"

"It's contraband, I know, but how can the Council expect an upstanding witch to function without her *Master Craft*?" She opened the book to the middle and began flipping pages, muttering, "It's like expecting a plumber to do his job without a wrench. Now, let's see, since Denver's spell bent a person's will, that crosses the line from craft to magick, which brings us to the serious spells."

"Will it be possible to reverse it?"

"Of course, any spell can be reversed," she said. "The question is, do you and I have the craft and the smarts to accomplish that?" She stopped at one page, read parts of the spell aloud, then shook her head and moved on.

I leaned close, trying to read over her shoulder, trying not to be a pest, trying not to think about the fact that my spellbound friend could be minutes away from eloping with a bestial warlock. Glancing at the names of spells, I noticed that there were dozens designed to reverse someone else's magick; however, this was no simple task. For the first time in my life I was sorry I hadn't paid attention during Divinations class.

"This one just might work." Aunt Gladys ran her finger

down the list of instructions. "Wooh-boy, this is going to be fun. 'Witches performing this spell must be skyclad to avoid vibrations and emotions embedded in fabric.'"

"Skyclad?" I thought back to the training they'd tried to drill into me. "They mean naked?" I let out a laugh. "Naked in Manhattan?"

"You see, the spell isn't exactly designed for this astral plane. We could remain clothed, but then we take a chance that it won't work, with the fabric blocking auras and vibrations."

I glanced over at the door. "We could lock the door and do it in here, quickly, before anyone comes in."

"No, no, my emerald, this spell is specifically divined to reverse unwilling love magick, and so it must be performed in the presence of the subject of that magick." She frowned at me. "We need to be with Judy."

I sighed. "Okay, so we head over to the party, drag Judy into the janitor's closet, drop our drawers, and perform the spell. Would that work?"

"Almost. The spell should be performed under the night sky, so the janitor's closet is out of the question."

I moaned. "Night sky and privacy are not compatible in New York."

Gladys slapped a palm against the table. "I have just the thing for New York naked." She pushed away from the table and disappeared into the wardrobe closet. "What size are you, sapphire? A five?"

"Six," I called, following her into the racks of clothes. "What? What are you thinking?"

She pulled out a hanger bearing a sheer, flesh-toned garment. "Body stockings!"

I felt nude, though none of the people we passed on Sixth Avenue seemed to mind. In fact, most of them didn't even notice.

"Don't be such a prude," Aunt Gladys had said as I'd braced myself to head down the stairs of the studio and into the midst of the revelers. "You're in costume, and that hair covers everything that matters."

The thick Lady Godiva wig fell over my torso like a poncho, the bright orange hair wavering down to my knees. Orange was definitely not good for my skin tone, but it helped to cover the bodysuit, which hugged my hips and chest with a provocative firmness.

Aunt Gladys's costume was a far more festive hula girl with coconut bra and charming silk orchid in her head, and she wore it well, her grass skirt shushing as she pressed into the crowd. The sidewalk of Sixth Avenue was now a crush of people lined up from the edge of the street to shop windows. Revelers stood atop mailboxes and newspaper vending machines, hooting and howling and shaking noisemakers even as they maintained their New York cool, the notorious I-don't-give-a-rat's-ass attitude that left barbs in the hearts of tourists. A fun party, but we weren't going to get anywhere through this crowd.

Ahead of me, Gladys pressed into the intersection, into a wall of dark blue uniforms. I could see her speaking to the police amid the surface of bobbing wigs and spiked hairdos. What was she telling them? I seriously doubted they'd let us past the barricades for a magick emergency.

A moment later my aunt turned back to me and pointed down the side street. "The officer suggested Fifth Avenue, and I think it's the only way. We'll skirt around the crowd and double back half a block to the New School. Now where is this party?"

As we hurried down Twentieth Street I told her about the rooftop venue. "Sounds perfect for a night-sky spell."

I held my orange locks to my tummy as I hopped up a curb. "What else do we need for this spell? An eye of newt or hair of an ogre?"

"Nothing so exotic, though we could use another handful of witches. Given more time I would have called in some of my gal pals from Ephemera, but since we're on the verge of losing your dear friend Judy, we'll have to wing it."

I thought of all my brothers and sisters on Ephermera. I'd grown up surrounded by witches and warlocks, had taken the swirling powers for granted, sometimes had resented my siblings. But right now I'd give up my closet of Ralph to have a few witches here. . . .

We hurried into the New School, rode up the empty elevator to the top floor, and pushed through the revelers who now spilled out into the hallway. Laughter and music filled the air as we cut through the main room to the outside balcony, where I scanned the crowd for my friends, hoping that Landon and Jeremy had been able to keep Judy here.

"I'll go check the perimeters for talismans," Aunt Gladys said. "We can't afford to have any charmed objects throwing off our spell."

"I'll find Judy," I told her as she scurried around two men in combat gear. Not far from the door I spotted a familiar-looking woman dressed as a Tyrolean maiden in lederhosen and blond braids. She was talking to the devil I'd passed before, an attractive tall man with dark eyes that penetrated his red mask. I was squinting at her, trying to make her out, when she stepped toward me.

"It's me, Mercedes," she said, lifting one blond braid.

"Oh . . . the hair threw me. And no glasses?"

"I'm trying out contacts. And you've got quite a hair thing going yourself."

I held two locks together at my throat, hoping they covered my breasts. "I'm Lady Godiva, and to be honest, I'm in a bit of a panic. Have you seen Judy and Landon and Jeremy? Judy is . . . isn't feeling well, and I'm really worried about her."

"As well you should be," spoke the devil. He plucked the mask and let it dangle at his neck, revealing his face.

Oh, great. My boss had crashed the party. "Simon, what are you doing here?"

He gave Mercedes a sharp look, and she moved off into the crowd.

"If you must know, I was summoned here by Mercedes, who detected a swirl of magick in the air."

"Mercedes is a witch?"

"Half-witch. She's my sister, and a more than adequate resource to report your activities. Tell me, do you and your friends ever think of venturing beyond that restaurant?"

"Mercedes . . ." That was how Simon knew the details of my life. "That little spy!"

"Consider yourself fortunate that the spy was here tonight, as we were able to divert your friend Judy from hopping on a jet to Vegas while you were out and about."

I put my hands on my hips. "I went to my aunt to . . ." What? To find a spell? But Simon would remind me that spells were unauthorized. On the other hand, I had no choice but to perform this spell, and what could Simon do, fire me? "I went to my aunt to get help with a spell," I said quickly. "Mercedes was correct when she sensed magick. Denver has put a bondage spell on Judy, and he plans to marry her before the Council can intervene. I'm going to stop him. Aunt Gladys and I are going to reverse his spell."

He folded his arms.

"I know, I know, against Council rules. But I'm not going to let Denver destroy my friend's life. So, Simon . . ." I stepped closer, so that no one would overhear. "Unless you want to be associated with the illegal use of witchcraft here, I suggest you leave. Now."

"I'm not leaving."

My heart sank as he unstrapped his mask and tucked it into a pocket of his cape. Was he going to try and stop me?

"Your spell will be more powerful with greater participation," he said. "Mercedes and I will join in."

"What?" I blinked.

"We're going to help you, Judy. Did you think we would turn our backs on such a gross violation of craft? Now stop acting so bewildered and let's get this craft in place."

16

"I found this near a planter on the balcony." Aunt Gladys held up a small crimson pouch, closed by a drawstring.

"May I?" Simon lifted it to his nose and sniffed. "Filled with clover and cornflower, I suspect; herbs dealing with love and psychic power. He's trying to capture her love by controlling her mind."

"Should we deconsecrate it?" I asked.

"I say we use the talisman in the reversal," Simon suggested.

"Excellent idea," Aunt Gladys said. "I know just where to fit it in. Now, are we all clear on the properties of this spell? We must be of like mind for the reversal to work."

"I think we're all on track," I said. "But what about the skyclad requirement?"

Aunt Gladys looked Simon and Mercedes up and down. "Good point."

"Oh, no!" Mercedes waved her arms. "I'm not going naked on this planet."

Simon laughed. "Is that why you two are wearing those silly costumes? Didn't anyone ever tell you that the rules of ritual change when you leave Ephemera? Skyclad is not required."

"Now you see that?" Aunt Gladys shook her head, the orchid in her hair bobbing. "All the more reason to have an Earth edition of the *Master Craft* book."

"Can we get on with this?" Mercedes prodded.

"Before Judy leaves the party with Denver," I added. We needed to catch Judy while she was still on the balcony, and she was now in the process of saying perfunctory good-byes to Landon and Jeremy, who told me they'd nearly ripped their hair out thinking up ways to keep Judy here while I was gone.

"All right, then." After years of directing seamstresses, designers, and actors, Aunt Gladys was accustomed to taking charge. "I'll lead the spell, and you three are to stand behind me, link arms, focus your powers."

"And hope like hell that the Council doesn't notice this spell opening up the earthly plane," Mercedes muttered as we linked arms and hobbled as a group over to Judy.

Landon glanced our way, cocking one brow. Jeremy leaned back, patting Judy's hand. When Denver noticed us, his face flattened in suspicion.

"What's going on here?" Denver snarled, pulling Judy toward him.

"Step away from her," Aunt Gladys ordered, "step away or risk banishment."

I knew the spell would require less power if Denver stepped out of sight. *Please back away,* I pleaded silently. *Just go . . .*

Of course, he refused to budge. "You can't do a reversal on Earth," Denver insisted. "Do you really want to attract all that attention to yourselves? Risk offending the Council?"

"The Council passes fair judgments," Simon said. "And I suggest you step aside and save yourself now."

Denver held tight to Judy, his eyes gleaming with malevolence. "You don't scare me, McAllistair. Bring it on."

Landon and Jeremy had scurried over to my side.

"Denver knows people on the New School Council?" Landon asked.

I shushed him and worried about the various horrendous ways it can backfire when you perform a spell in the wrong astral plane—the misfires and ricochets, the fallout to observers. I turned to Betty and Wilma and whispered, "You may want to take a few steps back."

Mercedes nudged me to pay attention, as Aunt Gladys had already begun chanting and dancing, moving in a circle around Judy and Denver, who stood in a pool of light. As Gladys chanted, the light rose, whirling and twirling up around their ankles, nipping at Judy's dark skirt as it twined around her legs.

All around us I heard conversations cease. Ripples of excitement passed through the crowd as people noticed my aunt's unusual dance and the spectral glow, but I tried to block out the distraction. They could think what they wanted; this had to be done.

Judy stared down at the growing halo, confused. She never liked being the center of attention, but she was unable to avoid this moment, held fast by Denver, who seemed to think he possessed the power to hold her in his command and ward off our spell. I felt his aura rising, a dark, acidic cloud over his head.

"He's rallying!" Simon called out. "Use the talisman!"

Lifting the pouch Denver had charmed, Gladys opened the drawstring and shook it. Tiny bits of herb shimmered out and flew into the gathering vortex; dark flecks turned to spun gold that surrounded Judy—only Judy—in a halo of light. Where was Denver? I couldn't see him in the swath of gold.

Although my aunt wasn't speaking to us, I could hear

her voice summoning Simon, Mercedes, and me. "Focus. Center. Focus." I channeled my energy into the shaft of golden light, my vision blurring as the light grew in intensity, throbbing and glowing, spinning around Judy like a cyclone. The light was the thing . . . only the light.

A shower of golden light sprayed over Judy, tiny sparks dancing on her head and shoulders, bouncing off her green gown, hopping around her feet. The tower of sparks shot up into the sky like a searchlight, far too evident to the people at the party, the people in surrounding buildings . . . the people of New York.

"Everyone in the five boroughs is going to see this!" I gasped.

But Aunt Gladys danced on, circling Judy, shaking her coconuts, rattling her grass skirt as if performing some ancient ritual. I wasn't sure where the witchcraft ended and the show began, but it didn't seem to matter to the revelers.

"Fireworks!" Jeremy shouted. "A most unexpected bonus."

"What are they doing?" someone behind me asked.

"It's performance art, by students of the New School," Landon answered as my aunt twirled around and shimmied to the ground to tap the tops of Judy's boots.

"Isn't that hula girl a little old to be a student?"

"She must be the professor," came the whispered answer.

I wanted to laugh, partly because of their comments, but mostly because of the feeling of joy that rushed through me in the glow of the golden light. The reversal had worked, I could feel the effects: I could smell the scent of freedom, sweet like the earth after a spring rain, and could feel the warm, sunny glow that wakes the soul after a dark night.

The shaft of light intensified, then popped off Judy and blew into the stratosphere.

Just like that, it was over.

Denver was gone, vanished.

Wincing, Judy looked at the crowd, then stepped forward and fell into my arms. "I don't know about you," she whispered in my ear, "but I'm staying away from wine for the rest of the night."

I hugged her close. "I am so glad you're okay. So glad."

"Where's Denver?" Jeremy asked.

"Yeah, he missed the performance art." Landon squinted toward the door. "I didn't even see him leave."

"I think he had to catch a flight," Simon said. "To Hades, I believe."

Judy stepped back and rubbed one temple. "I have to admit, I'm glad he's gone. He can be very smothering at times."

"Ha, ha!" Aunt Gladys did a little shimmy, then adjusted her coconut bra. "I say we crank up the music and do some real dancing!"

Jeremy smiled and swung his hands in a mini-twist. "You go, Bahama Mama!"

As the party swung back into action, Simon and Mercedes stepped away, giving me a chance to talk with Judy.

"It's odd, but I don't feel bad about Denver at all," she said, "and that's so unlike me, the queen of guilt."

"It just wasn't meant to be," I said with a huge feeling of relief. At least, if I had to go back, this one disaster had been avoided.

"So Simon's here," she said, her brows lifting suspiciously. "Are you two working something out to extend your gig?"

"Oh . . ." I didn't want to disappoint her. "I hope so." At least it wasn't a lie.

When I turned back to the dance floor, Aunt Gladys was dancing with sumo Bruce, the guy I was supposed to hook up with tonight. A minute later, Bruce was dancing with Mercedes, Jeremy with Landon, Gladys with Judy.

"Quite a motley crew you've assembled here," Simon said.

My friends . . . "I'll miss them."

"Yes, well, we really should talk about that." Simon checked his watch, frowning. "It's almost midnight. May I suggest a very early breakfast? I know an all-night diner a few blocks from here."

His suggestion jolted me back to reality. Almost midnight . . . so this would be my last meal.

17

Simon and I fit right in at the diner, where the waitress was dressed like Marilyn Monroe and the grill man wore Yankees' pinstripes. I was dying to shed my heavy, itchy wig, and Simon was kind enough to loan me his red cape, which seemed to keep other diners from staring. Watching Marilyn carry off our empty breakfast plates, I took another sip of coffee and wondered when the fading would begin. I felt surprisingly hearty for a woman who would be disappearing from this dimension shortly, but maybe each astral relocation got easier as you went along. I could only hope.

I looked across the table at Simon, who'd eaten his meal without the usual bravado. I wasn't sure when, if ever, I would see him again, and I knew that I owed him some thanks.

"It's hard for me to say this, but thanks for extending yourself." I reached across the table and squeezed his hand, surprised by the warmth I found there. Simon wasn't such a bad guy all the time, and tonight he'd really saved my skin.

"I know you took a chance, practicing magick without

permission of the Council, and I appreciate it. It meant a lot to me, saving my friend."

His eyes were wide and shiny and fixed on me as if he could draw some information by simply staring. "Really, the spell would have been justified considering the numerous violations Denver committed in trying to woo your friend. I'm glad I could be of assistance." He looked down at my hand in his, then cradled it between his palms for a moment.

I felt my eyes tear up over the small act of tenderness.

Silly sentiment, but there were so many things balled up under the surface—the sorrow over leaving here and the dread of life in Ephemera—that I couldn't bear such a simple act of kindness without crumbling.

"I need to thank you, too," he said, turning my hand to examine my fingernails. "You have always been honest with me, brutally honest, and despite my resistance, you've taught me a lesson or two." He took a deep breath. "While I've made great strides adjusting to this astral plane, I realize I am intolerant of human flaws. How did you put it? 'Lacking compassion.' It's something I need to work on."

He drew my hand to his lips and gently kissed the tip of my index finger.

I gasped, surprised at the soft gesture, surprised at the response inside me, the gentle implosion of my resistance to this man.

"I'm glad I could light the path for you," I said. "Will you come visit me in Ephemera? Bring me a half-burnt New York pretzel, or maybe a latte from Starbucks?"

"A three-dimensional postcard?" He released my hand and reached into the pocket of his pants. "Perhaps I can do better than that."

"Sure," I muttered, "maybe you can throw in an inter-astral shopping trip."

"Would you like to stay on Earth, Annie?"

I felt my jaw drop. "Do you mean . . . How's that possible?"

"This is a contract from the Council," he said, unfolding a paper. "They've agreed to grant you a visa to stay here, with an assignment as a cultural ambassador of sorts. They'd like you to research ways to broach the cultural divide between these two astral planes. Of course, we'd like to publish some of your observations in *Ephemera Online,* but those are details that we can work out as we go along."

"A new column?" And I was staying . . . "I'd love to do it, to write about people and New York. About the differences between life here and life in Ephemera."

"The Council sees it as a way to approach reforming immigration laws and lifestyles on Ephemera. Not to detract from witches who are happy with their lot, but they would like the rules to serve everyone, and you were not the only witch who complained of boredom in domestic paradise."

"I would love to be involved with some sort of reformation." I frowned. "But how did you swing that, when the Council didn't like my meddling? They wanted me to keep a low profile, to back away from—"

"Not all of that advice came from the Council," he said sharply. "I admit, after a certain point I found it difficult to watch you pursuing more and more men, ill-suited matches, the lot of them."

"It was my job," I pointed out.

He let out a breath and turned away. "Annie, I suppose I was wrong to interfere. Perhaps you would have found a man, eventually. But I could not bear to watch the cat-and-mouse play, the chase, the longing for attachment, when I realized that—now, don't laugh, please—I myself felt such a strong attachment toward you."

For the second time my jaw dropped; my heart was thudding in my chest.

"Well . . ." He sighed. "At least you're not laughing. But you seem surprised."

"You never let on. You were so hard on me."

"Trying to help you realize that those worthy men were all wrong for you." He reached across the table, this time extending an open palm an inch from mine. "They *were* all wrong . . . and Mr. Right was in the picture all along."

Simon. Simon. Simon. Each heartbeat seemed to echo his name as I realized the underpinning of his bad behavior, his stern advice, his snappish messages.

I lifted his hand, pointing his fingers skyward, then pressed my palm against his in an ancient, ritualistic greeting of witches and warlocks, a connection that signified equality and union, two hands and yet one common pulse at the base beating in unison.

This time his jaw dropped slightly. "I take this as a good sign. You no longer wish me dead?"

I smiled. "Not anymore." I linked my fingers through his, surprised at the heat on our palms. If we generated that much electricity just by holding hands . . . I swallowed, thinking of the activities we had to look forward to.

Simon stood up and pulled on my hand, bringing me away from the table, to my feet. He pulled me against him, pushing back his cape so that the flesh tones of my stockinged body pressed against him.

"So you don't want to kill me. Is it a mad leap to suggest that, in time, love is a possibility? The sort of love that, and I quote you: 'makes you want to shrivel up and die a little in his arms.'"

"Did I say that?" I felt myself warming to him. "I guess anything is possible."

"Yes, you've demonstrated that. You and your ninety dates, your crazy aunt, your compassion for men who make paper shoes and doctors who work with dead bodies and ladies who polish banisters. I must say, I was in awe to watch as you found redeeming qualities in so many of these humans."

"You shouldn't be so hard on them. You're half-human yourself."

"My worst quality."

"No, that would be your sarcasm."

He placed a finger under my chin, lifting my face up toward his. "Perhaps you can cure me of that. In time."

"We'd better start now," I said, realizing we were about to kiss and deciding to go for it. "It's going to take a lot of time."

He drew in a breath. "How encouraging. Perhaps we won't grow bored over the next hundred years?"

As his lips met mine, I sensed that boredom would not be an issue in our relationship. Not at all.

THE WITCH'S GUIDE
TO LIFE

Theresa Alan

1

The Witch and Family

Ariel sunk her fork into the moist chocolate cake. The rich, velvety frosting clung to her fork. Though Ariel's three-year-old niece was ordinarily a chatterbox, she didn't use words to ask for another bite. Since she had been a baby, she'd made a hand sign using the index and middle fingers of her right hand tapping against the palm of her left hand to indicate she wanted more. Ariel wasn't sure if this was a sign of precociousness, or if it made her niece the next Coco the Gorilla. Probably, like her Aunt Ariel, Rhiannon's love for food was such that she didn't want to have to stop chewing to speak. Using sign language meant she could keep stuffing her face without pause.

Ariel fed her niece another bite of cake. Rhiannon squealed with delight, her blond curls bouncing, her cheeks as pink as peonies.

Ariel used the bottom of her fork to press down on the last bits of cake, creating a bond that lifted the crumbs from the plate so she could lick them off the fork in a civilized manner, rather than giving the plate a tongue bath, as she would have done in the privacy of her home. Ariel closed her eyes and savored the last little bite of the soft, spongy cake. It tasted like heaven. The setting of the rapturous delight was less than celestial, however—they sat in the middle of an old-school diner with worn black-and-black-checkered floors, Formica tables, and battered red stools. The smell of grease hung thickly in the room.

"Rhiannon, try to get the plate to come to you without using your hands," Ariel coaxed. She hoped to see some signs of magical talent in Rhiannon. Ariel didn't want to be the last witch in the Walker family clan, and Rhiannon was her last hope. Rhiannon's mother, Faith, showed no inclination toward witchcraft whatsoever; neither did Faith's oldest daughter, Penny. With all the inter-marrying, the family knack for magic had become more and more diluted with each generation. Even Ariel's abilities were weak, despite her best efforts to strengthen them. She wanted to train her niece from a young age to help her grow into her full witch potential.

Rhiannon looked at her aunt with her face scrunched in confusion. She reached for the plate.

"No, don't use your hands. Just think about how you want the plate to come to you."

Rhiannon made an adorable expression, a face that asked, *What does this crazy lady want with me?* Then she stared at the plate for a moment, clearly lost in thought. Ariel watched the plate hopefully. It was trembling, wasn't it? Maybe? Maybe? Maybe not. Damn.

Ariel sighed and wiped the telltale crumbs from her niece's mouth. Faith would not appreciate that Ariel had fed Rhiannon chocolate for dinner, but Ariel was doing her sister a favor by babysitting, after all, and anyway, it really wasn't her fault. She always got severe chocolate cravings before an art opening. Her third show was coming up, and her nerves were thoroughly rattled. She had never sold a piece of her work, and if she didn't sell something soon, she wasn't sure a gallery owner would give her another opportunity to display her work. This could be her last chance.

Ariel nodded at the waitress when she dropped off the bill. Ariel reached for her wallet to pay, and that's when she saw him.

He was gorgeous, with dark brown eyes and thick dark hair. There was something about his eyes and expression that Ariel found captivating. His appeal wasn't a tingly, tear-the-clothes-off-my-body-and-do-me-now feeling. It wasn't simply about lust, it was about being instantly drawn to him, overwhelmingly intrigued to get to know him better.

It took her a moment to realize that she was staring. Her entire body was frozen with a powerful electric surge of desire. She forced herself to look away and peel a five-dollar bill from her wallet. Casually, she glanced back at him again, unable to stop herself. He was sitting with another man. Whatever they were talking about must have been funny, because Hunk kept smiling a heart-meltingly sexy smile.

You should go introduce yourself. You're a witch. Witches aren't passive. They go after what they want. They make things happen.

She considered ways to get him to notice her. He was only a few tables away. Maybe she could create a minor windstorm from her table to his, gusting napkins in his direction so he'd be distracted from his conversation and look her way. Ariel strained her memory to recall the spell to conjure wind. How did that go again? She remembered the words *gale* and *sail* and *commence*—she just needed to remember how to string them together in the proper phrases. After reviewing the spell in her mind a couple times, she closed her eyes and in a quiet voice said, "*Attention north-*

ern gale, kick up your sluggish sail. I bid you come hence, with forceful currents do now commence."

Immediately, the door to the restaurant thundered open and careened with a loud crash into the wall as a veritable tornado of wind blustered through the dining area. The wind was far stronger than Ariel had intended. Oops. Maybe she wasn't supposed to say "forceful"? What was the correct word? Damn! She couldn't remember. She gripped the table with one hand so she didn't go flying away and hugged her frightened niece to her side as chairs went toppling over, dishes became airborne, and the plate from Ariel's cake went tumbling through the air—landing on Hunk's head.

Just as abruptly, the wind stopped when a quick-thinking waitress managed to shut the door. Ariel watched in mortified horror as Hunk peeled the plate from his head, cake crumbs and sticky remnants of icing clotting in clumps in his otherwise gorgeous hair.

Ariel leapt up, holding her niece to her side like a koala bear clinging to its mother. She took a moment to smooth down her hair, which had been whipped up into something resembling a windblown haystack. She straightened out her tight red button-up shirt and rushed to his table.

"Are you okay?" she asked.

Hunk, looking a little stunned for a moment, smiled, then chuckled lightly. "I'm fine. What was that?"

"That was the weirdest thing," Hunk's friend said.

"Yeah, huh," Ariel said, with less poetry than she would have liked. "I'm so sorry about your hair. That's our plate that landed on your head."

"No problem. That's what shampoo is for," he said, fishing out little pieces of cake and icing with his fingers. "Anyway, it's not like it's your fault."

Ariel didn't say anything for a moment. Then, remembering herself, she said, "Right. Well, I'm glad you're okay. My name is Ariel Merrill, by the way. This is my niece Rhiannon."

Hunk nodded distractedly at her—he was busy trying to extricate the icing from his cranium.

"I wish there was a way I could make it up to you. Maybe . . . do you like wine?" she said.

"Huh?" Hunk asked.

"Wine, the drink, do you like it?"

"Yeah, sure, of course," Hunk said, confused.

"Me, too," Friend of Hunk said.

"I'm an artist and I'm having an art opening on Friday night at the MacLean Gallery. There will be free wine and cheese, so it's kind of fun if you don't have anything else to do. Both of you are welcome to come."

Hunk smiled at her. "That sounds like it could be cool."

"Art?" Friend of Hunk asked, looking at Ariel askance, as if trying to determine if she'd suffered a head injury of some sort.

But who cared about Friend of Hunk? Hunk was all that mattered. He seemed amused by her. Amused wouldn't do. She wanted him to be insane with lust for her, or at least interested enough to come to her art opening and get to know her better. She had to think of a love spell or a charm to cast on him, but right now her mind was completely blank. Oh, what a burden it was to be saddled with a pathetic short-term memory! Ariel closed her eyes for a moment, deep in concentration, trying to will the words to the spell from the deepest recesses of her memory.

When she opened her eyes, Ariel looked from Hunk to Friend of Hunk, noticing that they were both staring at her chest. She looked down to see that the top two buttons on her blouse had come undone, and her entire right breast was exposed for the world to see.

"Boobie," Rhiannon announced sagely as she poked her fingers into Ariel's breast, pointing to her find like an archaeologist would display a prize dinosaur bone he'd excavated. Quickly, Ariel pulled her shirt closed and tried to re-button it one-handed at the same time she was busy dying of shame.

She was mortified. On the upside, maybe this meant her niece did have magical abilities—Rhiannon had made her aunt's blouse almost disappear, after all.

"Right, then. Maybe I'll see you Friday. I'm going to go die of humiliation now." Ariel gave a weak smile and carried her niece out of the restaurant as fast as she could walk without actually breaking into a full-blown sprint.

Across town, Ariel's sister, Faith, had just gotten home from her job interview. She peered out the window at her neighbor's house, watching the UPS truck deliver yet another package to Bret's house. What was *in* all those packages?

From the beginning, there was something not quite right about Bret Halloran. Maybe it was the way he seemed just a little *too* nice. (Faith had read that Ted Bundy was an exceptionally charming man, and he used that charm to enlist the trust of his victims. Which just went to show, you couldn't trust *anyone*.)

Bret had moved in next door two years ago, and the shipments had started to arrive not long after he did. The packages came in a variety of sizes. Sometimes they came in a trickle, just one or two in a month. Other times—and not just around Christmas—they came in a deluge, one after the other. It wasn't like he worked at home and would be receiving work-related shipments; she knew he worked as a business analyst at Abbott Technologies in downtown Denver—he'd told her one day when they'd both been out working in their yards.

Bret's behavior was highly suspicious. Like the way he seemed to spend most of his evenings in his basement with the shades drawn and nothing but a weak lamp to light his way. Faith could see the faint glow from the basement windows that stuck out just slightly above ground level. On the evenings he was down there, Faith would casually walk over to her living room windows now and then, parting the curtains no more than half an inch, trying to see what exactly was going on. She hadn't seen anything yet, but she knew he'd slip up someday, and she'd be the one to expose what he was up to. Maybe he was another Tim McVeigh, and all those boxes delivered to his house were pieces of a bomb. Maybe he was an environmental extremist who wanted to protest the way the clean up of Rocky Flats Nuclear Power Plant was going, and he was stockpiling his weapons, preparing for a siege. Maybe he was a child pornographer, selling his wares over the Internet, and those boxes were filled with video and computer equipment. Whatever it was, Faith would uncover it. She'd make the cover of all the newspapers; she'd be interviewed on *Good Morning America*; she'd be a hero, known the world over.

Faith had to hand it to him, Bret did keep up a good front. From all outward appearances he seemed like an upstanding guy. He had a small but lovely garden. In contrast to his evenings spent furrowed in his dimly lit basement, he spent his weekends in the sun, tending to his flowers that lined the path to his front door or the small vegetable patch in his backyard. Gardening was a good cover for a murderer; it gave him the appearance of being gentle and nurturing, when he was actually probably a sadist who buried his victims' bodies in his floorboards.

She didn't trust him. He was much too good-looking to still be single in his early thirties. She'd read that serial killers rarely got married. The serial killer theory really explained a lot.

Of course, Faith was in her thirties and single, but not by choice. She'd had her eldest daughter, Penny, when she was sixteen years old. Then, about four years ago, she was married just long enough to get pregnant with Rhiannon. As soon as she'd told Casey she was pregnant, he couldn't get the divorce papers signed quickly enough. She'd had a lengthy court battle to get him to pay child support, but he rarely sent the checks he was required to send, and Faith just didn't have the energy to keep fighting. So she had to support herself and her two girls on her anemic salary as an administrative assistant. Most months it took some seriously creative math to get all of the bills paid.

Ever since Casey had left her, the thick tendrils of heartbreak had squeezed her chest in a tight vice, making it difficult to breathe.

Faith couldn't stand when people ordered her to have a nice day. She'd have a crap day if she felt like it, okay? She'd always been moody. In high school, Bobby McFerrin's "Don't Worry, Be Happy" song was played relentlessly on the radio, and people never tired of telling Faith that she should not worry and be happy. She wanted to beat them upside the head.

Faith couldn't have been more different than her sister, Ariel. Ariel was two years younger and always seemed to be generally happy. Ariel had a smile as big as bicycle handlebars and white teeth that could have starred in a commercial for a teeth-whitening product.

Ariel opened the door to her sister's house. "Hi, Faith. I just wanted to let you know you're raising Satan's spawn."

"Oh, believe me, I know. What did she do this time?"

Ariel recounted the story, and Faith laughed and gave her daughter a hug.

"Hey, don't do that; you're just encouraging her," Ariel teased, though she herself tousled Rhiannon's blond curls. Rhiannon was far too adorable to stay mad at for any length of time.

"Thanks for watching her," Faith said, looking her younger sister up and down briefly—jealously—before averting her gaze.

Ariel's tight red blouse stopped short of her jeans, letting her firm stomach and lower back peek out, revealing the ankh symbol she'd had tattooed there when she'd been in college. She had long blond hair that she wore straight; she tended to go heavy on the black eyeliner.

"How did the interview go?" Ariel asked.

"I don't know. I'm sure I didn't get the job."

"Faith, why do you always assume the worst of everything and everyone? Have you ever heard of the power of positive thinking?"

Faith rolled her eyes.

"I'll do a prosperity spell for you tonight, okay?" Ariel said.

Faith threw her sister an incredulous look. She didn't believe in spells or magic, which Ariel thought was a shame. If there was anyone who needed a little magic in her life, it was Faith.

"I know you don't believe in magic, but it can't hurt, right? Do you think you'd like the job if you did get offered it?"

"Definitely. It would be a huge increase in salary. And the lady I'd be working for seems really nice."

"You're going to get the job. I know you are. Look, I need to get going," Ariel said, looking at her sister's sad expression. "Faith, are you okay? I wish you would smile more."

"What's there to smile about? I've got a ten-year-old car and a crap job and credit card debt rivaling our national deficit."

Ariel frowned. It was so hard to see her sister gripped in depression. She'd done countless spells to ease Faith's sadness, but Faith's sorrow was so deep it was proving challenging to overcome.

"Thanks for watching Rhiannon."

"No problem."

Faith and Ariel hugged, then Ariel gave her Demon Child niece a hug good-bye, too.

Moments after Ariel left, Faith's fourteen-year-old daughter, Penny, arrived home from school.

"I thought you had newspaper tonight," Faith said.

"We finished early. Jim Peterson actually had the photos finished on time for once." Penny dropped her schoolbag on the floor and sprawled across a chair, her leg hanging over the armrest, her head bent at an ergonomically menacing angle, and her eyes closed in an exaggerated pose of exhaustion. Faith took another peek out her window at Bret Halloran's house.

"Have you caught Mr. Halloran in his plot to overtake the universe yet?" Penny asked.

"Penny, you have to admit that it's strange how he receives all those packages all the time."

"He is strange; I'm not arguing with you there. I'm just not convinced he's up to something sinister."

"Most murderers seem very normal. That's why so many literally get away with murder."

"I guess. What's for dinner?"

"I wasn't expecting you tonight. I was just going to make grilled cheese sandwiches."

Penny gagged theatrically.

Faith tried again. "How about a frozen pizza?"

"Well . . ."

"How about a frozen pizza, a bowl of popcorn, and an excessively sappy video that will make us cry our eyes out?"

"Yeah, okay."

"Rhiannon, are you hungry? Did you eat when you were with Auntie Ariel?"

"We got cake."

"You got cake?"

"Cake. Choca cake."

That was just great. Why did her sister feel the need to inject pounds of sugar into her daughter so that she'd spend her evening bouncing off the walls in a sugar-spun frenzy? Faith sighed.

Penny made the popcorn and poured the diet sodas while Faith heated up the pizza. They picked out a video that they'd taped from cable months earlier, and all three of them settled down beside each other on the couch with a bowl of popcorn, slices of pizza on paper plates in their lap, and a giant box of tissues centered between them. Rhiannon nodded off soon after the opening credits; Faith carried her to bed, then returned to finish watching the movie with Penny. They'd watched the video dozens of times before, but it never failed to make them weep copiously.

By the time the movie ended, paper plates with hardened pizza crusts lay on the end tables beside them, and used tissues lay on the couch and floor around Faith and Penny like a field of pink carnations. The bowl of popcorn had been reduced to nothing more than a few oily, salty, unpopped kernels.

They stared absently at the video rewinding at turbocharged speed, their eyes puffy and red.

"I'm going to crash," Penny said at last. She leaned over and gave Faith a good night kiss on the cheek.

"Night, honey."

Faith gave Penny a hug, her eyes still on the television screen. The video finished rewinding, and Faith realized she was staring blankly out at nothing.

When Ariel got home, she made herself a cup of cleansing mint tea. She had a number of medicinal and magical herbs, which filled her kitchen with vibrant colors and gave the room a homey feel. The scent of sage and lavender and lemon balm infused the air with a pleasing scent.

When her tea had steeped, she took her cup and went to her bedroom, where she sat at her small altar. There was a layer of blue silk covering it, and on top of that was one of her handmade candles, a small container of salt, and several crystals: carnelian for harmony, tiger eye for strength and courage, and aventurine for prosperity.

Ariel lit the candle, a special one she'd made herself that was the bright lime green color of peridot crystal. Green was the color of prosperity. She took a tourmaline stone, which was good for protection against negative influences, and set that beside the candle. She burnt pinches of dill in the flickering flame of the candle, which was a good trick for bringing in needed income. Then she took a thread and wrapped it around the candle, chanting her wish over and over again: "*Bring my sister happiness and prosperity. Bring my sister happiness and prosperity.*" She chanted this for several minutes with her eyes closed, visualizing her sister getting the new job and finding a guy who would love her. When she was done, she blew out the candle; the smoke swirled and danced around the room.

Ariel went to her small "studio," which was really just a second bedroom. The room was bare of furniture except for an easel and a stool and a small wood table covered in splattered paint. She finished up one of the last pieces she'd be showing at the gallery on Friday—it would have just enough time to dry before the opening—and with a satisfied smile, she stripped off her clothes and fell into bed where she fell asleep in just moments.

In the morning, she took time to do a spell for herself. It was the spell she performed most often—a spell to bring love her way. She boiled basil and orange peel in a small pot. Over the boiling pot she chanted, "*Somewhere be-*

tween the mossy woods and the turbulent seas there is a man for me. Clear the dark night skies and the thick forest of trees and let us find what is meant to be." She repeated this chant several times and then, with a sigh, she left for work.

2

The Witch and Work

Faith woke up in a bad mood, as usual. The world had lost its color for her, and she didn't know how to get it back. Ariel was always talking about the importance and significance of colors. If this day had a color, it would be something murky gray, or maybe purple and depressing like the stretch marks dividing the landscape of her thighs.

There were some mornings when she would have gladly stayed in bed all day if she didn't have two daughters to get off to school and a job to get to so she could ensure her daughters got enough food to eat. Once again, Faith forced herself to get up. She would get through her day as she'd gotten through every other day for the last three years: on autopilot.

Faith trudged out of bed and down the hallway to where little Rhiannon sat at the kitchen table. Rhiannon had the same blond hair, blue eyes, and coloring as her Aunt Ariel; Penny had brown hair like her mother.

"Mom, the Hello rang."

"The Hello" was Rhiannon's way of expressing the word

telephone. Rhiannon wasn't old enough to reliably answer the phone, but she rarely heeded Faith's request not to answer it. Usually Rhiannon would answer the question, "Is your mommy home?" with an affirmative "yes," and then slam the phone back in its craddle with a purposeful flourish. Faith figured it was probably just a telesalesperson anyway. She thought it unlikely that it was Publisher's Clearing House telling her she could kick up her feet and let the good times roll.

"What do you want for breakfast, baby?"

"Cimmin' toas'."

"Honey, we talked about this. That's not a healthy breakfast. What about some Cheerios?"

"Cimmin' toas'! Cimmin' toas'!"

"But Rhiannon—"

"Mom, you're drivin' me nuts."

Faith smiled. She had said that exact thing to Rhiannon when they'd been at the store the other day and Rhiannon wouldn't stop begging for candy. It was both amusing and a little surreal to have this little person mimicking her expressions.

Faith thought about it. A little cinnamon and butter on whole wheat toast wasn't completely without nutrients. And it would be so much easier just to give the kid what she wanted than having to argue with her. Feeling like a terrible mother, Faith caved and gave her daughter the toast. She had this vision in her mind of being a much better mother than she was, but most of the time she was much too tired to be the kind of mom she aspired to be.

Faith turned on the radio. Whenever Rhiannon heard music, she couldn't stop herself from dancing. With her half-eaten toast in hand, she hopped up and began dancing around, her blond ringlets bouncing about. It was so adorable, Faith laughed aloud.

"Dance, Mama!"

"Oh, no, I don't have time."

"Mama!"

"Honey . . ."

"Mama!"

"All right, all right, but just for a second." Faith took her daughter's hand and the two of them spun around and around. Despite herself, Faith had fun; she couldn't even completely suppress a smile. Faith felt a little better. For the moment.

Faith had gotten Ariel the administrative postion at the office where she worked several months earlier, when Ariel had been fired from her last job. The two of them sat near each other. Their jobs were to do administrative work that the executives and senior managers needed help with.

"Hi, Faith," Ariel said when she arrived at the office. Faith was already hard at work.

"Mornin'."

Ariel turned on her computer. As the computer groaned to life—the numbers and letters dancing across the screen like a baby suddenly awakened and blinking irritably into consciousness—Ariel swiveled around in her chair and surveyed the scene. She saw their boss, Barbara, approaching with a stack of papers that no doubt needed copying.

Ariel had long ago put a hex on the copy machine. Making copies was one of her least favorite jobs, so she'd cursed the copier. It was a longstanding joke that the machine simply would never work for Ariel. Her boss had actually stood over her and watched her try to use it; the machine froze or got stuck every single time. So Ariel had been permanently taken off copier duty. Score one for Ariel!

"Faith, can you make me fifty copies of these by noon?" Barbara asked.

"Sure thing," Faith said, taking the stack and setting it

on the desk. Faith smiled at her boss, but once Barbara turned and was out of sight, her fake smile faded.

It worked out well—Faith did things like copying and typing, and Ariel answered the phones and scheduled meetings. This division suited their personalities. Ariel was a people person, whereas Faith liked to deal with office machinery—it was more predictable and less temperamental than people were.

After work, Ariel came home and made herself a quick dinner. Just as dusk was turning irrevocably to night, Ariel walked to a small woods not far from where her apartment complex was. She found a clearing amid the trees and built a fire. She stared into the flames for several minutes, trying to clear her mind from thinking of anything but Faith. Ariel's psychic abilities had never been as strong as she would have liked, but most of her attempts of skrying (divination) had given her at least an idea of what was to come. But this was important, really important. She needed to be sure if things were going to turn around for her sister.

In a flash, the images appeared powerfully and unmistakably in the flames. There were three dolls whirling around on a wheel like the one that was spun on *Wheel of Fortune,* only this one was vertical and there were no colors or decorations on it except for the three dolls. One was a brunette, another was a blonde, and the third one was a redhead. Then, like a camera panning back, the image expanded. Ariel saw that the dolls were in a room in a house. Faith was there with a man. She was smiling.

Bam! As quickly as it had come, the image faded. Ariel fought to catch her breath. What did it mean? The blonde and the brunette could have represented her and Faith. But Ariel didn't think so. She thought the blonde was Rhiannon, and the brunette was Penny. The redhead was the daughter Faith hadn't had yet. Ariel smiled. She couldn't wait to tell her sister the news.

But first she needed to get through her art opening. Ariel returned to her apartment and changed into a red sequined blouse, a black skirt, and shoes that were so red and shiny they put Dorothy's to shame—three clicks of these babies wouldn't just get ya to Kansas, they could fly you to the moon.

The gallery was a modest space with white walls and white floors that wouldn't compete with art displayed in every possible inch of space. Ariel orbited the room with a wineglass in hand, smiling and thanking the patrons who complimented her work.

The art scene in Denver was a good one in some ways for a struggling artist. It was a small enough city that the pool of talent wasn't insurmountably huge. Here, skilled artists had a chance of getting their work seen. It wasn't like New York where you tripped over an artist everywhere you went. But in Denver, people tended to spend their disposable income on skis and snowboards and golf clubs, not art; in that way it was difficult for an artist to make a living at her art, as Ariel knew all too well.

Ariel liked the MacLean Gallery. Half the patrons were dressed up in fashionable attire, but the rest were sporting jeans. That was Denver for you: rugged individualism as expressed through wardrobe. There was no such thing as a dress code in the West.

Ariel did a lot of work with wax. She made thin wax creations that could be hung in such a way that let the light shine through the brilliant colors. She made candles of every different hue and scent, sometimes using multiple colors at once and making unusual designs by adding flowers and leaves. Ariel also painted with oils. She had two different series of paintings: her goddess paintings and her abstracts. The abstracts were composed of beautiful swirls of colors that evoked general emotions like sadness or happiness rather than depicting a specific scenario. Her goddess paintings showed various goddesses from Greek, Roman, and Indian cultures going about tasks that everyday modern women did. For example, Diana, the goddess of the hunt, was shown dressing a Thanksgiving turkey, and Ceres, the goddess of fertility, was rocking a baby to sleep.

Ariel sold the candles through local shops, and that was the only artwork she ever sold. People would come to her art openings and "ooh" and "aah" over her wax sculptures and oil paintings, but no one ever bought anything. There just weren't that many people out there with a few hundred extra bucks lying around with which to buy paintings. It was tricky to figure out how to price her work. It had to be expensive enough that people thought it was high quality (not to mention help Ariel recoup her costs for paint and canvases), but she didn't want to make it so overpriced that people couldn't afford it.

Ariel turned and stopped dead. Hunk was smiling and walking her way. Her heart leapt.

"You came," she said.

"It's not every woman who flashes me in the first two minutes I know her. How could I resist?" A strand of his dark hair fell in a wave across his forehead just above his eyes.

"I love my niece, but she's a little devil."

"I've got a nephew, so I know exactly what you mean. This one time I was babysitting him when he was about two or three years old. I ordered a pizza for us and the pizza delivery girl was really cute. I started chatting her up, thinking I was all suave. I was wearing sweatpants at the time and little Robby was tugging on them, trying to get my attention. I had my arms out to hold the box of pizza, and in a split second Robby pulled my sweats down to my ankles. There's nothing more damaging to your manhood than to be standing commando in front of the hot pizza delivery girl. We never did go out on a date, in case you're wondering."

Ariel laughed. "You know, you know my name, but I don't know yours."

"I'm J.T. J.T. Manning."

"It's nice to meet you, J.T."

"I really like your work."

"Yeah? Are you into art?"

"Into it? Not really. That's why I'm so impressed with your work. Normally I'm not a big fan of abstracts, but your use of colors... I don't know, your work has this wonderful energy. I think it's great that you can make a living as an artist."

"Oh, no, I wish. I've never sold a painting in my entire life. I've had a few openings, and it's a nice self-esteem boost to find gallery owners willing to display my work, but I just can't seem to convince anyone to buy a painting."

"Maybe I'll buy one."

"Are you joking?"

"Why would I joke?"

"That's nice of you, but you don't have to. Really."

"I'd like to. I need to decorate my place. I'm serious. I've got nothing but blank walls. I'm a guy, so I don't know anything about that sort of thing."

"Well, if you want to, that would be really cool of you." Ariel smiled stupidly at him for a moment, at a loss for words. After a few seconds of silence, she blurted out the first thing that came into her mind. "So, tell me about yourself. So far all I know about you is your name and that you have no future in interior design. What do you do for a living?"

"I'm a gym teacher and ice hockey coach at North High School."

An ice hockey coach—that explained his incredibly fit build.

"Gym was one of my worst classes," she admitted.

"I find that hard to believe. You look fit. You don't look uncoordinated."

"It wasn't that. It's that I don't have that competitive edge. I could never bring myself to care who won. I remember we'd have to play basketball in high school and the other girls had these long nails; whenever I had the ball, they would scratch up my forearms with their claws trying to snatch it away. I thought of the ball like a hot potato, something I wanted to get out of my hands as quickly as possible before these bloodthirsty Amazons carved me up. I would always think, 'People, get a grip on reality. This is *gym* class. Nobody is going to win an endorsement from Nike for this, so calm the heck down.'"

J.T. laughed, a rich, deep laugh.

"Do you like your job?" Ariel asked.

"Most of the time I love it. Teenage boys aren't easy though. There's lots of testosterone to deal with, but by and large, yeah, I like it a lot. What about you? What do you do when you're not painting?"

"I'm an admin assistant at a financial services company downtown. I actually work with my sister. She got me the job when I got fired from my last job."

"Fired?"

"They were really strict there. They wanted me to actually do work while I was there, and they were really picky about wanting me to show up on time, blah blah. It just wasn't a good fit."

He smiled. "Well, I think that I really should support the arts by buying a piece. Which one do you like best?"

"Are you seriously going to buy a painting? Are you just buying one because you want to go out with me?"

"I do want to go out with you, but that's not why I'm buying a painting. I just want to support the arts."

Ariel couldn't believe her luck. A cute guy was interested

in dating her, and she was selling her first major piece of art-work. To think that only a few hours earlier she'd been a sad working stiff who'd never sold a painting and didn't have any romantic possibilities in sight!

Ariel watched with pride as she sold her first real piece of art. He didn't actually get to take it home with him tonight—the gallery owner just stuck a red circular sticker near the price tag to indicate that it had been sold. J.T. would get to take it when the next exhibit took Ariel's exhibit's place a few weeks from now.

"Thank you. Thank you so much."

"Ariel, you can stop thanking me. I should be the one thanking you. Someday this painting is going to be worth millions, and I got it for a bargain."

"I can't help myself. I'm too excited. Do you want me to kiss your feet? At this stage in my career I'll happily kiss the feet of any soul kind enough to support my work."

"That's okay. Thanks, though, but I prefer to be the one doing the kissing."

Ariel had never had a desire to have her toes sucked or her feet otherwise serviced, but looking at J.T.'s teasing smile, she was suddenly willing to give it a shot.

"Ariel," Elise, the gallery owner said, "can I talk to you?"

"I'll be right there."

"I should get going," J.T. said.

"Oh." *No! No! Don't go! Please!*

"When can I see you again?" he added.

Yeah! Yeah! Yeah!

Ariel smiled. "Come to my place tomorrow night. I'll make us dinner." Ariel would cook a special dinner that included basil—the love herb that brought people together. "I'll walk you to your car." Then, turning to Elise, she said, "Elise, I'll be back in a minute, okay?"

The streets were empty. Only the stars and moon lit their

way. It was chilly out—winter hadn't quite given way to spring, though it had begun to lose the fight.

"This is me," he said, stopping in front of a silver Saab sports sedan.

"Thanks for coming tonight. And for the painting . . . and everything."

"My pleasure."

Ariel looked up at him, catching his gaze for a long moment, then said impulsively, "Kiss me."

J.T. looked around. "Somebody will see us."

"Only the moonlight will know."

He smiled and leaned close to her. He put his hands on her arms and kissed her. His lips were soft yet strong, tentative yet assured. She took in the smell of soap on his skin, his warmth, the slight taste of red wine on his breath. They kissed for several moments, then she pulled away.

"Bye," she said softly.

"Bye."

As Ariel walked back to the gallery, thoughts of J.T. swirled in the cauldron of her imagination. She smiled as she replayed the kiss in her mind—she could still faintly feel the sensation of his lips on hers. She thought of his dark eyes, his teasing smile, his sexy athlete's build.

She returned to the gallery feeling like she was in another dimension, hovering over reality. She picked up a glass of wine and stood smiling stupidly at the floor, wondering if this night was really happening to her.

"Tell me the inspiration for this piece," an older man said to her, pointing to one of her oil paintings of Vesta, the goddess of the hearth.

"What?" It took Ariel a moment to come back from la-la land. Ariel started to explain about how the woman shown in swirling colors of greens and blues cooking at the stove represented Vesta when she noticed something peculiar. There was a red sticker next to the price tag. But this wasn't the painting that J.T. had bought.

"Could you excuse me for just a moment?" Ariel said to the man. She hastened over to the owner of the gallery, Elise. "Elise, there's a red sticker on my Vesta oil painting, but that's not the painting J.T. bought."

"I know. Another patron bought it. And another patron bought *Rhapsody in Blue*."

"I sold three paintings?"

"I know, that's what I wanted to tell you. Isn't it wonderful?"

It was more than wonderful, and it was all thanks to J.T. He had lifted the curse. Imagine, people paying actual money for her work! People hanging her art in their homes! Ariel wasn't sure if she'd ever felt such a high.

"You'd better start producing more paintings," Elise said, "or you're going to run out of pieces for people to buy."

That was the most wonderful problem to have that she could possibly imagine.

The next morning, Ariel was still beaming with excitement. She went into her small second bedroom where she did her artwork. She sat in front of a blank canvas and wondered what she should work on. She'd been toying with the idea of doing something with Laksmi, the Hindu goddess of wealth, but what? And how? Ariel sat for several minutes trying to sketch something—anything—in her notebook, but nothing came to her. Oh well, she just needed to get the ideas flowing again. She was probably just too wound up with excitement over her date tonight to focus.

Usually she had too many ideas, more ideas than she had time to articulate on the canvas. Today, she would relax her mind and spend the day straightening out the house and buying ingredients for dinner.

But first she wanted to call Faith and tell her about the exciting night she'd had.

"Hello?"

"Rhiannon, it's Aunt Ariel, is your mother home?"

"She's dying."

"What?!"

"Hello?" It was Faith; she'd picked up the extension in her bedroom. Her voice sounded low and gravelly, as if she'd been run over by a truck.

"Faith, what's wrong? Are you really dying?"

"No, I just have a migraine." Faith was lying in her darkened room, her arm covering her eyes to shield them from every last trace of light. Waves of nausea ran through her. "I might be moaning so it sounds like I'm dying, but I'm not."

"Are you okay? Do you need me to come over to watch the girls?"

"Penny is taking care of Rhiannon. Everything's under control."

"Are you sure? I'm free all day."

"I'm sure."

"Okay. Oh, oh, I didn't tell you. I had a vision."

"A vision? Could you tell me about it later? My head is being cleaved in two by a chainsaw right now."

"I had a vision of you smiling happily with a man. You had three daughters: a brunette, that's Penny; a blonde, that's Rhiannon; and a redhead."

"A redhead? Where would I go and get myself a redhead?"

"You're going to marry a redhead, of course."

"I don't even like redheads." Faith thought a moment. That wasn't entirely true. She'd been attracted to a redhead a time or two in her life; such as her neighbor, Bret. He had a sort of reddish brown hair coloring, sort of a burnt sienna shade, and he was pretty cute if you could get over the fact that he was probably a serial killer.

"I'm just telling you what I saw. Feel better, okay?"

"I will," Faith said. Though, in truth, there were times she worried she would never get better, not really.

3

The Witch and Sex

Ariel spent the day bustling around her apartment getting it clean. She plucked fresh basil from her window herb garden and spent much of the afternoon baking fresh bread and making homemade pasta.

When J.T. knocked on her kitchen door that evening, she took a deep breath and tried to calm her heart, which threatened to explode.

"Hi, I'm glad you could make it," she said.

"Me, too." He leaned in and gave her a kiss on the cheek. "These are for you." From behind his back he pulled a bouquet of mixed flowers.

"Thank you. They're beautiful." She was being romanced! She loved it! She pulled a vase from her cabinet. It was dusty. That's how long it had been since a guy had given her flowers. She got asked on dates a lot, but in her experience, most guys weren't hopeless romantics, they were just hopeless. All signs were suggesting that J.T. was a keeper. After Ariel had washed the vase and filled it with water, she asked J.T. if he'd like a tour.

"Sure."

"It won't take much time." Her apartment had a kitchen that doubled as a dining room and a living room with a sliding glass window that led out to the balcony (with a charming view of the parking lot), and upstairs were her bedroom, the studio, and the bathroom.

"You have a lot of candles," he said as she showed him around.

"I make them."

"Ahh. What's this?" he asked when she showed him her bedroom.

"It's my shrine."

"Shrine?"

"I'm a witch." She braced herself for his reaction.

"A witch? Really?"

Ariel flinched. She'd lost more than one boyfriend because they thought her spiritual beliefs were too outré.

"Yes."

To her great relief, he didn't say anything mocking or go sprinting out the door. He just said, "When did you become a witch?"

"Not long after my parents died. I was about thirteen years old when they were killed in a car crash. The only family my sister Faith and I really had was our grandfather, so we were sent to live with him. He wasn't a very nice man to begin with, and he wasn't happy about having to look after two teenage girls."

"Man, that's rough. I'm sorry. But how did that make you a witch?"

"I'm getting to that. My grandfather had a sister who had Alzheimer's disease and lived in an old folks' home. Grandpa had something to do one day, so he dumped Faith and me there, pretending like it was just for a visit, but really it was to get us out of his hair. Aunt Mina had moments of lucidity. She sorted of flitted in and out of reality. Faith, Mina, and I were sitting around a table. We'd exhausted the kind of conversation you have with an older person you don't know very well, you know, the usual, 'How are you?' 'I'm fine, how are you?' type stuff, and we were sitting there in silence when suddenly Mina's eyes glowed—I'm telling you they *glowed* like lightbulbs—and she looked right at Faith and said, 'Be careful of shallow promises. All is not as it seems.' It freaked out Faith and me. Aunt Mina said that she could see the future. I said, 'Oh yeah, how can you do that?' She explained how Faith and I come from a long line of witches, but there has been so much inter-marrying with non-witches that our powers have been weakened. She told us a little bit about our famous witch ancestors. I was transfixed. Then Aunt Mina said, 'Who are you?' I said, 'Mina, it's us—Ariel and Faith.' She just kept repeating that over and over again, 'Who are you?' 'Who are you?'

"Anyway, when we left, I was all excited about being a descendant of witches. Faith just kept rolling her eyes and saying sarcastic stuff about how Mina was off her rocker. But I started reading everything I could about witches and witchcraft, and I found that I did have magical powers. They're weak, and they don't always work like they're supposed to, but I've been developing my skills ever since. As a witch, I have control over my future. It made sense to me that I had witch's blood running through my veins. I should have realized sooner that I had certain . . . powers. Cats were always following me around, and when I really put my mind to something, it seemed like I'd usually get my way. Like one time before I knew I was a witch, I forgot to study for a test. I wished and wished for something to happen to give me extra time, and what do you know, that day a water main broke at school and school was closed for the day. I ended up acing the exam. Faith never had luck like that. I think you need to believe that good things can happen, and then, more times than not, they do."

Had she gone too far? She believed in being honest, but

she didn't want to scare J.T. off before he even started to get to know her.

"I think that's a great attitude. That's the kind of winning attitude I try to get my players to adopt. I'm sorry to hear about your parents, though. That must have been hard."

"It was. Life's hard enough when you're a teenager. I escaped into my art. I think I felt this need to prove myself as an artist because my grandfather thought so little of me. I thought, basically, *I'll show you*. But then I didn't have any success as an artist, and for a while I was wondering if maybe he was right after all."

"Ariel, that's a terrible thing to think."

"I know but . . . you didn't know my grandfather. He was always putting us down. When you're a teenager, your ego is already so fragile. It's easy to believe the bad things people say about you. I think he's the reason Faith got pregnant at sixteen."

"Your sister has another child?"

"An older daughter, yeah. I think she was unconsciously looking for someone she could love and be loved by, so she had a baby she could love. Our grandfather was completely unsupportive of her pregnancy, of course. It was a really hard thing for her. I remember this one image in particular when I was walking behind her on the beach when she was eight-and-a-half-months pregnant. She was huge, just huge, enormous. She was so depressed, as if all the joy had gone out of the world for her. I can't get that image out of my mind."

"I'm sorry."

"Oh, no, don't be. It all worked out in the end. Well, sort of. Faith has two wonderful daughters, that's the important thing. Faith . . . she got remarried again a few years ago, but her husband left her when he found out she was pregnant. He could tolerate Penny because she was older and could do her own thing, but the idea of having to care for a helpless infant freaked him out. Faith has been depressed ever since. I've tried every happiness spell I know to help her get over it, but so far nothing has worked. Why are you looking at me like that? You think I'm a freak, don't you?"

"No, definitely not. I guess I don't know a lot about it. Can you do witchcraft?"

"Yeah, so be sure you don't break my heart, or I'll cast an impotency spell on you." Ariel laughed at his horrified expression. "That was a joke by the way."

"That's nothing to joke about," he said gravely, then smiled to show he was teasing.

"Sorry. Anyway," Ariel continued, "even if I did want to cast an impotency spell on you, I'm not very good at witchcraft I'm afraid. I haven't been able to help my sister yet. Maybe I just haven't tried the right spell."

"Maybe she should try a more traditional approach, something physical like a yoga class or dance lessons. Physical activity can really boost a person's spirits."

Ariel considered this for a moment and nodded. "I'll look into it. It certainly couldn't hurt. Are you hungry? I think dinner should be ready."

"For whatever you're cooking, absolutely. It smells great. What did you make?"

"Homemade pasta with fresh basil and roma tomatoes and fresh bread."

"Wow, homemade pasta? I'm impressed."

"Well, wait till you taste it before you make a decision on whether you're impressed."

J.T. followed her downstairs to the kitchen.

"Can I get you a glass of wine?" Ariel asked.

"Please."

Ariel poured them each a glass of chilled white wine, and they sat at her small kitchen table with one of her home-made candles flickering between them. She had a dimmer on her kitchen light and she turned the lights low for effect. As she served dinner, she smiled to herself. It was a big deal to her that he didn't judge her for believing in witchcraft and magic. She had had more than one boyfriend in the past who treated her beliefs as off-the-wall, quirky, and cute at first, but then when things started to get challenging in the relationship—and challenges, of course, always arose in any relationship—suddenly they turned her beliefs into a weakness that could be used against her. They declared that everything that was wrong with their relationship was her fault because she was too "weird" and not "normal." J.T.'s attitude made her feel safe. Thank the goddess she'd been craving chocolate cake and taken her niece to that restaurant. Thank the goddess that Ariel had taken a chance and introduced herself to him. Thank the goddess that he'd found her attractive and intriguing enough to show up at her art opening. If any one of these things hadn't happened, she wouldn't be here right now, feeling so happy it seemed as if her entire body were smiling, as if her heart and her mind and her blood were fused with a cosmic energy that made her body float someplace between reality and some happier ethereal kingdom.

They had a few bites of their dinner and looked across the table at each other, smiling shyly with the newness and excitement of it all. He assured her that her cooking was delicious.

He asked her about her candles and how she made them. She explained about how she could make them different colors and how adding pure oils to the melted wax created the different odors.

"I've always loved candles, so I decided I wanted to make them myself," she said. "What about you? How did you become a hockey coach?"

"I played hockey in college, but I knew I wasn't good enough to go pro, so I majored in education with the intention of finding a school where I could teach phys ed and coach hockey. And that's what I did."

"You seem surprisingly un-battered for a hockey player. Like why aren't you missing most of your teeth?"

"Caps," he said, tapping one of his front teeth and then an incisor.

"You're kidding! Those look so real." She leaned across the table for a closer inspection—not noticing that her hair was draped over the candle's flame. J.T. and Ariel smelled the singed scent of burning hair before they actually noticed that she was on fire.

Ariel screamed, leapt up, and thrashed ineffectually at her flaming hair, hopping from foot to foot as if doing a Hopi rain dance. J.T. flew into action, flipping the table over to get it out of the way—pasta went flying everywhere, sticking to every available surface, while the clatter of broken dishes echoed through the room—and hustled her over to the kitchen sink, drenching her head under the faucet.

As quickly as the excitement had started, the fire was put out. Ariel, with her head and shoulders soaking wet, surveyed the damage and slunk down to the floor, resting her back against the lower kitchen cabinets. J.T. sat next to her. Fortunately, when J.T. had upended the table, the flame of the candle had gone out so her entire apartment complex hadn't been set ablaze. Eyeing the destruction, Ariel started giggling. J.T. joined her.

"I don't normally set myself on fire on a first date. Or even any date, typically."

"Well, then I feel very honored that I could be here when it happened."

"Sorry about dinner," Ariel said.

"I got half a meal. I won't die of hunger. Let me help you clean up."

"Thanks."

J.T. started straightening up the kitchen and doing the

dishes while Ariel dried her hair and changed out of her wet blouse. Afterward, they went into the living room and relaxed on the couch. They talked about music they liked and concerts they'd gone to. J.T. told her about his sister and her two sons, including Robby, the kid who'd disrobed him publicly. They talked about food they liked and didn't like (neither liked beets—borscht, yuck!—but they disagreed on olives—she loved them, he hated them). He asked her about her art. She asked him about the pros and cons of coaching versus playing. They talked until they fell asleep together on the couch, wrapped in each other's arms. Ariel woke up first and watched J.T. sleep. He had long, dark eyelashes. When his eyes flickered open, Ariel said, "Good morning."

"Mmm. Mornin."

"I'll make us some breakfast. Do you like eggs?"

"Eggs? Sure."

She whipped up a quick tomato omelet with cheddar cheese, and they sat at the kitchen table, eating hungrily.

"Do you want to go skiing today?" he asked her.

Oh dear. Ariel was not much of a skier even in the best conditions, but when winter gave way to spring, the snow was often icy and hard from being packed down from hundreds of skiers racing over it without fresh snow to rejuvenate it. Those were poor conditions for even the best athletes. However, things were so new with J.T. that she was still in the stage where she wanted to pretend she was perfect: She could cook! She could paint! She could race down a mountain on skis like another Picabo Street!

"Sounds like fun," she lied.

Though it hadn't snowed in Denver in a few weeks, the mountains still had snow. As Ariel suspected, the snow wasn't in optimal shape for skiing. On her first run down, her ski caught on a rough patch of snow, came off, and she stumbled forward, twisting her left ankle painfully and landing hard on her knee.

J.T. was right behind her. "Are you okay?" he called, swooshing to a stop beside her, a spray of snow arcing out as he did so.

Ariel pressed her lips together and moaned quietly. Outwardly, she said, "I'm okay! I'm fine!"

Ariel continued to ski a few more runs despite the blinding pain in her ankle. She didn't want J.T. to think she was a wimp. He was a jock; it would do no good for him to know that she was an uncoordinated wuss, at least not at this early stage in their relationship.

"Having fun?" he asked her when they were at the bottom of the hill, heading for the ski lift.

Ariel smiled through gritted teeth and nodded.

"I'm getting hungry. What do you say we make this our last run, and then go grab something to eat," he said.

"Oh, sure. That sounds good," Ariel said nonchalantly, while silently thanking the goddess that she could end the charade at last.

After their last run, J.T. had said he wouldn't mind showering before they had dinner. "Do you mind stopping at my place?"

"No problem."

J.T. lived in a two-bedroom condo with hardwood floors. It was neat and clean, but he had been right—it needed some decorations to spice up the pristine planes of the white walls.

"Your painting is going to go right here," he said, indicating the area on the wall above his couch.

"That is a blank space begging to be filled with decorations," she agreed.

"I know. I can't wait. I'm going to hop in the shower. You take a look around, okay?"

Ariel meandered around the house, checking out the place. She listened to the chugging of the water through the pipes and pictured J.T. testing the temperature, then shedding the clothes from his sweaty skin. The sound of running water paused, then let loose in a firm peal. The shower curtain swooshed closed. She imagined what he looked like naked, the water cascading down his flesh. For a moment, she was tempted to hop in the shower with him, but that would be far too bold a move at this point in their relationship. Instead, she decided she would take this opportunity to inspect her ankle.

It was swollen, but it didn't look more serious than a sprain. She went to his kitchen and emptied an ice tray full of ice cubes into a plastic sandwich bag, which she only found after opening every conceivable drawer where it could possibly be. Then she went into the living room, sat on the couch, and propped her injured leg on the table. She draped the plastic bag over her ankle.

She didn't know how long she had been asleep, but she woke up when she sensed a presence moving in front of her. It was J.T., who was removing the bag from her ankle. The ice had melted completely.

"Sorry, I didn't mean to wake you, but it was leaking out all over the place. You hurt yourself?"

"I'll be fine."

"Let me take a look. I have a lot of experience with sports-related injuries." After dumping the melted remains of the ice cubes in the kitchen sink, he returned to inspect her ankle. "Ahh, yes, you definitely have a sprain. But you'll be okay in a few days. Just make sure you keep icing it. When did you hurt yourself?"

"On the first run down," she admitted sheepishly.

"Ariel! Why didn't you tell me?"

"I was trying to impress you with my dazzling fortitude."

"Silly girl. You don't like skiing, do you?"

"No, it's not that, I'm just not very good at it."

"Why didn't you tell me? I could have given you some

lessons. Or we could have gone to an art museum or to the movies or something. Ariel, promise me you'll always be honest with me."

"I'll be mostly honestly with you, I promise."

"What's that supposed to mean?"

"Come on, everybody lies a little when you first date. You wear better underwear than you normally do and spend more time looking good, that sort of thing. Am I right?"

"I suppose."

"So that's what I mean. I'll be almost completely honest, but I'll pretend I like red thong underwear until you've fallen for me, and then I'll pull the underwear rug out from under you and go back to my cotton undies I love so well."

"Deal. You look pretty beat. Why don't I order us in a pizza and we can just relax right here?"

"That sounds perfect."

They continued to get to know each other as they waited for their pizza to arrive. Ariel told him about her day job and how she didn't love the work, but besides art, she didn't really know what she wanted to do with her life.

"I know that there is very little chance I can make a living as an artist. I have no illusions about that. But I don't know what else I can do for a living."

"What about being an art teacher? Have you ever thought about that?"

"What, you mean like to grade-school kids?"

"Sure. Or high school. College even."

Ariel thought a moment. "That might be fun. I do like kids. At least I like my nieces. I wonder what I'd have to do to become a teacher."

"Do you have a Bachelor's degree?"

"I barely squeaked by with one, but yeah, I have a degree."

"Then it would take a year of course work to get certified."

"Huh. I'll think about it. That does sound better than answering the phone all day. It's not a bad job, but it's not exactly a career that challenges my mind, you know."

Their pizza arrived, and they gorged themselves happily. Half an hour or so after they were done eating, Ariel stood to clear her plate. "Ouch!" she said as all the muscles she wasn't used to using went rigor mortis; she could practically hear the splintering sound of her body tightening up on her.

"What's wrong?"

"I'm not used to using these muscles. They're a bit sore."

"That's natural. Exercise causes inflammation, which leads to an increase in the production of immune cells. These cells, in turn, produce bradykinins and prostaglandins, which make the pain receptors in your body more sensitive."

"Aah, yes, those damned brady-somethings and prosta-whatevers."

"Would you like a massage? It might help."

"Sure."

"I don't mean to be a perve, but my bed is probably the best place."

Ariel nodded and shuffled geriatrically to his bedroom. She collapsed stomach-first on the bed.

He started with her neck, shoulders, arms, and back. His hands were large and strong, and she melted under his touch. Here was a man who knew a thing or two about sore muscles. He skipped over her butt and massaged her hamstrings and calves; Ariel moaned aloud with how good his touch felt.

"Thank you so much," she said when he had finally managed to loosen every kink in her body. "You have gifted hands. Can I return the favor?"

"Yeah? Sure, I guess, if you want."

He assumed the stomach-down position, and Ariel began to rub. His shirt kept bunching up around his neck. "I think it might be better if you took off your shirt," she said.

"'Course." He sat up and pulled off his shirt. Ariel was taken aback by his beautifully sculpted physique.

"You are in damn good shape," she said admiringly.

He laughed. "I work out a lot."

"Yeah, I'd say you do. Oh, I'm staring, aren't I?" Ariel pried her eyes away from his muscled chest and looked into his smiling eyes. For a long moment, their gazes held, with hints of smiles turning up at the corners of their lips as they anticipated what was to come.

He closed his eyes, tilted his chin ever so slightly, and brought his lips to hers.

As their kisses grew more intense, Ariel's nipples swelled. She longed to have his mouth and hands on her—she couldn't pull off her shirt fast enough. She snapped her bra off. Immediately, he cupped his hand around her breast and took her nipple in his mouth.

As they slowly shed their clothing and discovered each other's bodies, she forgot entirely about the pain in her ankle.

The first time they made love was slow and sensual. They looked into each other's eyes as if they needed confirmation that what was happening was real.

Afterward, they lay in each other's arms. Eventually, thirst forced Ariel from her warm, comfortable spot. She hobbled to the kitchen to get a glass of water, and when she returned, they made the kind of athletic love that involved jumbles of limbs being tossed around. It was thrilling—Ariel felt like they were making their way through the entire *Kama Sutra* that night. At one point, J.T. had her in the wheelbarrow position: her legs were wrapped around his waist as he stood; their only contact with the bed was

Ariel's two hands. Unfortunately, when J.T. thrust just a little too exuberantly, Ariel's hands slipped and she went sailing right across the bed—and into the wall, wrist-first.

"Aag! My wrist!" she moaned, clutching her right wrist.

"Oh, God! Ariel, I'm sorry! Are you okay?"

"No. Ow. Ow."

"I'll take you to the hospital."

She nodded, fearing she'd broken it.

In the emergency department, she told the doctor about the skiing injury, blaming both her wrist and her ankle on that. She didn't feel the need to let the crotchety old male doctor know that her new boyfriend had fucked her clear across the room.

"How did you manage to injure your left ankle and right wrist?" the doctor asked.

"Uh . . . I fell two different times."

"Not much of a skier, eh?"

"Not really."

Fortunately, she hadn't broken her wrist. It, too, was just a sprain. The doctor wrapped up her wrist and ankle in Ace bandages, advised her to apply ice compresses every four hours, and encouraged her not to go skiing for several weeks. "And you might want to consider taking lessons when you do!"

J.T. dropped her off at her apartment, looking contrite. "I'm so, so sorry," he said.

Ariel startled giggling. Her giggles morphed into a full belly laugh. "Don't worry. I had fun, a lot of fun. Right up until the end there."

"I'll make it up to you. I promise. I have to coach tomorrow night, but I could pick you up in time for a late dinner."

"Sounds like a plan." She kissed him good night and hobbled her way into her apartment complex. She was so happy the throbbing pain of her wrist and ankle were barely noticeable.

On Monday morning, Faith asked how Ariel's art show had gone. Faith couldn't make it because Penny couldn't babysit Rhiannon.

Before Ariel could answer, Faith noticed Ariel's bandaged limbs. "What the hell happened to you?"

For a moment, Ariel considered not telling Faith about J.T. She didn't want to seem like she was bragging or rubbing it in that Faith didn't have a special guy in her life while she did. But she couldn't lie about something so big.

"Um, well, it all began with the show Friday night. I sold a couple paintings and I met a guy. We went skiing yesterday. That's how I hurt myself."

Faith nodded. "I'm sorry you got hurt, but I'm glad you met someone."

"Really? Because you don't look happy."

Faith sighed. "I'm sorry. It's just that I haven't heard about the job I interviewed for. I'm just worried that means they've chosen another person for it, that's all."

"Faith, I was thinking that maybe one way you could start feeling better would be if you took a dance class or something. I remember how much you enjoyed taking dance when you were younger. Doing physical things can really lift your spirit. You know, connect your mind and body."

"Who would watch Rhiannon?"

"I would watch her, or if Penny was free, she could watch her. I printed some information from Body Moves studio's website this weekend. They have beginning and intermediate dance classes on Tuesday and Thursday nights. It's not very expensive."

Faith took the printout Ariel was holding and looked at

it. Ariel was right, an eight-week class for $80 was very reasonable. She could get in shape . . . it might be fun.

"The next class starts next week, so you'd better sign up right away," Ariel said.

"I don't know . . ."

"Faith, you have to do something to cheer yourself up. Do something nice for yourself. Don't you remember how much you used to love to dance?"

Faith considered this for a moment. It was true that there had been a time when she loved nothing more than soaring across the dance floor. Maybe Ariel was right. She had to take steps to shake off her dark mood.

"You know what? I think I will."

Ariel smiled. "Excellent!"

After work, Faith stopped by the studio to check it out. Little girls with rounded bellies and pink tights and leotards bobbled around and across the dance floor in an approximation of ballet. Faith approached the front desk apprehensively and cleared her throat.

"Hi," she said.

The woman behind the desk was praying mantis skinny with black eyes and black hair pulled back into a taut bun. She was elegant rather than pretty. "May I help you?"

"Um, maybe. I . . . was sort of thinking of maybe taking a ballet class?"

"You're in the right place."

"Well, but, I was wondering . . . are all your classes . . ." Faith leaned in and said in a whisper, "you know, full of little kids?"

The woman's condescending laugh made Faith feel like an idiot.

"No, no. Our afternoon classes are strictly for children. Our evening classes are for adults. Now, what level are you interested in? We have a Beginners, an Intermediate I, Intermediate II, Intermediate III, and an Advanced."

"Well, I've taken some dance before, so I guess maybe the Intermediate I? If I get bored I can always advance a level."

The woman gave Faith a cold smile. "Certainly. Just so you know, we do have some students who take classes carte blanche."

"Carte blanche?"

"It means they can drop in for any class they'd like. So every now and then advanced students take an intermediate class just for fun."

"Oh, okay."

Faith filled out a form and signed her check. The woman gave her a "pass" that was really just a blue square of paper with sixteen squares drawn on it that the teacher would mark off for each class she attended.

A few days later, Faith arrived early for her first class so she could stretch. She had once been extremely flexible, being able to go into the splits on both her right and left legs (though she'd never quite mastered middle splits). She'd once been able to bend forward from her waist and wrap her arms tightly against her legs so that her nose was pressed against her knees. Tonight, she bent from the waist and was unable to stop herself from whimpering aloud after getting only as far as an L shape, with her back parallel to the floor. Faith pretended like that was as far as she'd wanted to go, like she'd never had any intention at all of touching the ground with her fingers. Next, she sat on the ground with her legs splayed out in a V shape in front of her. She attempted to bend from her waist over her right leg with her left arm extended in a curving line above her head. She managed to go from 90 degrees to about 88 degrees before a splinter of pain shot down her side and froze her in that position for several moments. In her petrified, statue-like state, she had nothing else to do but watch the other students warming up before class. They were all preposterously thin with body–fat ratios hovering a few percentage points above certain death from malnutrition. They draped their upper bodies over their legs with rag-doll ease. Faith watched one woman in the splits reach back and grab her back leg, pulling her head down so it touched the leg that was behind her.

"Ouch!" Faith murmured quietly, wincing at the mere thought of such contortionist moves.

"All right class, let's begin," a man said, clapping his hands. He was slightly older than the rest of the class with a thick swatch of black hair styled in something of a tribute to Donald Trump's hairdo. He had a slight lisp and the beginnings of a paunch, though he was still clearly in great shape from his years as a dancer.

He started the class off with barre exercises. Faith stood in position, back straight, with one arm on the barre. Then the teacher rattled off commands like gunfire, "*Plié, demi-plié, cambré*, four *tendus* to the front, *plié*, four *tendus* to the side, *plié*, *battement frappe*, Frappaccino, Al Pacino, café au lait, Bain de Soleil! . . ." Something like that. Faith lost track. She tried valiantly to mimic the woman in front of her, lofting her arm about in what she hoped was a graceful manner and *pliéing* and shuffling her foot around the floor in a way she hoped was convincingly passable. Faith realized with horror that every last one of the students in the class must be in the carte blanche program. These were professional dancers just here to keep their limbs limber until their real class began, and Faith was stuck in the middle of them.

Faith was sure she couldn't be any more embarrassed. Then they started the floor work, and her humiliation was complete.

The teacher once again listed off four zillion things in

French. The rest of the class briefly turned their eyeballs inside their heads as they quickly engraved the series of exercises into their memories while Faith looked around the room in bewilderment. Apparently, she didn't remember as much from her childhood ballet lessons as she thought she did. The rest of the students scampered into position, forming two lines in the back corners of the studio. Faith did her best to follow what the people ahead of her did, but failed spectacularly. She could feel all eyes on her as she flailed about. It was too cruel, being surrounded on all sides like this amid a roomful of lithe, fat-free beauties. Faith felt fat and recklessly ungraceful.

When everyone had flitted (or in Faith's case, flopped) across the floor, the students once again lined up at the back of the room. From the commands the teacher gave, Faith for some reason thought she was supposed to do a small lunge to the left and then a little spin. Out of nowhere, bodies were leaping, pirouetting, and doing triple backflips, at least so it seemed to Faith. After she crashed into her third soaring ballerina, tripped over her own feet twice, and finally just stood still for the safety of herself and all those around her, the teacher noticed she was having some minor difficulties.

"If you're having trouble with the sassafras-something-or-other, you can substitute it for the blah-blah-blah-thing-a-ma-jig."

Which turned out to be less than helpful.

Faith came home feeling worse than ever. She couldn't believe how out of shape she'd gotten. She had been humiliated. This was why she didn't try new things. No good could come of it.

Faith changed into her pajamas and got in bed. She stared at the ceiling for a long time. Tears leaked out of her eyes, falling sideways on either side of her face into her ears.

There were so many things she wished were different in

her life. She wanted more money and a different job, she wanted to be in shape without having to diet or exercise, she wanted adventure and excitement. But most of all, she wanted love. True love.

She had believed that she'd loved the man she'd lost her virginity to. They had sex three times before he left her for another girl. It had taken her months to get over that rejection, and it didn't help her sadness to realize she was pregnant. She'd realized later that her feelings toward Cam had only been infatuation. But with Casey she was no longer a kid. She was an adult who'd weathered some tough times. She had been well and truly in love with Casey, and when he asked her to marry him, she was certain her luck was finally changing.

He'd never been exactly thrilled about Penny being a part of their lives, but he and Penny seemed to get along all right. Penny had always been a precocious child. She was bright, and she had been able to take care of herself from an unusually young age. She was a solitary child happy to spend time alone, and she could be a fun kid when the mood struck her. Faith and Casey had never talked about having children of their own. Faith didn't even want to think about more kids until their finances were in better order and they weren't always scrambling to pay the rent or get groceries on the table. Kids were expensive, that was all there was to it. But she'd gotten pregnant within a month of their marriage—the new diaphragm she'd gotten wasn't quite the right size, a fact she learned when it was too late to do anything about it.

Faith wanted to tell Casey about the pregnancy in a way that wouldn't freak him out. One night Faith arranged for Penny to spend the evening at her friend's house. Faith made an extra nice dinner. When Casey came home from work and saw the candles on the table and the special meal, he looked askance at Faith. "What's going on?"

"Why would you say that? Can't I make a romantic dinner for my husband?"

He looked incredulous, but he dug in. Halfway through the meal Faith said, "I have something to tell you."

"I knew it. What is it? Did you lose your job? Get in a fender bender?"

"No, it seems that when I got my new diaphragm, it wasn't quite the right size. I know we didn't plan for this, but . . . I'm pregnant." Faith swallowed hard, giving him a moment to absorb the news. "Isn't that great? I mean it might be tough, but we'll have our own little baby together, yours and mine."

"No, that's not fucking great. We can't afford a kid. Are you insane? I can't believe you let this happen."

"*Let* this happen? I told you, it was an accident. Just let the news sink in a little. It's a shock, I know. It came as a shock to me, too."

But if the news ever did sink in, it didn't bring Casey a sense of joy and wonder but rather of fear and responsibility. Not only did he divorce Faith as fast as he could, but soon after the divorce, he moved three states away to distance himself from his child as much as possible.

Faith had thought their love was something really special—a once-in-a-lifetime thing. Faith finally realized that while her love for him might have been that strong, her feelings weren't returned. She'd started to believe that she wasn't worth loving. What about her was special? She wasn't particularly pretty, she wasn't particularly smart, she couldn't cook . . . what was the point? The only thing that kept her from ending it all was that she had two daughters, two wonderful daughters who needed her, as flawed as she was.

4

The Witch and Sports (Ha! As if)

J.T. and Ariel had been dating for two perfect weeks. Ariel was blown away by the magnetic pull he had on her. She wanted to spend every second with him, and he felt the same way about her. The only problem was that spending so much time with him meant that she wasn't working on her art like she should have been. Even on the nights when he had to coach late and they couldn't get together, she felt completely frozen, unable to sketch a line or paint a single stroke. She'd sit in her "studio" feeling panicked. She tried to convince herself that it was just that she was in the incredibly overpowering first throes of love and that things would soon get back to normal. Soon she would be able to think straight and paint again.

Some nights Ariel would cook for J.T., and sometimes he'd cook for her. Tonight, he'd taken her to a relentlessly hip new Thai place for dinner, and then suggested a new Johnny Depp movie. Even though they were full from dinner, they waited in line at a concession stand to buy some popcorn and soda because, to Ariel's way of thinking, there simply wasn't any point in going to the movies if they didn't gorge themselves on movie popcorn.

"What size soda do you want?" he asked her.

"Hmm," she surveyed her options. "Holy crap! Look at the whammo size." The drink options went from small, to medium, to large, to extra large, to whammo, which was the size of a barrel. "Do you think that comes with your very own harness to carry it to your seat? A personal Sherpa maybe?"

J.T. laughed. "I love you," he said.

Stunned, Ariel stared at him. "What?"

"You heard me. I said I love you."

"Really?"

"Really. I love how you make me laugh. I love how beautiful you are. I love your positive attitude. I love that you believe in magic. I love you."

She was too taken aback to say anything in return. The feelings she'd had for him had been overwhelmingly powerful. She'd suspected "love" might be what she was feeling, but it was so soon. It was both thrilling and a little scary to hear him say the words. She was so unnerved she couldn't return the sentiment . . . yet.

"Hey," he said, as they inched forward in line. "My team is playing in the semifinals tomorrow. If they win, they go on to the finals: if they lose, that's it for the season. I thought it might be fun for you to see my kids play."

"Oh, sure, that'd be great." Would now be a good time to tell him she knew absolutely nothing about hockey? Nah. She could fake it. Right?

Ariel went to the skating rink just minutes before the game started. She watched J.T. talk to his team in the . . . what was it called? Huddle? Box? She didn't know her sports terminology. If things worked out between them—

and all signs indicated that they would—she'd have several months to study up before the next season began.

When the game started, she tried very hard to pay attention to what was going on. She squinted as the players zoomed from one side of the rink to the other. She knew this much: She was cheering for the boys in the red jerseys and against the boys in the white jerseys. J.T. had explained to her that high school ice hockey wasn't the violence-filled blood-festival that pro hockey was. Still, Ariel flinched every time one kid rammed another kid into the wall. Ariel couldn't believe that there were parents in the world who would allow their children to be tossed around like crash test dummies. Then the thought occurred to her: *What if J.T. and I get married and have kids together? What if we have a son?* No doubt J.T. would want his son to follow in his hockey-playing footsteps. What would she do then? Live in a perpetual state of mortal fear for the safety of her son no doubt.

Something happened, because all around her people were jumping up and cheering. Ariel looked around, confused.

"What just happened?" she asked the teenage girl sitting next to her.

"The Devils scored a goal."

The Devils? That was J.T.'s team. Belatedly, Ariel cheered, which earned her strange looks from all around her. She would just have to pay closer attention. She focused once again on the zipping bodies carving up the ice with their skates. But it was no good, in moments she fell once again into a trance-like state. Thoughts of J.T., of her art, of her sister—they all competed for time in her imagination, and all were far more interesting to her than the game that was being played in front of her.

Ariel was once again shaken from her reverie when a

loud chorus of "Boos!" and plaintive "ohhhs" were shouted out by everyone in her section.

"What just happened?" Ariel asked the same teenage girl.

"The Mad Dogs scored."

"I see. Would you mind elbowing me when the Devils score so I can remember to cheer?"

"Not much of an ice hockey fan, huh?"

"It's just sports in general. I have nothing against hockey in particular."

"Do you have a nephew or a cousin on the team or something?"

"I'm dating the coach."

"No way! You're dating Mr. Manning?"

"Yes. Why do you sound so surprised?"

"Oh nothing. You're just the envy of every girl in this high school, that's all."

"He is pretty cute, isn't he?"

"He's a total babe. I have to say, I always pegged him for the kind of guy who would fall for some bimbo-y type. You're much cooler than I was expecting."

Ariel had to think a moment. Had she been complimented or put down? She wasn't sure which. "Is that a good thing?"

"Very good. It just means Mr. Manning has character. He's not a stereotype."

Ariel smiled.

"My guy, he plays right wing, number eleven," the girl continued.

Right wing? She may as well have been speaking Urdu. Ariel hadn't a clue what she was talking about.

Ariel spent the majority of the game in her trance, thinking of things that were more important to her than a game. This included everything from trying to remind herself to clean the bathtub to wondering whether expensive eye cream really was better than inexpensive eye cream, or if it was all about marketing. The one shot she did catch came during the second period. It was shot into the goal where the Devils had scored in the first period. Ariel stood and cheered, almost as much from the excitement of having been alert enough to catch the play as happiness that her team was winning. But she immediately felt a tug on her sleeve from the girl sitting next to her. Ariel sat down again. "What? Didn't we just score?"

"The teams switch which nets they guard after every period. The Mad Dogs just scored."

Ariel sighed. She would never get this strange world.

"I'm Karen, by the way."

"I'm Ariel, and I'm completely confused."

There a came a point in the game when Ariel was so beyond bored she couldn't even muster important internal debates such as the eye cream dilemma to keep her entertained. "How many innings are in hockey?" she asked Karen.

Karen laughed. "There are periods, and there are three. We're in the third period. There are four minutes remaining."

Four minutes! Instantly, Ariel was revitalized. She could get through a mere four minutes! She looked at her watch.

"No," Karen said, "you can't follow your watch. Follow the clock on the scoreboard."

Ariel looked up. The clock was stopped at 3:56. "Why has it stopped?"

"The Devils have called a time-out."

The next "minute" took five. What cruel world was this where a "minute" took five times as long as it should? Ariel studied the clock eagerly. When the seconds zipped along, her heart rejoiced. When it stopped again, it felt like her heart stopped right along with it.

"What now?"

"Mr. Manning called his last time-out. They need to score two points in the next three minutes or they're going to lose."

Lose? Oh no! She had to do something. She had to muster every last magical power bequeathed from her ancestors. Ariel closed her eyes. She cleared her mind of all thoughts and imagined the Devils cheering, J.T. pumping his fist in the air victoriously, and the scoreboard reading: MAD DOGS = 3 DEVILS = 4. She breathed in the cool air of the rink, filling her body with silvery light. Then she breathed out, unleashing the light across the rink, through the crowd, into the players, and finally, to J.T. himself.

Ariel was jarred by the thunderous screams all around her. Karen elbowed her. "They scored! The Devils scored!"

Ariel stood and cheered, pleased with herself. "So now what?"

"Well, it's tied now, so if one team or the other scores in the next minute and a half, that team wins. Otherwise, they'll go into sudden death—overtime basically."

"*Over*time? You mean, the game will last even *longer*?"

Karen nodded. Ariel sprung into action. She had to get the Devils to win in the next ninety seconds. Once again, she closed her eyes, breathed in the silvery light, imagined the Devils winning, and then breathed out.

Unfortunately, Ariel didn't quite manage to keep her mind focused on the outcome she wanted. She accidentally let an image of having sex with J.T. enter her mind. It really wasn't her fault. Everyone knows that when you first fall in love with someone, you live your life in a perpetual state of desire and you think about sex nearly every moment of the day.

So instead of scoring as she'd wanted the team to do, the offense began jerking about. Ariel thought their twitching movements were strange—until she realized that what they were doing was thrusting their pelvises as if they were having sex.

Oh dear. She'd turned J.T.'s players into Chippendale's Dancers on Ice.

Their erratic grinding movements were nothing short of obscene. It was like a pack of dogs in such frenzied heat they were humping the air around them.

At least their pelvic thrusting had one good outcome: It so confused the Mad Dogs that they were too frazzled to score either, and the game was forced into sudden death.

Ariel rolled her eyes at cruel fate. Before she could attempt to use her powers to help the Devils once more, a thunderous booing and riot of shouts disrupted her.

"The Mad Dogs scored. It's over," Karen said.

"What?"

"The game is over. The Devils lost."

"Damn!"

Magic didn't always work, Ariel knew that. There were many forces in this universe with far more power than Ariel and her will. Still, it was always disappointing to envision an outcome so strongly only to be disappointed when it didn't turn out that way at all.

Ariel shuffled to the hallway outside the locker room where J.T. had told her to wait for him. She waited an entire hour, watching player after player clear out before J.T. finally emerged. He was smiling a tight, dejected smile.

"I'm sorry, J.T."

"It happens. We should have beat them. We were the better team. I just don't understand what happened out there tonight. All of a sudden my players started doing some kind of crazy chicken dance or something at the most critical point in the game. It was like they were purposely trying to lose or something. They claim they don't know what happened, but it had to be something they planned. I just don't get it."

"You seem to be doing pretty well under the circumstances."

"It's disappointing, but all we can do is try harder next time. The bad thing about coaching high school is the parents. The boys take losses in stride, but the parents, if we lose, they blame me and want me strung up on a stake."

"Doesn't that bother you?"

"I don't love it, but I try not to worry about it. When people are critical, it's just their own shit. Let's not talk about hockey anymore. Let's go home and make love until we collapse in exhaustion."

Ariel smiled. A man who dealt with loss admirably—unbelievable! J.T. was her needle in a haystack, her winning lottery ticket. "Yes, let's."

Ariel awoke wrapped in J.T.'s arms. They lay with limbs entangled for several minutes in a silence broken only by the sound of their breath until J.T. said, "I love you."

Without hesitating, Ariel said, "I love you, too."

They sat in silence for a few more minutes, then Ariel, laying on her side, rested her head against her hand so she could look J.T. in the eye. "Have you ever been in love before?"

"I've dated some other really nice girls, girls I really liked a lot, but I never felt like I'd been hit by Cupid's bow or anything. With you, it's like I was hit by Cupid's canon or Cupid's M16 or something. What about you? Have you ever been in love before?"

"I don't think so. At least, I've never felt about anyone the way I feel about you. But I have a confession to make."

"Uh-oh. What is it?"

"I'm not actually that big of a fan of hockey."

"That's it?"

"Yeah, well, you know, it's a huge part of your life, and I don't know a single thing about it."

"Maybe if you learn a little more about it, you'll be able to appreciate it more. I can teach you if you're willing to learn."

"I won't have to get on the ice and get battered into the wall to learn about it, will I?"

He chuckled. "No, I'll teach you about it from the safety of the sidelines."

"Okay, I'd be up for that."

"How about me? Should I join a coven? Begin casting spells?"

"No, definitely not. We're allowed to have our differences. We click in the areas it's important to get along in. We'd good in bed together, for example."

"Absolutely."

"We laugh at the same jokes."

"True."

"We like the same movies."

"Also true."

"And we get along with each other's friends."

"And that's not easy to do."

"Exactly. So you don't have to practice witchcraft unless you feel you need to for a spell for something. Then I'd be happy to help you."

"Like a spell to win a game?"

She thought about how her spell had turned his team into well-padded humping machines on ice skates. "Okay, I'm sure we could work on something for that."

"I'll never lose a game again! This witchcraft thing is going to be great!" he teased, wrapping his arms around her and nuzzling her neck with his mouth, kissing it with machine-gun rapidity all over as he tickled her.

Ariel shrieked with laughter and attempted to tickle him back.

"I love you, I love you, I love you," J.T. said as he attacked her with light, pecking kisses.

Ariel managed to push him on his back, straddle him, and pin his arms down with her legs. "I love you more."

She bent over and kissed him deeply, letting her tongue gently explore his mouth.

The romantic moment was interrupted by the shrill ringing of the phone. Ariel hesitated.

"Go ahead and answer it, to shut it off if nothing else," J.T. said.

Ariel nodded and picked up the receiver. "Hello?"

"Ariel, it's Elise. How are you coming along with those new pieces?"

"Oh . . . I'm making progress, you know, incrementally."

"Well, kick it into high gear. We sold two more of your pieces. We'd like to extend your exhibit. How long would it take you to get us four more pieces?"

If she'd been working as hard and as prolifically as she sometimes could, she might be able to get two canvases done in the next three or four weeks. But the only time she'd ever pulled off a feat like that she'd been single. "I'm not sure really. A few months?"

Elise tsked. "Ariel, you're on fire right now. You don't want to lose that momentum. See what you can get done by the end of the month."

"Okay. Hey, thanks, Elise. For everything." Ariel hung up the phone feeling panicked.

"What is it?"

"Elise from the gallery wants me to produce some more work. She sold two more pieces."

"That's great."

"Yeah, the only thing is that it means that I'm going to have to spend more time on my art, which means less time with you."

"Just when I was going to have more time since I won't be coaching. Oh well, don't sweat it, your art is important."

"Thank you for understanding."

"What do you want to do today?"

"Actually, I was thinking I might paint."

"Oh, yeah, of course. I'll get out of your hair." He gave her a quick kiss, hopped out of bed, and pulled on his clothes.

He kissed her good-bye one last time. When she was alone, she went into her studio and sat in front of her easel. Images of various goddesses flickered through her mind, but as she contemplated ways to execute her ideas into a narrative whole, her inner critic started hollering that her ideas were "derivative" and "uninspired." She wondered if a real critic might write something about her in a newspaper. She knew exactly what the critics would say. She could see all of the flaws in her work before she even brought a brush to the surface of the canvas.

She went into her bedroom, sat on the floor in front of her altar, lit a candle, and closed her eyes. She needed to open up her mind and get her creativity flowing again. She took slow, deep breaths and imagined inhaling blue light, letting the color filter through her body. She tried to clear her mind of all extraneous thoughts and just breathe. Normally she had no trouble getting to a meditative place, but today, she couldn't clear her head from a loop of thoughts and images. It was no good, she could never quite peel away reality and get to a mystical place. She blew out the candle, feeling defeated. She had never been blocked like this before. She had also never been in love before. The two things were obviously related. Being happily in love was making her creatively constipated. She had to decide what was more important: J.T., or pursuing a career as an artist.

It was a horrible choice to have to make.

5

The Witch and Heartbreak

Over the next two weeks, Ariel used every excuse she could think of to avoid seeing J.T. so that she could focus on painting. But even all the time she had alone wasn't helping. She couldn't doodle, sketch, or finger-paint for that matter. The more she stressed about not having anything to give Elise, the more she felt unable to think of what to work on.

The problem was obviously that she was unable to focus. Her thoughts were being pulled in too many directions. There was nothing else she could do. She had to break up with J.T.

For two days Ariel didn't return his calls as she worked up the courage to break up with him. She tried to figure out what she would say to him, but the words never came. At last she just picked up the phone and blurted, "I'm sorry. We can't see each other anymore. We have to break up."

"What? I don't understand. Things are going so well between us."

"I know, J.T. It's just that . . . well, you know the stereotype. Artists are always unhappy. If they were happy, they wouldn't have anything to paint or write about or sing about, you know? When I'm with you I'm ridiculously happy, and it's keeping me from being creative."

"Ariel, you strike me as a person who is generally pretty happy most of the time."

"That's true, I am, but when I'm with you, I'm *too* happy. You make me content. I don't feel like I have any voids to fill when I'm around you. I need to feel a little emptiness to create." Ariel wasn't sure that she did, but she didn't understand what else could possibly be making her mind and body freeze every time she so much as contemplated painting or drawing.

"You're being superstitious. What you're saying makes no sense. Can't you just do some creativity spell or something?"

"J.T., don't tease me, not about this. You don't have to believe in witchcraft, but don't knock my beliefs, okay?"

"I wasn't knocking your beliefs. I asked if you couldn't do a spell to help you out."

"I have, believe me. They just haven't been working."

"If you can't see me for the next few weeks while you catch up on your work, I understand, but please tell me you're not breaking things off for good."

"I'm sorry, J.T. It's over—for good."

"If you don't see things working between us, well, I have to deal with that, but I don't think you should use your art as an excuse."

"I'm not. You just don't get it. Look, I have to go. I've had fun with you, really, I just can't be with you at this point in my life. It's just bad timing."

Ariel hung up the phone with a sinking feeling. She knew without looking that her aura was black, the color of negativity and depression—the color that billowed around Faith most of the time.

She collapsed on the bed. The whole situation was heartbreaking. She was sad that she'd had to cut things off with

J.T., but she just didn't see another way. She wasn't sure she'd ever been as attracted to another man as much as she was attracted to him. She had never felt such a connection. There was something so vital and exciting about him. He inspired her to try new things and grow and expand as a person. Granted, her desire to do such things led to sprained ankles and maimed limbs, but the important thing was that she was trying.

But life was all about choices. She'd wondered for the past several years whether she had any talent as an artist, or if art was something she should do just for fun for herself in the privacy of her own home. Selling several paintings in the last few weeks had persuaded her that she must have at least some skill after all. She had been trying to hone her abilities as an artist for the past twelve years. Now that she was finally getting somewhere, how could she just give up?

Finally, she forced herself to get up. She cast another creativity spell. She lit a white candle and a yellow candle. Yellow was the color of inspiration and optimism, and white was the color of purification. She chanted the words, *As this candle burns, let creativity burn within me. Let my imagination loose and my intuition run free. Fuel my spirit with ideas and my mind with inspiration. Stimulate my artist's eye and heed the words of this incantation.*

When she was done, she went to her studio and stared at the blank canvas. It couldn't have frightened her more if it had fangs and claws that threatened to devour her. Her heart actually pounded with fear. This was ridiculous. Why was her magic failing her? Why was she choking like this?

Over the next several days she repeated this and other creativity spells to no effect. She bought a few books on creativity, as well as books on goddesses. She hoped reading about goddesses would inspire her to want to paint one. She read and read and read, but inspiration still didn't come. If she were a character in a movie, her block would eventually end with a scene where she was buying a baguette or getting a cup of coffee and suddenly the lightbulb would go off in her head; she'd race home and paint furiously until she had her masterpiece. She kept waiting for the lightbulb to go off, but she was beginning to fear that the electricity fueling her creativity had been shut off permanently.

Maybe her sister's Eeyore-type attitude on life had finally rubbed off on her. Faith had gone to a few more dance lessons—taking the beginner's class after that first humiliating time—then she made up a lame excuse for why she couldn't go, and finally she just kept on making excuses and never went back. Faith gave up so easily. Was it any wonder life for Faith had lost its magic?

Faith was grumpy day in and day out, and now Ariel was also puttering around with a frown and a bad attitude. Being blocked creatively was stressful, but more seriously, painting and artwork was always how she'd processed any dark thoughts or bad feelings that came her way. Without that outlet, all the negative emotions churned within her like a tar-dark witch's brew, oily and sticky and impossible to break through.

6

The Witch and Magic

Faith was driving home from work and just about to pull off the highway when the dashboard lights flickered, and then her car just died like a candle that had been blown out—poof! Gone, just like that. The car had just enough fumes to coast onto the shoulder of the highway.

Faith didn't have a cell phone, so she waited in her car for a police car to drive by and notice her predicament, or for some kind stranger who did have a cell phone to take pity on her.

She waited and waited and waited. The whole time all she could think about was how much money it would cost her to get her car fixed. Money she didn't have. Why did everything bad always happen to her?

She still hadn't heard about that job for which she'd interviewed. She'd continued to send out résumés, but so far she hadn't landed any more interviews. She would be stuck at her dead-end job forever. Things would never get easier. Life would always be hard work.

These were the things Faith was thinking as the sky went from sunny, to charcoal gray, to so dark Faith couldn't see more than a few inches in front of her face. If she couldn't see, she certainly didn't know how anyone else was going to notice her. She was just about to abandon her car and begin walking to the nearest gas station she could find when finally a "courtesy patrol" tow truck came by. The courtesy patrol was meant to keep traffic flowing smoothly despite accidents or cars breaking down and getting in everyone's way.

The tow truck took her to a mechanic's shop in town, which was now closed for the day. At least the mechanic had a pay phone in the front, that she used to call Ariel and ask for a ride.

By the time Faith got home, the girls were already in bed. Faith fell into her own bed and mentally crunched numbers, trying to figure out a way to pay her monthly bills, as well as the repairs to her car. What more on earth could she cut back on? She cut coupons, she scrimped, she budgeted. She hadn't bought herself a new bra or a new pair of shoes for two years. She and the girls almost never went out to dinner or the movies. What more was she supposed to do?

Faith wanted a man in her life to deal with getting the repairs done on her car. She knew Ariel wouldn't approve of Faith thinking this way—Ariel would say Faith needed to find the goddess within herself and not wait around for a man to take care of her. But here was the thing: She worked all day, she cooked, she cleaned, she took care of the kids, and it would just be really, really nice to—just once—let someone else take care of *her*.

Faith barely slept all night—she was too busy worrying about money. Since Faith's car was in the shop, Ariel picked her up and took her to work the next morning.

Ariel wasn't a morning person, so Faith thought nothing of the fact that Ariel drove her to work in silence.

If Faith hadn't been so tired and grumpy herself, she

might have noticed that her sister was unusually blue, but she didn't notice.

Faith's day seemed to last forever. She was bored out of her mind with making copies. She needed to go back to school or at least find a job that challenged her more. She'd never gone to college because she'd been a broke single mother. But maybe now that the girls were older, she could look into student loans or something. The job she had interviewed for would have its share of menial work, but she would also be in charge of putting together the office newsletter, writing articles and doing the layout. Ariel wasn't the only one in the family with an artistic bent. Faith needed to use her creativity more. But she hadn't gotten the job, damn it.

After work, they walked out to Ariel's car together.

"You know, Faith, I know you're going through a hard time, but your self-absorption is getting a little old. It would really be nice for you to notice that I'm going through a hard time myself right now."

Faith looked at her sister. "What's wrong?"

"I broke up with J.T."

"But why? I thought things were going so well between you."

"Things were great between us. That was the problem." Ariel drove across town and pulled up to Tots and Toddlers, the daycare center where Rhiannon went each day.

"We'll talk about this when I get back, okay?" Faith said, getting out of the car to pick up Rhiannon.

Ariel said nothing. She was in a terrible mood, and for once, she didn't feel like being the strong sister, the sister who could smile through the hard times and always look on the bright side of things. She looked at the parents coming out of Tots and Toddlers. Sometimes she envied the little kids. At Tots and Toddlers, joy was relentless. There was never a crisis that couldn't be resolved with a red balloon or a chocolate chip cookie. She wished a cookie could fix all her problems.

Rhiannon jabbered the whole way home. Ariel pulled into the driveway and the three of them walked inside where Penny was, as usual, bent over her homework, studying furiously. Faith bribed Penny with twenty bucks to take her sister to McDonald's and a movie so she could talk with Ariel. She didn't really have the money, but she was in so much debt already, another twenty bucks wouldn't make any difference.

When they were alone, Faith said, "What's going on? Why did you break up with J.T.?"

"I told you how J.T. broke my curse of not being able to sell anything. But falling in love with him brought me a whole new curse: I couldn't paint anymore. I was too happy. Artists need to be a little unhappy."

"Ariel, you've always been happy."

"But I was too happy. I was completely blocked with J.T. I couldn't think of any ideas. I wasn't inspired."

"So now that you've broken up with him you're painting again?"

"Well, no. But that's because now I'm too sad."

"So your creativity is like Goldilocks's porridge? Everything has to be just right?"

"Don't be dismissive. You've been depressed and bitchy for three straight years, and all I've ever done is try to be supportive and help you." Ariel was grouchy, and she didn't feel the least bit guilty about it. It was her turn, damn it.

"You're right. Let's think about this. You said you met J.T. at the art opening?"

"I met him briefly before that and invited him to the opening, but the night of my show was really the first time we talked. That was the night I actually learned his name."

"That night he bought a painting and two other people did, too?"

"Right. And then the gallery owner told me I should get busy painting more stuff; but instead of cranking out more pieces, I haven't been able to paint a single brushstroke. I haven't even been able to make candles."

"Was the night of your art opening the night you fell in love with J.T.?"

"Love? Well, I'm not sure if it was that exact night. That *weekend* was magical. The roots of love were being sewn right from the beginning. I don't know the specific moment I knew that I loved him."

"Hmm." Faith thought a moment. "What was it like for you to sell your first painting?"

"What do you mean what was it like? What do you think it was like? It was the most thrilling feeling ever. . . ." Ariel's voice trailed off. She frowned.

"But?"

"But . . . nothing. Well, I mean, I guess it was also a little scary. What if the work I do in the future isn't as good?"

"Ariel, I don't think loving J.T. is your problem."

"Oh, so what is my problem?"

"You're afraid of success."

"What are you talking about? That's ridiculous."

"No, I don't think it is. When you finally sold a painting, that put you in a different league. Suddenly, you weren't just a wannabe artist, you were an actual, real-live artist. You started worrying about what critics would say about your work. You started worrying about what people would think."

Ariel was taken aback. She *had* thought those exact things. "How did you know I'd been thinking that?"

"Because I know you. You screw off at work because if you ever do anything right everyone is pleasantly surprised.

You never tried very hard in school because you didn't want anyone to expect you to do well. You like to set the bar low so there is less chance that you will fail."

Ariel shifted uncomfortably. Faith's thesis made a little too much sense. "Well, I don't know, maybe you have something, but what am I supposed to do about it? How am I supposed to get over my fears and get back to painting?"

"You need to give yourself permission to paint crap."

"What?"

"Don't worry about sitting down and creating the next masterpiece. Just sit down and paint. If something good comes of it, great, if it's total crap, then that's okay, too. You just need to get back to it. It's the only way to get over your fears."

Ariel considered the idea, then nodded glumly. "Maybe you're right. I'll try," she said with a shrug. Then, inspired, she added, "But only if you'll do something for me."

"Uh-oh. All right." She sighed. "Let's hear it."

"Faith, you need to let a little magic into your life. You need to be open to love and to the possibility of happiness. I want you and me to perform a spell together."

"Absolutely not."

"Come on. If you don't believe in magic and spells anyway, what's the harm?"

Faith rolled her eyes. "If I let you perform one of your little . . . *spells* on me . . . you'll call J.T. and tell him you want to get back with him? You'll start painting again?"

Ariel hesitated only a moment before agreeing, "Yes, I promise."

"All right then. Cast away."

"Awesome!" Ariel stood and started heading outside. "Well, come on!"

They walked outside into the cool night breeze. The sky

was crowded with twinkling stars. It was a perfect spring evening, warm but not yet hot.

"Faith, you have to listen closely to what I'm saying. Block everything else out. You have to focus, okay?"

"Fine."

"Close your eyes and hold my hand," Ariel ordered. Faith rolled her eyes but then complied, taking Ariel's hand in her own.

The two women stood with their eyes closed, feeling the caressing winds of the night air.

"*Every chrysalis must escape her cocoon,*" Ariel intoned. "*Every infant must leave the security of the womb. Every scribe must find her voice. Every woman must make her choice. To lead a life filled with love, laughter, and magic. To live deeply and love strongly.*" Ariel repeated the incantation several more times. Faith cleared her mind and focused on what Ariel was saying.

"Okay, now, Faith, I want you to think about what's been making you sad. Just really focus for a moment."

Faith did as her sister instructed. She thought about the first big choice that had changed the course of her life forever. She loved Penny more than anything in the world, but getting pregnant at sixteen meant Faith had never really gotten to be young, and sometimes, that made her sad. Then there was Casey leaving her when she told him she was pregnant with his child—how could she ever forgive that? She wanted to share her life with a man who she loved and who loved her, and there were times she worried it would never happen for her again. She worried that she'd been hurt too many times and it had made her heart hard, developing a protective sealant that wouldn't let any emotions in. And finally, she was sick of always being broke, of always having to work so damn hard. She was exhausted by the perpetual stress of being strapped for cash.

Ariel continued, "I want you to imagine releasing all your sadness into the night sky. Let the goddess and the universe swallow your sadness. Imagine your hardships floating up and away and letting joy and happiness take their place."

Faith did what Ariel said; she tried to imagine letting go of the depression that had lodged inside her. She pictured the tight knot of stress melting and her insides turning as pliable as Play-Doh.

Ariel continued, "Breathe in the life-giving oxygen. Remember that the Mother is here to take care of you and nurture you. Sometimes it seems like life is just an endless parade of mundane tasks, but when life seems drab and dreary and just too hard, you need to sit back and think a moment about how miraculous it is that you are here at all, that somehow your ancestors were able to avoid floods and hurricanes and mountain lions and famine to live long enough to mate and give birth to the next generation, who somehow managed to survive long enough to give birth to the next generation and so on and so on, until your mother finally gave birth to you, an individual whose DNA and dreams and thoughts are yours alone—unique in all the universe. Think about laughter and love and first kisses and watching your daughters grow and the smell of the forest just after the rain. Stop a moment and remember that each day is a gift that is yours to make into any thing you choose." Then Ariel returned to chanting. "*Every chrysalis must escape her cocoon. Every infant must leave the security of the womb. Every scribe must find her voice. Every woman must make her choice. To lead a life filled with love, laughter, and magic. To live deeply and love strongly.*"

Faith was sure she was imagining it—she was probably hallucinating from being so tired—but it did feel like something was loosening in her chest. It felt like she could breathe a little more deeply than usual.

Faith and Ariel stood outside for a long time, holding hands and breathing in the comforting night air.

When they broke apart, Faith felt strange. She felt lighter. It wasn't a drastic difference, but it was a nice little lift.

"So, when do all my dreams come true?" Faith asked sarcastically. She didn't want Ariel to think she'd bought any of this for a second.

"Making dreams come true is an ongoing process. Otherwise, life would be boring, don't you think?"

"Mmmm," Faith muttered.

"I love you, Faith, even if you are a grump."

"I love you, too. Very much. More than you could ever know."

Ariel went home and sat at her easel. Oil paints and canvases were expensive, so she didn't like to waste any supplies without having a good idea of what she wanted to paint, but tonight she wasn't going to worry about expenses or whether what she was doing was any good. She was just going to paint.

She mixed red and blue and white together to create a pale violet color. She swirled the color on the canvas. She had no idea where she was going with it, she just let the paintbrush lead her way, caressing the canvas with circular strokes. She painted a large pale violet oval on the canvas, but still hadn't a clue what she wanted to do with it.

She cleaned her brush and highlighted the oval with opalescent white that made the oval shimmer and come to life. Once again, she sat back and surveyed her work. And that's when she knew what she was painting. It was an ice rink.

Cue the lightbulb going off.

Ariel smiled and attacked the painting with renewed vigor, trying to bring to life the energy she'd seen on the players that night she watched J.T.'s team play. She painted the players as abstract blurs of motion with white or red jerseys, black skates, and helmets that matched the colors of their jerseys. She painted goals and goal boxes and fans cheering in the stands.

Ariel painted all night long until she was so tired her eyelids felt weighted by anvils and the morning light seemed to hit her with spotlight brightness.

She looked critically at her painting. It wasn't a masterpiece, but it wasn't bad. Or at least it didn't seem bad— though she was delirious from lack of sleep and her eyes could barely focus, so she couldn't be sure.

Something was missing. What was it? Damn it. What was she forgetting?

She tried to conjure up memories of going to the game. She remembered cheering at the wrong time, cheering for the wrong team, and aching for it to be over . . . that was it! The scoreboard! That's what she'd forgotten.

Ariel painted a scoreboard with the words HOME and AWAY on it in red lights. Under AWAY she painted the number zero. Beneath HOME she painted IS WHERE THE HEART IS. She suspected that once she'd caught up on her sleep she'd find that sentiment to be greeting-card cheesy. If so, she could paint over it and try again. For now, her bed was calling to her.

Before she collapsed into bed she had the wherewithal to call her boss and leave a message saying she had food poisoning and had spent the night draped over her toilet, so she couldn't come to work today. Then Ariel took her phone off the hook and fell onto her bed on top of the covers, fully clothed. She was sound asleep within seconds.

Ariel woke up at four o'clock that afternoon. She made herself a cup of tea and gave herself a little time to wake up. She glanced at the clock. J.T. would be home from school by now. Biting her lip, Ariel plugged her phone back in and dialed his number.

He answered on the fourth ring. "Hello?"

"J.T., hi."

He didn't say anything for several seconds.

"It's me, Ariel."

"I know who it is. Why are you calling?"

He didn't seem happy to hear from her. Shit. "I . . . wanted to say I'm sorry . . . if I hurt you."

He expelled a loud breath of air. "It's a little late for that now, don't you think?"

"Yeah, I just . . . the thing is, I think I was scared. About falling for you, about my career in art, about a lot of things. I freaked out. I panicked. You were caught in the cross fire of my stupidity. And I'm sorry. That's all I wanted to say."

Neither of them said anything for an uncomfortable stretch of time. Ariel was beginning to wonder if they'd been cut off when J.T. finally said, "So how have you been?"

"Awful, really awful. It's a little unclear to me why I thought breaking up with you would solve my problems. I haven't been this sad in a long time. I was talking to my sister yesterday and she suggested that maybe my being blocked wasn't so much about being too happy because I was with you but about being too scared that, I don't know, my art might get slaughtered by critics or people wouldn't like it and I'd never sell another piece. I think she might have been right. I painted last night. I haven't looked at it in the light of day, but last night when I was in a sleep-deprived trance I thought it wasn't terrible."

"Good. I'm glad to hear you're painting again."

"Thanks. So . . . how are you?"

"You know, the same. Not a lot going on here. School will be out for the summer soon. I was thinking I'd take an extended trip, maybe up the Pacific Northwest. I'll hit San

Francisco, Portland, Seattle, Vancouver, and then swing up to Alaska. I've always wanted to go to Alaska."

"That sounds great. That sounds like a lot of fun. I'm happy for you." Ariel chewed thoughtfully on her lip. "Um, so, this isn't my business, so feel free to tell me to keep my big mouth shut, but, um, well, I was just wondering . . . are you seeing anybody?"

J.T. laughed scornfully. "Ariel, what the hell? You think I fall in love with a girl one day, get dumped, and start dating somebody new the next day? Jesus. No, of course I'm not seeing anybody."

"Oh. Me neither. I'm not seeing anyone I mean."

"What's your point?"

"Point? No point. I don't have a point."

Again, silence. Awful, awkward silence.

"Well, thanks for calling," J.T. said. "It's good to hear from you. Really."

"It was good to talk to you. Have fun on your trip, okay?"

"I will. Good-bye, Ariel."

"Good-bye," she said, but he'd already hung up.

Ariel couldn't let this get her down. She'd just have to find a spell that would make him fall back in love with her. She deserved a second chance! She *needed* a second chance.

Ariel raced into her living room where she had a small bookshelf filled with books on spells and witchcraft. She hadn't used the books in years, and they were covered in dust. For the most part, she liked to create her own magic, which may have something to do with her success rate—or lack thereof. But for this she needed help. She needed to get this one right.

She blew a thick layer of dust off a heavy leather-bound book and delicately leafed through the thin, yellowing pages looking for an appropriate spell.

She was so absorbed in perusing various spells that she almost didn't notice that her phone was ringing. When the rings finally pierced her consciousness, she ran to the phone and answered it, dazed and distracted.

"Hello?"

"Ariel?"

"J.T.! What's up?"

"When you called me just a second ago, you didn't . . . want to see if we could try to work things out between us, did you?"

"Well . . . I called to apologize, that's why I called, but . . . yes, I guess my ulterior motive was to see if you might give me—us—a second chance."

"I might be willing to try again."

"Really?"

"Really."

"Oh, thank God. That will save me from trying to cast a spell on you to get you to fall back in love with me."

"It's too late for that. I've been under your spell since the moment you invited me to your art opening."

Ariel touched her fingers to her smiling lips. "I'm glad to hear that. Very glad. Because I've never been particularly good at casting spells. You might have ended up as a giant condom or a walking dildo or something."

"Yeesh! Don't cast any spells on me then, okay?"

"Okay, I promise. But let me take you out to dinner. And afterward, we'll just have to see what kind of magic we can make together."

Faith watched the five o'clock news while waiting for the water to boil so she could throw the spaghetti noodles in. Penny was sitting at the kitchen table doing her math homework when the phone rang. Faith had never had to bug Penny to do her homework. Penny loved to learn and brought home A grades like clockwork. Faith felt supremely lucky that the heavens had seen fit to send such a diligent, intelligent daughter her way.

"Hello," Faith answered.

"Hello, may I speak to Faith Merrill?"

"This is she."

"Faith, this is Muriel Dowling from Dowling, Henner, and McCain. You interviewed for a job a few weeks back?"

"Yes?"

"I'm sorry I didn't call you sooner. We've had some internal organizational changes that we needed to resolve before I could extend you an offer."

"An offer?"

"If you're still interested in the position, that is. You were clearly the best candidate for the job." Muriel explained the pay and benefits program. The pay was significantly more than what Faith was making now. She would have to wait for three years' worth of raises to make that kind of money at her current job. She would be able to pay off the repairs on her car in just a few weeks without borrowing any money from her sister! Hallelujah!

"Are you interested?" Muriel asked. "If you need some time to think—"

"I'm interested. When can I start?"

"When would you like to start?"

As soon as possible. Right this second. Tomorrow morning at the absolute latest! "Well, I guess I should give two weeks' notice to my current employer. How does Monday the eighteenth sound?"

"Perfect. Faith, we're so excited to have you join us. We really think you'll be a valuable asset to the team."

"I will do my best, you can count on that. Thank you so much for this opportunity. I look forward to working with you."

Faith hung up the phone and whooped with joy.

"What is it, Mom?" Penny asked, her big brown eyes looking up from her homework spread across the table.

"I got the job! I got the job! It's a big raise! Really big!"

"Mom, congratulations! Good for you." Penny leapt out of her chair and gave her mother a hug.

A knock at the door made Faith look up. Her heart raced when she saw that Bret Halloran was peering at her just outside her unlocked screen door.

Faith released Penny and opened the door just a crack. "Yes?"

"Hi. Sorry to impose like this, but I am having my parents over for dinner, and I can't seem to find my vegetable peeler. I wonder if I could borrow yours."

Faith hesitated a moment. "Sure, yeah, I'll get it."

Faith watched Bret out of the corner of her eye. He seemed nervous.

"What are you making?" he asked.

"Just spaghetti. I'm not much of a cook I'm afraid." Faith struggled to keep her voice from wavering.

"That's for damn sure," Penny agreed.

"Penny!" Faith looked at her daughter, her eyebrows raised in a how-could-you? look, but Penny didn't seem to notice. She had returned to her place at the table and was once again absorbed in her studies.

"I love to cook," Bret said. "Maybe . . . would you like to come over for dinner sometime?"

"Oh, that's sweet, but Penny is just so busy with school, and Rhiannon—"

"Maybe *you* could come over for dinner sometime," Bret interrupted. "I'm free tomorrow night."

Penny's pencil stopped abruptly. Her gaze met her mother's, then Bret's. Faith thought quickly. How long had he wanted to ask her out? Usually if he tried to talk to her, she found something urgent she needed to do in the house, and then race inside. Maybe he'd been plotting to get her alone for a long time. But really, what were the chances that he would murder her when her daughter could report her whereabouts to the police? If she went to his place for dinner, she might be able to find out what was in his basement once and for all. This wouldn't be a date exactly, it was just about being neighborly. Maybe if she became friends with him, he'd somehow find a way to spare her life when he went to destroy the neighborhood.

"All right," Faith said.

Penny gasped.

Bret smiled. "Come over around seven."

The next day, Faith found it difficult to concentrate at work. There were so many things that could go wrong. What if he fell for her, but she didn't return the feelings, and he began stalking her, threatening to kill her, making her life a living hell. It would certainly be easy for him—he lived next door! Or what if they didn't hit it off at all and the evening was one long, awkward, social disaster.

But mixed in with all her usual worries, Faith felt something she hadn't felt in a long while—hope. She had done a budget based on her new salary, and as long as she was careful, she would be able to treat herself and her daughters to some new clothes and finally get serious about putting money into a savings account. It was amazing what having a little extra cash on the horizon did for her spirits. Plus, getting asked on a date bolstered her ego. Granted, she'd been asked out by a man who was probably a serial killer, but beggars couldn't be choosers. Anyway, it still felt good just to be asked.

Today, Faith felt like she could do anything. She thought she might even start taking dance lessons again. She would start slow, but eventually she would get into shape again. She would become as limber as she had been when she was young, and in no time she'd be gliding across the floor like a ballerina!

After work, Faith surprised herself by how carefully she prepared for dinner with Bret. She showered, shaved her legs, applied extra lip gloss and mascara, and put on her favorite sundress, just as if she were getting ready for a real date.

"Have a good night," Faith told Penny as she went to leave.

"Don't get murdered and gutted," Penny said. "I'm just kidding. You look good."

"Yeah?"

"Yeah."

It was a short walk from Faith's back door to Bret's.

"Good evening," he said, "come on in."

Faith stepped inside tentatively.

"Would you like some wine?" Bret asked.

"Sure. What are you making?"

"Mushroom stroganoff. It's a specialty of mine."

"Sounds great."

What was she doing here? This was ridiculous, thinking she could covertly discover his secrets as if she were a character in a movie. Sandra Bullock or Julia Roberts could comically bungle their way into solving the mystery, but Faith, she didn't have a script to protect her. One false move and she'd be spending the rest of eternity six feet under.

Bret poured two glasses of wine and handed Faith a glass.

"Cheers," he said.

"Cheers." Faith sipped her wine and surveyed the kitchen. She knew that all of the homes in the area had been built around the same time. Bret must have had his kitchen remodeled, because it didn't have the unfortunate avocado green appliances and worn floor with which Faith was saddled. His kitchen gleamed with top-of-the-line appliances and expensive stone-tile flooring.

"You are going to love this recipe. I learned to cook in

Europe. I was stationed over there for a couple years, and after I got out of the Marines I stayed there for a while, working as a sous-chef."

"How long were you in the Marines?" Faith asked. Bret was preparing food, so he had something to occupy his hands, but Faith didn't know where to put hers. The hand without the wineglass felt awkward on her hip. She drank the wine too quickly just to have something to do.

"For five years. Those were some good times."

"What sorts of things did you do? What sorts of assignments?"

"Oh, this and that. A lot of it was training and waiting. It could get pretty boring sometimes. We found ways to entertain ourselves. We tested weaponry . . . I got paid to blow things up!"

"I see." He seemed a little too happy about his destructive past. "Well, that certainly sounds interesting."

"It was. It was quite a lot of fun."

"I've never been one for firearms or explosives of any sort."

"It's a guy thing. Every guy I know used to light things on fire or blow things up as a child. I used to build mounds of dirt and stick those little green soldier men in it and blow them up with firecrackers. What you do is . . ." He stopped cutting vegetables and gestured with the paring knife in hand.

Faith abruptly cut him off with a wave of her hand to indicate that he'd provided enough detail already.

"I don't mean to be a wimp, it's just, not, you know, my kind of thing." Great. Now Faith had identified herself as a sissy, an easy target.

Bret smiled. "Sorry. Dinner's ready anyway, it's good you stopped me from babbling too much. Take a seat."

Faith sat at the table. He refilled her wineglass. It occurred to her that he might have slipped something into the wine, but since he poured another glass for himself from the same bottle, she dismissed the theory as quickly as it came.

Bret set a loaf of bread on the table, poured olive oil on a plate for the bread, and served each of them some stroganoff.

"Thank you so much," Faith said. "It's so nice to have a home-cooked meal that I don't have to cook."

"Well, it's been a long time since I had someone to cook for."

The explosives thing was a little worrisome, but he was far from the strangest man she'd ever dated. And he could cook; the meal was delicious. He was good-looking, and he seemed nice. As long as he wasn't hiding corpses in his basement, he just might be a good catch.

"Not lucky in love?" Faith asked, dipping the bread into the olive oil. The bread was crispy on the outside, soft and warm on the inside. Faith closed her eyes, savoring the taste.

"I was once. We divorced."

Faith nodded, but she was taken aback. She hadn't envisioned him as ever having been married.

"Were you ever married?" he asked.

"Once, briefly."

"Tell me if I'm getting too personal . . . I don't see Penny or Rhiannon going off with their dad on weekends or for the summer."

"Their fathers are long gone."

"Did you ever want more children?"

"Sometimes I think about it. Kids are work, but they are worth it. My daughters are my pride and joy." Faith looked at the dish of olive oil and the leftover bread crumbs, bloated and soggy, marooned in the small, golden lake of oil. Why was she telling him this? The wine must have loosened her tongue.

"Never found another guy, huh?"

"I've gone on a lot of first dates, but not so many second

330 / *Theresa Alan*

dates. I didn't want to bring a man into the girls' lives if I didn't think he'd be a good enough father for them. I know from experience that it's better not to have a father than to have a bad one around. I sound like a country singer, don't I?"

"No, no, it's great. It's great to, you know, really talk to you. I've wanted to get to know you better ever since that day we were working outside together. I kept hoping I'd see you again, but it was almost like you were in hiding."

Faith had done her best to avoid him, that was true. "You wanted to get to know me better?"

"I've always thought you were so pretty. And your girls are just adorable."

Pretty? He might not be a serial killer, but he was clearly deranged. "Do you like kids? Did you want kids of your own?"

"Absolutely, I love kids."

"Do you want a boy or a girl?"

"It doesn't matter to me, although one thing I'll say about girls is that they are much neater and they tend not to blow things up or set them on fire."

Bret reached across the table and touched her arm lightly. His touch sent a jolt through her. It took her a moment to recognize what she was feeling. Then she remembered. It had been such a long time since she'd felt these sorts of emotions: excitement, attraction, and confusion about feeling the excitement and attraction in the first place.

Faith stood and began clearing off the table.

"Leave it," Bret said, "I'll get it later."

"No, no, you cooked this wonderful meal, the least I can do is clean up."

Bret walked over to the sink where Faith was stacking the dishes. He put his hand on her forearm. "Leave it," he said gently.

"Okay. So . . . how about a tour of the place?"

"Sure, follow me."

They walked into the living room. He had brand new carpeting, a large-screen television, an expensive-looking sound system, and shelves filled with books that lined the walls from top to bottom. In the study, there was more computer equipment than Faith had ever seen in her life.

"I do all my shopping in here," Bret said. "I hate dealing with crowds. Thank god for online shopping."

"So that's why the UPS truck is always at your house. I get maybe a handful of deliveries a year at my birthday and Christmas. I was feeling bad about not having more friends."

"Oh yeah, Amazon.com is a close friend of mine," he said with a smile, closing the study door before they moved on. Faith peered in for a quick glimpse at his bedroom, then a passing look over the bathroom. She found nothing untoward in either room. One door hadn't been accounted for.

"What's in here?" Faith asked.

"Oh, that's the basement. It's a mess."

"Can I take a look around?"

"No!" he said too quickly. "I mean, it's just a basement. It's really such a mess."

"I know this is going to sound strange, but it would mean a lot to me if you'd let me see your basement."

He looked slightly ill. Too nervous. "I guess." He hesitated.

Faith's heart pumped ferociously. Maybe once she saw whatever was down there, it would be like having been bitten by a vampire or getting on the wrong side of the mob—there would be no going back.

She followed him to the basement door and down the treacherously narrow stairs into the dimly lit basement. Faith was taken aback by the unpleasant but not unfamiliar odor. It didn't have a cadaverous smell, she noted with relief, but she couldn't quite place it. She clung to the handrail, feeling her way down the stairs. Something strange was definitely going on, dead bodies or no. Why was it so dark?

At the bottom of the stairs, Bret told her to stay where she was. Faith could barely make out his figure moving across the room. Bret flicked on the light. When Faith's eyes adjusted to the light, her gaze focused on a large framed photograph on the wall of bizarre, red-capped trees with sponge-like trunks radiated by an eerie yellow glow.

There were several tables lined with shallow boxes draped in some kind of strangely textured cloth. Faith pulled the cloth away quickly, revealing some kind of sickening alien growths sprouting from beds of manure, dirt, and wood chips. Was Bret conducting some kind of extraterrestrial experiment? Raising some illegal, poisonous plant to sell to terrorists?

Faith didn't dare speak. Her eyes continued roaming until she saw another large photograph. After studying it for a moment, she was able to discern what she was looking at, and her tension evaporated. "These are *mushrooms?*" she asked.

"I'm a bit of an amateur mycologist," he said.

Faith studied the photograph. The row of mushrooms looked like bedraggled, cream-colored brides carrying lace umbrellas.

"Did you take these photographs?" she asked.

"No, I bought them at a conference. I know it seems like kind of a strange hobby, but mushrooms can be really beautiful. Look at this one." He pointed to another photograph of a fallen tree in a forest drenched in sunlight. It looked like a spiral of orange butterflies was splayed across its trunk. "And they hardly take any time to raise. Some of them only take two weeks. They grow in darkness, and you just need to keep them moist."

"Are they poisonous? Psycho . . . psychedelic?"

He laughed. "None of these is poisonous or psycho-active. That's the best part. You can eat them. We had some with dinner tonight."

"You raised those, huh?"

"I've never shown anybody down here before. It doesn't smell very good I'm afraid. My ex-wife was the only one who knew about this crazy hobby of mine, and she thought I was a maniac. It is a little strange, I guess."

"No, it really isn't. I think it's kind of neat," she said.

Faith reached out to stroke a mushroom's spongy surface and looked out over the rows of mushrooms. It was a small, strange, enchanted forest.

She looked back up at Bret and smiled. She couldn't be-lieve how happy she felt.

It seemed almost like magic.

Epilogue

Two Years Later

Faith and Bret's home looked like a Halloween decoration supply store. Together, Faith and Ariel had scrubbed the house clean and decked the place out with construction paper witches and ghosts and gauzy cotton stretched and hung to look like spiderwebs. Pumpkins lined the front walkway like flickering sentinels; bowls of candy rested on the credenza by the front door for trick-or-treaters; and, best of all, the baby girls were decked out in outfits so adorable that Faith wished it could be Halloween everyday.

Faith's baby, Serena, was dressed like a pumpkin. She wore a puffy orange top with a green leaf felt collar, orange pants with footies, and an orange cap topped with a green leaf and stem. Serena's fiery, sienna-colored hair peeped out just a little from her orange cap. Ariel's daughter, Sabrina, was dressed like a monkey in a brown suit with footies, a wired tail that she took great pleasure in tugging on, and a faux white hair trim that fanned out around her face like extra-long whiskers.

"You be good for your daddy and Uncle J.T.," Faith said to Rhiannon, who was dressed like a fairy with a headband of pink roses, a pink ballet top, and a beautiful iridescent mauve skirt with mauve, blue, and pink flowers around the waist. Rhiannon hopped up and down excitedly, unable to contain her joy at the night that lay ahead—an entire night devoted to collecting free candy. It was definitive proof that there was such a thing as heaven.

"Ready to go, my beautiful girl?" Bret asked.

"Yes, Daddy!"

She took her stepfather's hand with her left hand and went to reach for her Uncle J.T.'s with the other, only to discover that she'd run out of hands, because she needed one of them to hold the large cloth bag her mother had given her to hold the candy that she would collect.

"Would you like me to hold the bag for you?" J.T. asked.

Her eyes grew round. "No, I'll hold Daddy's hand for five minutes, then your hand for five minutes. You can trade."

"That's a very fair and precise decision," J.T. said.

She nodded, agreeing that her plan was sage indeed.

"Bye, sweetheart!" Faith called.

Rhiannon waved and smiled back at her mother and aunt.

"I can't wait till these two are old enough to take trick-or-treating," Ariel said, tugging gently on Sabrina's toe.

Faith nodded. "There's such a small window of opportunity. Before you know it they're sixteen and too cool to dress up. They'll just bug you for twenty bucks so they can go spend the evening hanging out with friends," Faith said, referring to Penny, who had left earlier in the evening.

"True," Ariel said, picking up the colorful cloth octopus that Sabrina loved to hurl to the ground and handing it back to her daughter so Sabrina could once again perform her experiments on the force of gravity. It was truly amazing how Sabrina never seemed to tire of this game. If Sabrina had asked her mother's opinion on this particular activity, Ariel might have gently suggested it was a *smidge* monotonous. But Ariel continued her octopus retrieval duties and let her gaze wander around the room, coming to a stop at one of her own paintings, which decorated the empty space on the wall above the television. Since giving birth to Sabrina, Ariel was a full-time mom and part-time painter. Her artwork sold sporadically. It was nice having the extra income, but she and J.T. couldn't retire and go sailing around the world on their luxury yacht quite yet.

The shrill of the doorbell filled the room. "Our first trick-or-treater of the night!" Ariel said. "I'll get this one."

Ariel stood, walked across the room, and flung open the front door. Disappointingly, it wasn't a group of adorable little toddlers standing there but five preteen boys with sacs big enough to trap rhinoceroses. They had barely even made an effort to dress up. Fake fanged teeth here, a little frightening make-up there; it was all so clearly a chocolate pirating excursion. Hmphf.

Oh well, she'd get cute little kids next time. She put a smile on her face and looked at the two bowls of candy Faith had put out. One had Snickers, which had always been Faith's and Ariel's candy bar of choice. Once upon a time that had been the only thing Faith had given out on Halloween, but then one year a mother accused her of trying to murder her son, who was allergic to peanuts. Ever since then, she had offered an alternative treat; this year it was Jolly Ranchers watermelon candy sticks. Ariel put one Fun Size! Snickers bar into each of their cavernous sacs.

"That's it?" one of the boys said.

"What do you mean 'that's it'?"

"Just one piece of candy? Those things are little. The Wilsons are giving out whole candy bars."

"Look, kid, the appropriate response is, 'Thank you,' not, 'Is that it?'"

He sighed and shook his head. Ariel watched the five boys turn and walk away, and for a moment she wished she had been able to study transfiguration from Minerva McGonagall and could have turned the boys into rats; but then she remembered that one day her own daughter would become an ungrateful teenager, too, and it was best to just bite your tongue, remember you had once been just like them, and wait for them to grow up a little.

Ariel walked back to the living room floor toward the girls, who were happily kicking in their bouncy chairs. Unfortunately, she only made it halfway across the kitchen floor before her stockinged feet went slipping under her on the overly slick surface of the newly scrubbed floors; she landed with a hard thump.

"Ow," she moaned, lying there for a moment like a dead body waiting to be outlined in chalk.

"Are you okay?" Faith asked.

"The floor jumped out and attacked me out of nowhere," Ariel explained, picking herself up.

The doorbell rang again moments later. "I'll get it. You can rest your bruised butt," Faith said, rising to answer it. There on the porch were three angelic toddlers—a little boy in a firefighter hat, yellow coat, and black rubber boots; a little girl dressed like a snowman with a plastic carrot nose and a black hat on her head at a jaunty angle; and another little girl in a tiger costume.

"Why, aren't you kids just the cutest things ever? Which kind of candy would they like?" Faith asked their father (at least, she figured he was the dad to at least one of these kids).

"Chocolate, definitely."

Faith nodded. Snickers were so clearly the ideal Halloween

candy for kids of any age. She dropped some candy into each of their bags and waved good-bye.

"Bring some Snickers over here," Ariel said as Faith closed the door, "a big handful."

"Don't you think you should pace yourself?"

"It's not Halloween if you don't end up puking up cheap artificial chocolate products half the night."

"You'll get one for now."

"I'm a mother now. Are you ever going to stop acting like my bossy older sister?"

"Never."

Faith handed Ariel a piece of candy and unwrapped one for herself. "Hey," Faith said. "What are you doing giving the girls candy?" Faith pulled out a mini Snickers bar from where it was wedged in between her daughter's pudgy body and the edges of her beloved bouncy chair.

"I didn't give the girls candy. I swear! Don't look at me like that. I may be a lot of things, but I'm not some candy pusher forcing sweets on helpless infants—give me a break!" Ariel plucked a piece of candy from beside her own daughter and held it up as evidence. "Maybe Rhiannon thought she was being helpful bringing her sister and cousin candy that they couldn't get themselves."

Faith considered this for a moment and then nodded; it was a plausible explanation. She picked her daughter up to see if there was any more candy contraband hidden beneath her and found none.

Ariel tore open the wrapper and smiled at Sabrina, who reached up with her chubby little hand as if trying to grab it. "Sorry, my sweet girl, this isn't for you."

The doorbell rang again, and once again Faith answered it. Standing at the door was an adorable girl who looked to be four or five and was dressed to look like a gingerbread man. She had chubby chipmunk cheeks and a big, broad grin.

"Here you go, sweetheart."

"Sank you."

"You're welcome." Faith watched the little girl go, then closed the door and returned to Ariel and the girls. "Ariel, what the heck? I asked you not to give the girls candy."

Ariel looked up. Serena was sucking on the end of an opened Fun Size! Snickers. Her jaw dropped. "I didn't give them any, I swear."

"Oh, and I suppose she just ripped it open herself? She can't even find her own nose yet, I don't think she has quite enough dexterity to open Snickers' packaging."

Ariel smiled. "Maybe the girls have a little Walker magic in them."

"Oh, for God's sake, Ariel, that's ridiculous."

"How else do you explain the time I'm sure I put her stuffed hippopotamus on the shelf, but when I came back he was in the crib with her?"

"Easy. You're an overtired young mother who forgot you left Mr. Hippo in your daughter's crib and in your sleep-deprived delirium you made up fanciful tales about your daughter's magical talents."

"Okay, well how do you explain the way the chimes in Sabrina's room begin to jingle even when her window is closed and she has no breeze?"

"Fine. Fine. Your daughter is a witch. But I don't have any magical skills, and neither does my daughter."

"Sometimes it skips a generation."

Faith rolled her eyes and snatched the illicit chocolate booty from her daughter's hands.

The doorbell rang. Faith gave one last huff, and then stood to get the door.

"Well, we know the truth, don't we, girls?" Ariel said.

Some might say that what happened was mere chance. But Ariel knew that in life, not everything could be explained away by logic and scientific fact. Take love, for instance. Faith had spent her life falling for the wrong guys and thinking she was unlucky in love when, in fact, fate was just seeing to it that she was ready for Bret. Television witches might be able to wrinkle their noses and make a guy fall for them, but in real life, sometimes romance didn't happen simply because you wished it would. Sometimes destiny had other plans. Your job was simply to trust fate and be ready to see the opportunities presented to you.

Faith was a stubborn one. Even though Ariel had predicted that she would give birth to a red-haired daughter more than a year before she did, Faith held fast to the idea that it was merely coincidence.

When the doorbell rang again, Ariel rose and said she'd get it.

"Be careful of the floor," Faith cautioned. "It's been known to move right under your feet."

"I'm laughing on the inside, Faith," Ariel said dryly.

Ariel greeted the gaggle of children who ranged in age from three to eight years old, while Faith picked up Sabrina's octopus toy from the ground and handed it back to her niece. Then she turned and shook Serena's rattle as Serena squealed with delight and bounced in her chair with great enthusiasm.

"Faith," Ariel said as she resumed sitting Indian-style on the living room floor.

Faith shook the rattle again. "What?" Faith turned to look at her sister.

"How do you explain this?" Ariel picked a candy bar up from where it was hiding under Sabrina's tail.

"Very funny. You're not—" Then Faith saw the candy in Serena's hand.

How the *hell* did that get there? There was no way Ariel could have slipped it past her. . . .

All right, all right, thought Faith, *maybe these two babies are special*. Since Bret and Serena had come into her life, she'd never been happier. There were times when Faith looked at her family and wondered just what she'd done to get so lucky. In the past two years, there had been moments when Faith grudgingly conceded that maybe there were some things in this world that science couldn't explain. Not that Faith would ever admit that to her younger sister. "Gotcha," she said instead.

Ariel narrowed her eyes. Faith usually wasn't a practical joker. "*You* put those candy bars here?"

"Of course."

Ariel's expression was doubtful. Faith just smiled. It was Halloween, the night when ghosts and goblins—and witches, of course—came out in droves. Who was to say that witches couldn't come in tiny, adorable packages, smelling of baby powder and Johnson's shampoo? After all, was there anything more magical than a newborn baby?

This, Faith thought, looking at her daughter and niece, *will just be our little secret, what do you say?*

The babies giggled in unison, and Faith knew that witches or not, these two had her under their spell.